PEGGY'S DISCOVERY

Richard E. Haskard

To Marilyn

All the best —

Dick

ISBN: 978-1514313114

Cover photo courtesy of NASA
Published by Richard E. Haskell, Inc.
Printed by CreateSpace, An Amazon.com Company

To Peggy, and everyone like her

1

Standing in her second-floor bedroom window, looking south over neighborhood rooftops as the early afternoon sun reflects from the Portsmouth High School building in the distance, Peggy Leach wonders what college she will be attending a year from now. She smells the Thanksgiving Day turkey baking in the oven. This is her favorite holiday, for as long as she can remember, her Uncle Sam has joined them for Thanksgiving dinner, always asking her what she has been doing in school, telling fascinating stories about being an electrical engineering professor at the University of New Hampshire in nearby Durham, the kind of spirited conversations Peggy loves.

Since submitting her early admission application to Dartmouth, Peggy keeps picturing herself walking across the Dartmouth Green on the way to classes. But will she be accepted? She will know in a couple of weeks, but the uncertainty is driving her crazy.

Peggy's reflections are broken by her mother's yell, "Peggy, come down and set the table?"

"I'll be right down."

Peggy pulls on her Portsmouth High School sweatshirt, goes into the bathroom, and brushes her bright, shoulder-length brown hair. She puts her hair in a ponytail when playing PHS basketball games, where she is the starting forward, but otherwise prefers to wear it down. At 5' 9", Peggy is not the tallest girl on the basketball team, but she jumps higher than anyone else does.

"Peggy, are you coming?"

"Ok, mom, ok!"

She bounds down the stairs, hears the click-clack of her mother cutting up vegetables, opens the bottom buffet drawer, and asks, "Sterling silver today, right?"

"Of course, it's Thanksgiving!"

"How many will there be?"

Her mom counts. "Well, let's see, there's you, me, your dad, brother, Uncle Sam, Aunt Laura, and the new nurse from the hospital, Connie Baker, who I invited. So there will be seven altogether."

"How come we have to have someone nobody knows?"

"Well I know her! She just graduated from nursing school and we hired her in September. Her parents live in Texas, and Connie has to work today until 3:00. She lives by herself in Dover, so I invited her to have Thanksgiving dinner with us. I think you'll survive."

Peggy's mother Katherine – everyone calls her Kate – is a nurse in the Pregnancy & Birth Department at the Portsmouth Regional Hospital. Peggy resents Connie sharing attention with Uncle Sam, but she knows her mother is right.

"You are so thoughtful, mom."

Kate's smile and dimple in her right cheek display a warmth and sense of caring, suggesting an affectionate nurse. Peggy knows that her mother's hairdresser keeps any gray hairs from sneaking into Kate's light brown hair, highlighted with a hint of blond. Her mother and Peggy have always been close, easily sharing their feelings with each other. Peggy never knew her grandmother, Uncle Sam's sister, who died when Kate was in the ninth grade, making Kate the 'mother' of the family when she was barely a teenager, growing up on her dad's small farm in Rochester. After school and on weekends, Kate would help at the farm's vegetable stand, selling corn, beans, and tomatoes to local residents. Peggy has a vague memory of spending time at the farm, before it was sold after Kate's dad died when Peggy was six.

Where are dad and Matt?" Peggy asks.

"They both ran in the Rotary 5K Turkey Trot around Portsmouth this morning and are probably still at Prescott Park hanging out with their friends. They should be home anytime and your aunt and uncle will be arriving soon, so let's get the table set."

Peggy hears a car door slam. Moments later Matt and her dad come in through the back door.

"How did you do, Matt?" his mom asks.

"I was disqualified." Matt is a sophomore at PHS.

"Why?" Peggy asks.

"I took a short cut through someone's back yard."

"Why would you do that?"

"It was shorter."

"What a jerk," Peggy says.

Peggy likes to tease her younger brother, about the origin of his curly red hair, as no one else in the family has red hair, about not being as tall as she is, about his trumpet playing scaring away the crows, about spending too much time playing video games, about generally being a jerk.

"How did you do, Joe?" Kate asks.

"Oh, I came in the middle of the pack. There were three other teachers from the high school and we all sort of stayed together." Peggy's dad, Joseph – everyone calls him Joe – has taught American history at PHS for the past 17 years. Peggy thinks his slick black hair combed straight back looks like a black bowling ball and the small gray patch on the left side looks like the hole in the ball.

Joe met Kate when they were both students at the University of New Hampshire, he majoring in history, she in the nursing program. They married right after graduation, Kate's nursing job supporting Joe while he got a master's degree in education. Peggy arrived the day Joe accepted his teaching job at Portsmouth High School. Kate quit her nursing job to stay home with Peggy, not returning to work until Peggy started school.

Sam and Laura Woodbury park behind Joe's car in the driveway, a driveway leading to a single-car detached garage in the back yard. The Leaches have only one car that Kate drives to work at the hospital, while Joe and the two kids walk under a mile to school.

Sam raps at the back door, opens it, and lets Laura go in ahead of him. In his booming voice, he asks, "Anyone home?"

Peggy runs up and gives Sam a big hug. "I haven't seen you since summer. You missed our first basketball game."

"I'll try to make it to one in January. Let's go sit in the living room and get caught up."

Sam's 6′ 5″ frame fills the over-stuffed easy chair, his dark brown hair growing gray around his temples, matching his pointed goatee, making him look like the distinguished professor Peggy pictures him to be. Laura is a foot shorter than Sam, her hair salt and pepper – heavy on the salt. Peggy thinks it is unfair for short women to pick off all the tall guys. Even so, she likes Laura a lot.

"So Peggy, what colleges are you applying to for next year?" Sam asks.

"Well, I've already applied for early decision at Dartmouth – the Thayer School of Engineering, as well as UNH. But I really hope to get into Dartmouth."

Peggy has tried to keep her enthusiasm for Dartmouth in check and not to get her hopes too high. However, the small, intimate campus beckons her; the students she met were engaged; the faculty members she met were truly interested in her future. Peggy has no doubt; her heart is in Hanover.

"Excellent choices," Sam says. "I know some of the faculty in the Thayer School and their Engineering Science program is first rate."

"That's what I liked about it. You get a broad engineering background not focused on only one discipline like electrical or mechanical engineering. The program is also very project-based, and the students have access to computer-controlled milling machines and computer-aided design equipment just as we did in your summer program. In fact, they were very impressed by the projects I did in your program. Their students were doing similar projects in college."

"I got some of my ideas from them. The Thayer School also has an entrepreneurial bent, which I think will serve you well.

"I really hope I get in, but even if I do, I'll need a lot of scholarship help because Dartmouth is very expensive. Dad thinks it's not 'cost effective' and UNH would be a better bargain."

"Well, let's wait to see what happens. I'll bet you get into Dartmouth. They would be stupid not to take you."

About 3:15, a third car pulls into the driveway and everyone is surprised to hear the front door bell ring. Usually, no one uses the front door – neighbors and relatives always use the back door.

"That must be Connie," Kate says. "I'll let her in."

Kate introduces Connie, a striking 5' 7" blond with fair skin, twinkling eyes, and a terrific figure. Matt whispers to his Dad that if he were sick, he would want her to take care of him!

"I think we are almost ready," Kate says. "Joe, can you come and carve the turkey?"

Everyone takes a seat at the table, Joe and Kate at their usual places at each end, Sam and Laura on one side, and Connie squeezed in between Peggy and Matt on the other side. Matt thinks he has died and gone to heaven.

Peggy says, "You know, everyone, these are all my favorite foods – roasted cider brined turkey with Madeira gravy, mom's special stuffing with apples in it, chai-spiced orange-cranberry sauce, green beans with caramelized onions, marshmallow fruit salad, pumpkin bread, and best of all, grandma's sweet potato casserole with orange sauce that has Grand Marnier in it. Connie, wait until you taste the sweet potato casserole."

"I can't wait. Everything looks so good! Thank you for inviting me. I really appreciate it."

"We're really glad you came," Matt says.

"Were there any babies born this morning at the hospital?" Kate asks Connie.

"Yes, Mrs. Rogers had a 7 lb. 2 oz. baby boy around 10:00 this morning."

"Oh, she was in my Lamaze class. In fact, her last class was just on Tuesday night. She must have been early. How did she do?"

"She did great – no anesthetics at all. Came in around 6:00 this morning with contractions about five minutes apart and had the baby about four hours later. I think she was a couple of weeks early, but she and the baby are doing great."

"That's terrific. I will try to stop in to see her tomorrow before they discharge her. I should take her some left-over turkey since she missed

Thanksgiving."

"Connie, what is your schedule at the hospital?" Joe asks.

"I work three 12-hour shifts a week, Thursday, Friday, and Saturday from 3:00 a.m – 3:00 p.m. I am the new hire, so I get the weekend shift. But I don't mind it. I'm off at 3:00 pm on Saturday and then have four days off."

"What time do you get up?" Matt asks.

"About 2:00 a.m. I try to get to bed by 7:00, so I can't stay too long after dinner."

Sam helps himself to another helping of sweet potatoes.

"Tell me, Peggy, what are your favorite classes this term?"

"I'm taking AP physics and pre-calc. I like them both. I'll take calculus next term."

"Don't think this means you don't need to take Calc-1 when you get to college. This is the biggest mistake I see students make – skipping Calc-1 because they think they learned it all in high school. No one learns calculus the first time. Calc-1 in college is a lot different from what you take in high school. You will want to take the time to go as deeply into each topic as you can.

"You know, Peggy is a straight-A student," Joe says.

"All the more reason to make sure you know the fundamentals of a subject. Remember, no one learns calculus the first time. I have been teaching college classes for over 35 years, and I do not learn anything well until I have to teach it. That is what I love about teaching. I am always learning new stuff. I have taught dozens of different courses over the years and developed many new courses from scratch. Those are the most fun."

"And he usually ends up writing a book about them," Laura says.

"That's true," Sam says.

"How many books have you written?" Connie asks.

"Not sure, over two dozen."

"Wow," Matt says.

"I think I'd like to be a college professor," Peggy says, "maybe teach engineering like you do."

"I can certainly recommend it. If you find the right place to teach and can stay away from university politics."

"I tried to tell her that she should become a nurse, like her mother," Joe says. "Healthcare is only going to grow in the future."

"Maybe she should do what she wants to do," Sam says, "what she's passionate about. That's the most important thing."

Peggy is annoyed. "Yes, Dad, I want to invent something, do something big, and I hate the sight of blood."

"You can't go wrong studying engineering," Sam says.

Sam majored in electrical engineering at Rensselaer Polytechnic Institute in Troy, NY and then stayed on at RPI to get a master's degree in mathematics and a Ph.D. in physics. He and Laura met when he was an undergraduate at RPI and she was majoring in art at Skidmore. They got married while Sam was in graduate school and moved into Rensselaerwyck, the married student-housing complex, long since replaced with a new football stadium and athletic fields.

Sam continues, "I've always told my students – and liberal arts faculty – that an engineering undergraduate degree is a more liberal education than a liberal arts degree. That is because it closes the fewest doors. With its strong math and science background and the problem solving skills you acquire, you can really go into any field you want. Classmates of mine who graduated with an engineering degree from RPI, in addition to becoming engineers, went on to become physicists, medical doctors, lawyers, salesmen, stock brokers, clergymen, generals, bankers, congressmen, actors, and many went on to start their own companies. There really isn't anything you couldn't do with that background. The trick is to learn the fundamentals, learn problem solving skills, and learn to know when someone is trying to pull the wool over your eyes."

"I know," Peggy says. "I sometimes think that some of my teachers don't know what they are talking about."

"It's not only your teachers," Sam says. "I gave a talk a couple of years ago in which I introduced *Woodbury's Law.*"

"What's Woodbury's Law?" Matt asks.

"Well, it's something that I think I always suspected to be true, but decided that it was time to elevate it to a universal truth. Woodbury's Law is *Conventional wisdom is wrong most of the time.*"

"That's wild," Peggy says. "Do you think it's really so?"

"There are lots of examples," Sam says. "For example, in horse racing the favorite wins only a third of the time. So the conventional wisdom of which horse will win is wrong two-thirds of the time. This means that you can't make any money always betting on the favorite."

"You wrote a computer program some years ago," Joe says, "that produced a horse racing tip sheet that we used to take to the Rockingham track."

"I did. We used to have a lot of fun with it."

"Did you really bet on horses, Dad?" Matt asks.

"Well, not that much. But your Uncle Sam's tip sheet gave us an edge, and we did have fun."

"How did you come to write the horse racing program?" Peggy asks.

"Well there was this guy at the university, who was a big horse player at Rockingham Park, and he knew I had developed a pattern recognition program that I was using to predict the stock market. He asked me if it could help him win more at the track. I told him we would need past performance records of the horses that were running. We found a company in Lexington, KY, which daily produced computerized performance data for all horses that ran that day in every track in North America. This was in the days before the Internet and before Windows, so my home PC was running the DOS operating system."

"No internet!" Matt says. "I can't believe it."

"So I wrote this program that would automatically dial the phone, upload the data into my computer through the phone line, run my pattern recognition program, and print out a tip sheet for any track in North America. We mostly used it for Rockingham Park."

"Did it work?" Matt asks.

"I think it was the best tip sheet at the track."

"You told me about the Kentucky Derby race in 1992," Joe says. "Do you remember?"

"How could I forget? The 10th race was a simulcast of the Kentucky Derby, where the odds-on favorite was going off at 1-3, a French horse called Arazi, who was number six on my tip sheet. I thought Arazi had no chance of winning. My number one horse was Lil E. Tee, a long shot at 17-1, definitely worth my $20 bet."

"Who won the race?" Matt asks.

"We were all gathered around the TV monitor, yelling as the horses came down the home stretch, not knowing who was in the lead, until the TV monitor flashed the winner – Lil E. Tee, who paid $35.60 on a $2.00 bet, making my winnings for this race $356."

"So how did Arazi do?" Peggy asks.

"Arazi came in 8th – way out of the money, just as I expected."

"Did you always win money at the races?" Matt asks.

"Oh no, some days we would win, some days we would lose. We probably broke even over the long run, but we had a lot of fun. But they no longer run live races at Rockingham Park."

"That's a good thing," Laura says. "I think you were getting a little too addicted to the track."

"What programming language did you use to write your horse racing program?" Peggy asks.

"I actually wrote the program in Forth, a little known programming language developed in the late 1960s, which was easy to implement on early microprocessors. As a result, it was not uncommon for Forth to be the first high-level language to show up on new microprocessors – months before others got around to writing C compilers, for example."

"How come I've never heard of Forth?" Peggy asks.

"Because the conventional wisdom of the main-stream computer science community thought it was a lousy language, because it didn't follow their rules. For example, it gave the programmer complete control over the hardware and memory stack of the computer. This is a no-no with the computer science elites because they don't trust the programmer not to crash the system all the time. But this is just what the Forth types like. They want to have control of everything so they can do whatever they want with no constraints. It is like having a chain saw to cut down a tree. It cuts down the tree quickly and it's up to you not to cut into your leg."

"Does Forth code look like the code of other programming languages?"

"Not at all! Some call it a write-only language that is hard to read. But you can get used to it. "

"Is it hard to debug?"

"It's actually very easy to debug because you can test each word when you define it. It is the ultimate in bottom-up programming – exactly the opposite of how programming should be done according to conventional wisdom."

"You're such a rebel, Uncle Sam," Peggy says.

"That's the whole secret," Sam says. "Remember the last verse of Robert Frost's poem, *The Road Not Taken*:

> "I shall be telling this with a sigh
> Somewhere ages and ages hence:
> Two roads diverged in a wood, and I,
> I took the one less traveled by,
> And that has made all the difference."

"There's plenty more turkey," Kate says. "Anyone want another helping?"

"Oh, I'm stuffed," Peggy says. "I've got to save room for pumpkin pie."

Matt's interest perks up. "Uncle Sam, what are some more examples of Woodbury's Law?"

"Well, there are lots of examples from physics. James Clerk Maxwell, who was born in Scotland, discovered the laws of electrodynamics in the 1860s when he was a professor of natural philosophy at King's College in London. These laws predict that electric and magnetic fields produce waves and that light is an electromagnetic wave. Most scientists of the day did not believe it. No one knew how to generate such waves or how to detect them. It wasn't until around 1887, after Maxwell had died, that Heinrich Hertz, working in Germany, first generated and detected electromagnetic waves."

"Are these what radio waves are?" Matt asks.

"Yes, but not only radio waves. Microwaves, infrared, visible light waves, ultraviolet light, X-rays, and even gamma rays are all electromagnetic waves. They only differ in their frequency. Now getting back to Woodbury's Law, in the late 1800s, when people started generating electromagnetic waves, they believed that the waves must propagate through some invisible ether that permeated the entire universe. But in 1905, Einstein wrote a paper in which he asserted that there was no ether and that absolute uniform motion couldn't be detected by any means."

"Is that his theory of relativity?" Peggy asks.

"Yes, his special theory of relativity."

"We talked about that in our physics class," Peggy says, "and it doesn't make any sense to me."

"That's because you really didn't study it carefully. Most people found the theory hard to believe when Einstein first proposed it. But it has been shown to be consistent with subsequent experiments."

"I still don't understand how it makes any sense."

"Well next term I'm teaching my graduate class in electromagnetic theory, and at the beginning of the course I go through special relativity very carefully using an easy to understand graphical method that even a smart high school senior could understand. It only takes a couple of lectures and the class is taught in the evening, so if you want to attend those classes, you can, and become an expert on special relativity."

"Maybe I will. I find it very intriguing. Why do you teach special relativity in an electromagnetic theory course?"

"It turns out that from special relativity and Coulomb's law of the force between two charged particles, you can derive all four of Maxwell's equations, which are the basis of all of electrodynamics. This derivation clarifies the intimate relationship between electric fields and magnetic fields – a relationship that even many electrical engineering professors don't seem to understand."

"Another example of Woodbury's Law," Peggy says. "Isn't there another theory of relativity?"

"Yes, in 1916, Einstein published his general theory of relativity, which is really a theory about gravity."

"Our physics teacher also told us about quantum mechanics."

"Now that's another story altogether for another day."

"How many different theories are there?" Matt asks.

"Well, the Holy Grail in physics is to try to combine all physical theories into a single Theory of Everything, but so far that hasn't happened."

"Bill and I are going to see the movie, *The Theory of Everything*, tomorrow night," Peggy says.

"Who is Bill?" Sam asks.

"Bill is Peggy's boyfriend," Matt says.

"Do I know him?" Sam asks.

"Yes," Peggy says, "he's Bill Parker. He's in my class and we worked together in your summer program for high school students last summer."

"Oh, I remember Bill. Nice guy. A real computer hotshot programmer. You will like the movie. I saw it last week."

"What's it about?" Matt asks.

"It's the story of Stephen Hawking, a famous theoretical physicist at Cambridge in England, who has struggled with Lou Gehrig's disease since he was a student at Cambridge. His goal since that time was to discover a Theory of Everything. I won't give away any more of the movie, but let me know what you think after you've seen it."

"I will," Peggy says.

"Ok, it looks as if everyone is ready for Peggy's pumpkin pie," Kate says. "Peggy baked the pumpkin pies this morning using grandma's special recipe."

"Unlike brownies," Peggy says, "all the pieces are the same, so Uncle Sam won't have to worry about getting the center piece."

"Remember how you faked him out with the brownies at the lake?" Laura asks Peggy.

"What happened?" Connie asks.

Peggy starts to laugh. "When we bake a pan of brownies, Uncle Sam always has to have the center piece. So one day last summer, Uncle Sam is sitting on the porch up at the lake and I bring him a plate of brownies with only the four corner pieces."

Peggy is now laughing so hard she cannot continue.

Laura picks up the story. "Peggy had taken out the center piece, left it in the kitchen, and had one of the side pieces in her hand when she brought the plate of brownies to Sam. She told him that there were only corner pieces left and that she has the center piece as she bites into it. Sam goes ballistic and tries to grab the piece out of her mouth. Everyone is roaring with laughter. Finally, we tell him that his precious center piece is in the kitchen. It was really funny."

"I don't think it was all that funny," Sam says with a smile.

"Professor Woodbury," Connie says.

"Please call me Sam."

"Ok. What was your summer program that Peggy was talking about?"

"It's a two-week intensive summer program that I have been running for the past decade for high school students who have just completed their freshman, sophomore, or junior years. Its purpose is to get them interested in science, math, and engineering as possible career paths."

"How many students are in the program?" Connie asks.

"There are a total of 45 in the program, divided into five groups of nine students, each group containing four freshman, three sophomores, and two juniors."

"Students go for three years," Peggy says, "so the sophomores were freshman the year before, and the juniors were there the two previous summers. There is some attrition each year."

"Sam, how do you select the freshman?" Connie asks.

"They have to be recommended by their teachers, and we accept those who we judge to be the top twenty applicants. There is no cost to the students. We raise money from local industry to fund the program. Each group has to complete a competitive project by the end of the second week."

"What kind of projects?" Connie asks.

"They all use samiPhones, spelled s-a-m-i," Peggy says as she pulls out her smart phone.

"What's a samiPhone?" Connie asks.

"It is this smart phone," Peggy says. "It looks like a regular smart phone, but it is a lot more. Uncle Sam gets the phone companies to donate old used phones. He then tears them apart and installs his own computer chip that he designed. It keeps all the old functions of the phone, including the camera, but adds a programming feature so the student can write new programs to make the phone do almost anything, like control robots."

"I assume Sami is you, Sam," Connie says. "Were you called Sami when you were young?"

"Well, when I was a little boy, my family and relatives called me Sammy, with a *y*, but when I started school, I switched to Sam, and my classmates and teachers always called me Sam. However, some of my relatives always called me Sammy. So when I developed my modified smart phone, I guess I got a little nostalgic, and started calling it a samiPhone, where I used a shortened version of Sammy."

"Where did you grow up?" Connie asks.

"I grew up in Moultonborough, NH and went to high school there where I was on the basketball team. In fact, I was the center. At 6′ 5″, I was the tallest boy on the team. My father ran a poultry farm on Long Island. A bridge connects Long Island to Moultonborough Neck so it is really part of the mainland. The old farmhouse sits on a hill and our land goes down to the water where we look south and west across the broads of Lake Winnipesaukee. My grandfather originally bought the land long before it became so super-expensive as it is today. My father built a lake house by the water's edge, a four-bedroom traditional lake house with wrap-around porch with part of the front porch screened-in. I still own the property and have always spent summers there."

"That sounds fantastic," Connie says. "Getting back to your samiPhones, what kind of projects do the students do?"

"Well, three years ago when Peggy and Bill were in their first year of the program, the project was to build a bowling robot that they could control wirelessly from their smart phone. The competition was to have the robot roll a small bowling ball across the gym floor and knock down the ten pins. The regular rules of bowling apply. Each group bowls an entire game, letting each player in the group bowl at least one frame. The highest score wins the competition and each student in the winning group gets $100."

"Does second place win anything?" Matt asks.

"Nope, it is winner takes all. No 'everyone is a winner' in my projects!"

"Getting them ready for the real world," Joe says.

"Where do they get the robots?" Connie asks.

"They make them," Sam says. "During the first week, the freshmen learn how to use a computer-controlled milling machine for making metal parts and a fused deposition modeling machine for making plastic prototype parts. The sophomore and junior students help them design a robot that will do the job. Meanwhile, the sophomores write the computer code that will control the robot from the samiPhone. The juniors help them with this. The two juniors in each group serve as co-project managers and are responsible for the overall design of the project"

"What computer language do they use to program the samiPhone?" Connie asks.

"It's a language I invented just for this purpose. I call the language *Samuel.*"

"Not too subtle," Laura says.

"It has some similarity to Forth in that the students program bottom-up, designing small tasks that can be tested separately, and then stringing multiple tasks together to produce the entire program. It is a very simple language that the students pick up right away. At the end of the two-week session, each student gets to keep their samiPhone and they can program it throughout the year to do all kinds of things – play games, communicate with their friends, control almost anything. When students return as sophomores or juniors, we begin by having each student demonstrate the coolest program he or she has written since the previous summer. The students in each class vote for the best program – they can't vote for themselves – and the student with the winning program gets a second samiPhone."

"Do you remember that Bill won last summer?" Peggy asks.

"How could I forget," Sam says.

"What happened?" Joe asks.

"Well, at the first meeting of the entire group, Bill came to me and asked if he could introduce all of the returning sophomores and juniors to the new freshmen. I said, of course. So each returning student walks to the front of the room in turn and stands next to Bill. Bill tells everyone the student's name, what high school he or she goes to, the project they worked on last year, what sports, if any, they play and what hobbies they like. Bill has no notes and appears to have remembered all of the returning students and their backgrounds. It was a virtuoso performance."

"You say 'appears to'," Joe says. "Was it a trick?"

"Well, Bill had his samiPhone hanging on a lanyard around his neck with the camera lens facing the audience. Over the winter Bill had written a facial recognition program for the samiPhone, and when each student walked toward him Bill would say 'Hello', which caused the samiPhone to capture a video frame, locate the face, recognize the person, and tell Bill, through a small wireless earpiece, all the information about the person. He fooled everyone, including me."

"He sounds like a very talented person," Connie says.

"He is," Peggy says.

Peggy thinks she is attracted to Bill because he shares many traits with Uncle Sam: smart, funny, self-deprecating, a certain restrained ambition, interested in science, technology, and her. Her favorite childhood memories are from those two weeks every summer, which her family would spend at Uncle Sam's farm on Lake Winnipesaukee, where Uncle Sam would always teach her new things. She was always told that a daughter looks for someone like her father; but while Peggy loves her dad, he is totally different from Uncle Sam, and she is definitely looking for an Uncle Sam.

"Peggy, what was your project last summer when you were a junior?" Connie asks.

"Bill and I were in the same group, so we were the co-project managers."

"Is that when the romance began?" Matt asks.

"Matt, I've known Bill since we were in kindergarten. The homecoming dance in October was our first real date."

"So what was the project?" Connie asks again.

"It was a kind of robot scavenger hunt. Five unknown objects were 'hidden' around the campus. We were given the GPS coordinates of each object. The robot had to find all five objects on its own using its built-in GPS device, and take a picture of each object. You could find them in any order, but the goal was to do it in the fastest time, so you tried to find the shortest path to get to all objects."

"Did you win?" Connie asks.

"Actually, we did. So Bill and I each won $100. This was at the end of August and that's when Bill said why not use our winnings to go to the homecoming dance together."

"How romantic," Matt says. "Did he kiss you?"

"No, Matt, I kissed him!"

"Sounds like another example of Woodbury's Law to me," Sam says.

"Why don't you all move into the living room while I clear the table and put the food away," Kate says. "I'll be right in and we'll worry about doing the dishes later."

Joe starts a fire in the fireplace while everyone finds a comfortable place to sit.

"So Peggy tells me she wants to go to Dartmouth," Sam says.

Joe says, "I told Peggy that there is nothing wrong with the engineering program at UNH. After all, Kate and I went there, you teach there, and it would be a lot less expensive."

"That's true," Sam says, "but the Dartmouth experience would be unique and I think Peggy could benefit greatly from it."

"Yes," Peggy says, "I just have this funny feeling that I belong there, that I'll get the most out of it, and that it will change my life."

"Sometimes we can't get everything we want," Joe says. "Sometimes we can only get what we can afford."

"Where there's a will, there's a way," Sam says.

"I agree," Peggy says.

"Let's just hope they come through with a good scholarship," Joe says.

Peggy can't believe that her father just doesn't get it; how important Dartmouth is to her; how her heart is set on it; how, sometimes, money just cannot be the deciding factor.

Kate comes in from the kitchen and pulls up a chair next to the fireplace. "Have I missed any more Woodbury's Laws?"

"I think a very important example," Sam says, "is how teaching is done at both the high school and college levels. For decades, students sit and listen to someone stand up in front of them and lecture. Half the students can't keep up and get lost, and the rest of the students are bored and start to daydream. Only the teacher is keeping up and enjoying it. Now I have been as guilty of this as anyone over the years, but at least my lectures, in my opinion, are more interesting and exciting than most. But I can see that sometimes students get bored, and that is the biggest sin of all – being a boring professor. So students are not learning as well as they should, and the conventional way of imparting knowledge through lectures is clearly wrong."

"So how *should* classes be run?" Kate asks.

"Things should be flipped. Instead of giving a lecture and then assigning homework problems on that material to do at home, the students should first view several short 5 – 10 minute video clips of the material before they come to class, which they can stop and rerun as much as necessary in order to understand it. Then the class time can be used for doing the homework and discussing the material. Students are then actively engaged during class time and can't fall asleep."

"Do you teach this way?" Peggy asks.

"I do in my digital design class. I wrote the book for that class and have recorded over 100 video clips of the material, which are posted on YouTube. The students are assigned particular clips to view before coming to each class, and then we do problems in class and I design particular circuits on the computer right in front of them."

"How can you design circuits on a computer?" Matt asks.

"Today digital circuits are implemented in large integrated circuits. One type is called an FPGA, or Field Programmable Gate Array. This chip, containing millions of transistors, is configured to be reprogrammable. To design a circuit, you write a computer program in a hardware description language – we use VHDL in my course – and when you compile the program it configures the FPGA to be your particular digital circuit. You can even design a complete computer to fit on a single chip."

"Have you done that?" Peggy asks.

"Not only have I done it, but in my computer hardware design class, I have the students design a complete single-chip computer, called a Forth engine, which will execute Forth words in a single clock cycle. Then, the students write a computer program in high-level Forth, like I did for the horseracing program, compile the program using a compiler I wrote, download the program, and execute it on the computer that they had just designed from scratch."

"That sounds really cool," Peggy says.

"It is, and the students learn a lot by doing everything for themselves."

"But the current lecture method of teaching is so entrenched, how do you think it can ever be turned around?"

"Well, it will be difficult. Learning is hard and good teaching is more difficult than it looks. Students pay tens of thousands of dollars a year to go to college, and I tell my students that everything they are going to learn is in the books in the library. All they have to do is go read them. It would be free. The question is, what books to read, and in what order. And the dirty little secret is that most textbooks are hard to read and not very good. And they are way too expensive."

"I've got an idea," Peggy says. "If all the books in the library could fit in a single chip, as I have read they can, why not put all the books needed for your entire 4-year college curriculum on a single chip that would fit in something like your iPad that you could read?"

"You know, I think you may be on to something," Sam says. "I never really liked reading electronic books on something like a Kindle, because you can't skip around quickly. However, there are some online books that I've seen in which words are hyperlinked, which makes it easy to jump back and forth to exactly what you want to know at a particular time. Dynamic books like this with embedded video clips are, I think, the future. But it is all a matter of content. You have to get the content right for them to be of any use. When I was in college, I took notes in a small notebook during class, and then I would go back to my room and recopy all of the notes very carefully in a large loose-leaf notebook, making sure that I understood every step in a derivation."

"And he still has all of those college notes in our basement," Laura says.

"When I go to college," Peggy says, "I'm going to make my own electronic hyperlinked version of my class notes and homework problems for each class to help me learn the material."

"That is a terrific idea," Sam says. "We need to talk about this more, perhaps at Christmas time. Laura and I are planning to spend Christmas at the farm on the lake and stay through New Year's Day. Our son, Dave, and his wife Eileen will be there as well as their son, Wayne. You're all invited."

"I haven't seen Wayne since he got his Ph.D. at MIT two years ago," Peggy says. "What's he doing now?"

"He's living in Dover and started his own company in Rochester to develop and market his smart electronic pen that he invented when he was in graduate school. It looks just like a regular ballpoint pen and writes on paper in exactly the same way. But inside are microcircuits that measure the exact movement of the pen and wirelessly send data to a computer. Artificial intelligence software is used to recognize your signature and I think that may be his first big application. He calls it a U-Pen and it is quite an impressive device. He'll have to tell you all about it."

"Wayne's a real athlete," Peggy says. "He's 6 feet 4 inches tall and almost made the Olympic ski team. Christmas at the lake sounds great. Let's make it a skiing vacation and we can all go skiing at Gunstock between Christmas and New Year's."

"Sounds great to me," Joe says, "let's do it."

"Do you ski, Connie?" Peggy asks.

"I love to ski."

"Then you'll have to come too, at least for some of the time."

"That would be a lot of fun. You all are so nice."

"And you could ski with Wayne," Matt says.

Connie blushes and Peggy rolls her eyes.

"There will be plenty of room for everyone," Sam says. "The big farmhouse on the hill has five bedrooms and the lake house on the water with its four bedrooms will also be open."

"Then it's settled," Joe says. "Christmas and New Year's Eve at the lake this year."

Peggy wishes that Bill could have been here for what, otherwise, was her best Thanksgiving ever. She can't wait to tell him all about it tomorrow.

2

"Sorry I can't stay and do the dishes tonight," Peggy says, getting up from the supper table, "but Bill will be here any minute to pick me up for the movies."

"What movie are you seeing?" her mother asks.

"We are going to see *The Theory of Everything* at the Cinemagic on Lafayette."

"What time will you be home?"

"We are going out for ice cream afterward. I will be home by midnight. I think I hear Bill coming."

Peggy grabs her jacket, opens the back door and lets Bill in. Bill is just six feet tall, Peggy's unofficial minimum for a boyfriend. His blond wavy hair is a natural for his athletic build. Unlike Peggy, Bill doesn't enjoy competitive team sports, preferring to ski in the winter and play golf with his dad at the Portsmouth Country Club.

"Hi, Mr. Leach," Bill says. "Peggy tells me you're writing a book on the history of Portsmouth. How's it coming?"

"I am. I have it about half done. It is a series of stories about real people who were important to the settling and growth of Portsmouth. Hopefully, it will get students interested in history."

"I can't wait to read it."

Peggy grabs Bill's arm. "We've got to run. See you later, Mom."

"Have fun."

Peggy closes the back door behind them.

"That Bill is a very nice young man," Joe says.

Peggy jumps into Bill's 12-year old Ford Taurus, a car Bill bought last summer with money he earned teaching older people in their homes how to use various computer applications. They talk about their fears of not getting into the colleges of their choice, Peggy into Dartmouth and Bill into RPI.

"You missed a great conversation yesterday with Uncle Sam. I'll tell you all about it after the movie."

"I can't wait."

As they walk out of the theater, Peggy asks, "How did you like the movie?"

"I thought it was good. It is hard to believe that someone with such a debilitating disability could accomplish so much."

"It sure is. We were going to go out for ice cream, but are you really hungry?"

"Not really."

"I've got so much more I want to talk to you about and it's pretty warm and a really clear night, why don't we drive down to Prescott Park where we won't be disturbed?"

"Sounds great to me."

As they head toward Prescott Park, Peggy tells Bill about Woodbury's Law and about Uncle Sam's horseracing program. She tells him about how physicists have repeatedly been shown to be wrong throughout history, with new theories replacing old theories.

Walking from the entrance of Prescott Park toward the waterfront, hand in hand, Peggy realizes how much her feelings for Bill have changed, from the little boy in kindergarten who beat her at marbles, to someone who listens to her, someone who understands her, someone who shares her desire to make a difference, to do something big, someone who instills in her a feeling of hope, a feeling of adventure, a feeling of excitement, a feeling of affection, a feeling she likes. They pick out a park bench near the water, their arms wrapped around each other, watching a big harvest moon.

"I love looking out over the water at night," Peggy says.

"Me too."

"Look at those stars. Do you think the universe is expanding like the movie said? It doesn't make any sense. "

"That's what all the scientists say."

"I know, but remember Woodbury's Law, they're wrong most of the time. I think none of it makes sense. In the movie, Stephen Hawking calculated the rate of expansion and then ran the clock backward to predict that the universe started with a big bang almost 14 billion years ago. It doesn't make any sense. How can a single point just go bang and start exploding to make the entire universe? Did God just snap his finger and say 'Go!'? What was God doing just before he snapped his finger?"

"I don't know. It is sort of weird."

"If the universe has been expanding for billions of years, and at an ever increasing rate, why can we still see stars? Wouldn't they all have disappeared by now and the sky would just be black?"

"I suppose."

"Just look at the stars," Peggy says. "Do you think people live on other planets in the universe?"

"Probably. You wouldn't think it would make sense that we were the only living creatures in the universe. Why would someone make the entire universe just for us?"

"But do you think they would be like us, or something else like ET?"

"They're probably quite different. Remember we had big dinosaurs here long before any humans."

"Maybe dinosaur-like creatures on another planet got smart enough to think like us, and maybe they came up with their own physics equations to describe their world and the universe. What is the chance that their equations would look anything like our physics equations?"

"Not very likely, I would guess. Heck, their entire mathematics might be different."

"It makes you wonder if anything is really real," Peggy says laying her head on Bill's shoulder.

"You're real," Bill says, pulling her close.

Peggy sits up straight. "Oh, I didn't tell you that Uncle Sam is having everyone up to his farm on Lake Winnipesaukee for Christmas and New Year's Eve. We are going skiing at Gunstock during that week. Can you come skiing for some of the days and stay for New Year's Eve? Uncle Sam says there is plenty of room as both the farmhouse and the lake house will be open."

"I'd love to. Let me check with my folks and see what plans they have for Christmas."

"You've really got to come. You're needed at the lake and on the slopes!"

"I'll try. I really do want to come."

Peggy goes on to tell Bill about the discussion they had yesterday about teaching methods and the idea she has for making some kind of multimedia electronic hyperlinked book for her class notes in college. She tells him that that is going to be a big discussion topic over Christmas at the lake. They talk about college and how she really wants to get into Dartmouth. Bill tells her that he wants to study Computer Science at RPI, and has applied for early decision.

"You're really good at programming in Java," Peggy says.

"You're not bad yourself."

"With a lot of help from you."

They talk a lot about their high school years and then Peggy recalls a sad time earlier this year. "I still can't believe that Donnie Marshall died of leukemia last summer."

"Me neither. He was the only student in our class who has died. He was such a good friend, a member of the computer club – really a good computer programmer. I just don't understand why he died."

"I know, it is so sad. His sister, Lucy, is on our basketball team, and I feel so bad for her. I sometimes don't know what to say to her. I can't imagine what it would be like to lose a brother."

"I know what you mean. Everyone was crying at his funeral."

"I hated seeing him in the open casket. He is the first dead person I have seen in an open casket."

"I saw my grandmother two years ago, but I hate it too. Why do you suppose that they open some caskets?"

"I don't know. Maybe it is closure for some people, but I think it is ghoulish."

"Me too."

"Do you think I could ever discover a Theory of Everything?"

"I think you can do anything you put your mind to. Maybe if you discovered a Theory of Everything, it would explain what causes leukemia and would lead to a cure so people like Donnie wouldn't die."

"Do you think Donnie went to heaven?"

"I don't know. I don't know what heaven is."

"Do you think a Theory of Everything would explain what happens when we die?"

"It wouldn't be a Theory of Everything if it didn't."

Peggy thinks about this. "Do you think a Theory of Everything would explain consciousness, emotions, and feelings?"

"I'm not sure it could explain how I feel about you?"

"How is that?" Peggy asks.

"I just feel like I always want to be with you." Bill squeezes her hand.

"Well my Theory of Everything will have to explain how we feel about each other.

"That would be some Theory of Everything."

"Do you think it would also explain God?"

"I would say, by definition, it couldn't."

"Well maybe it will be a Theory of Almost Everything."

Peggy looks directly at Bill. "I really want to make a difference – do something big. Don't you?"

"I guess."

"And I really feel that going to Dartmouth will help me to accomplish something big and important. But I'm afraid my family is just not going to be able to afford all four years. Even if I get in with some scholarship help, we probably have enough money for only one or two years. You're lucky your dad owns a real estate agency and can probably afford to send you to RPI."

"He has saved a lot for my college education, but I have also worked and saved quite a bit. You know, having computer skills makes it easier to earn money. You are pretty good with computers. Maybe we should think up a good computer app that we could sell. If it really took off, it might help with your college expenses."

"Do you really think we could do something like that?"

"The hard part is coming up with a great idea that nobody else has done."

"I don't know how we could ever do that."

"We just need to keep thinking and keep our eyes open."

"Or closed," Peggy leans her head on Bill's shoulder.

"You know, Peggy, I could talk with you forever."

"Me too, but it is almost 11:30 and I have to get home."

Bill turns into Peggy's driveway at about quarter to twelve, pulls the car up to the back door, and turns off the ignition. "I really had a lot of fun tonight," Bill says.

"Me too."

"I have a question. Is your real name Margaret, or is it really Peggy? My mom says that Peggy is a nickname for Margaret."

"It is really just Peggy. I am named after my great-great grandmother, whose name was really Margaret, but she went by Peggy. My parents didn't like Margaret but they did like Peggy and they knew it was not that popular a name anymore, so I would probably be the only Peggy in my class, and that has turned out to be the case. They said they wanted me to be recognized by only my first name, like Madonna! The name Margaret comes from the Greek and means pearl and when I was small, my parents always called me their pearl."

"I'm going to call you my pearl," Bill says. "You know, I thought of another good example of Woodbury's Law."

"What's the conventional wisdom?" Peggy asks.

"People who have known each other since kindergarten never end up marrying each other."

Peggy stares at him for several long seconds.

"You've got to be kidding."

"Peggy, some day I'm going to marry you."

Peggy smiles, gives Bill a quick kiss, jumps out of the car, and runs into the house.

3

Peggy has five more days of school before the Christmas break. Every day for the past week, she has hurried home to see if a letter from Dartmouth has arrived. Today she opens the mailbox and removes several letters. The top letter is from the admissions office at Dartmouth College. She runs into the house. It is finally here. No one else is home. She sits on the sofa for a few moments, wondering if she should wait for her parents to get home, but the suspense is too much. Slowly, she starts to tear the envelope open, inch by inch, moving her finger along the flap until the final edge of the envelope pops open. She carefully removes the letter, her heart racing, and a thousand butterflies churning in her stomach as she slowly unfolds the letter. She looks down and begins to read.

"Dear Miss Leach, We regret to inform you that your application for admission to Dartmouth College is denied."

Her heart sinks and tears cloud her vision as she continues to read about how the freshman acceptance rate at Dartmouth is ten percent, and that many very qualified applicants must, of necessity, be denied.

Peggy feels a queasy knot in her stomach. Although she had tried not to get her hopes too high, she has pictured herself as a freshman on the Dartmouth campus, on her way to discover a Theory of Everything. Now it is not going to happen. She sits there in a daze, tears running down her cheeks, sobbing, trying to imagine what is going to happen to her life's dreams. *Is this just someone telling me my life is not so perfect after all, or is it just a little bump in the road? What if I don't get into UNH either? Then, what will I do? Do I even want to go there? It was expected that I apply to UNH, and I didn't want to hurt Uncle Sam's feelings by not applying, but I thought of it as my safety net. Now I feel like all the doors to my future are being slammed in my face. I thought it would be my choice as to which college to attend. Oh, snap out of it, Peggy. I hate being here all alone feeling like my life has hit a wall. I wish Mom and Dad would get home soon. I could sure use their hug and support now.*

Peggy hears a car door close and her mother talking to her father. *Mom must have picked up Dad as he was walking home from school.* When the back door opens, Peggy is already in the kitchen with tears running down her cheeks. "I didn't get into Dartmouth."

"Oh, no." Kate wraps her arms around Peggy and holds her tight.

Joe takes the letter from Peggy's hand and reads it. "I know you really wanted to go to Dartmouth, but now we'll have to go to Plan B."

"I don't even know what Plan B is," Peggy sobs. "I won't hear from UNH until the end of January. Do you think I should apply somewhere else?"

"Why don't you call Uncle Sam," Kate says, "and see what he thinks."

"Ok."

Peggy calls Uncle Sam and tells him the bad news. He suggests that he and Laura stop by to chat, saying he will pick up a couple of pizzas on the way.

Just then Matt walks into the house and senses the dark mood. "What happened?"

His mom looks up. "Peggy didn't get into Dartmouth."

Matt thinks, *Well I guess perfect Peggy is not so perfect after all.* "So does that mean you're going to UNH?"

"I guess."

"Well, at least you won't be that far away."

"Uncle Sam and Aunt Laura are on their way over," Kate says, "and they're bringing pizzas. Why don't you get washed up and set the table?"

"Ok," Matt says. "Sorry about Dartmouth, Peggy."

Joe opens the back door to let in Sam and Laura.

"Get a piece of pizza while it's hot," Sam says.

Peggy shows Sam the letter from Dartmouth.

"I didn't realize that their acceptance rate was so low," Sam says.

"Do you think I should apply somewhere else?"

"With your high school record, you will certainly be accepted at UNH. In fact, I would think your chances of receiving some type of merit scholarship are very good. Moreover, if you go into one of the engineering or science programs, you will certainly get a solid education. UNH is much larger; probably more than three times the number of students. Nevertheless, I would think that the campus life at both places is very good. So unless you want to go to a much smaller school – I certainly wouldn't go to a much larger one – then I don't see any real reason to apply somewhere else."

"That's what I thought."

"Dartmouth doesn't take many transfer students, but they do take some. So you can always apply to transfer after your freshman or sophomore year and see what happens. So all paths to Dartmouth haven't been cut off yet."

"I hadn't thought of that."

"Remember," Sam says, "it's much less important where you go to college than most people think. What you get out of college depends entirely on what you put into it. You can get a lousy education at a top-notch university, or an exceptional education at an average one. And UNH is above average, or I would not have been here so long. It is all up to you."

"Thanks, Uncle Sam. I feel better already, and am beginning to get excited about going to UNH."

Peggy lies in bed thinking about this awful day, her past, and what lies ahead for her. *My life has been perfect: a loving and supportive family, the top of my class at school, one of the top players on my basketball team, winning the project competition in Uncle Sam's summer program. Why isn't that enough to get into Dartmouth? What will my friends say when they learn that I was rejected by Dartmouth? I wanted two letters of acceptance and be able to choose myself. Now I have to wait to hear from UNH.* Peggy presses her face into her pillow and cries.

4

Sam's son, Dave Woodbury, and his wife, Eileen, are on their way to the lake to spend Christmas at the farm for the first time since he was a kid. Plows have cleared the roads following six inches of new snow overnight. Dave's ski hat covers his nearly bald head. Eileen makes up for Dave's deficit with her long, straight, dark auburn hair. When Eileen wears her hair up, her height becomes the same as Dave's six feet.

Dave is an architect who, like his dad, went to RPI. He worked for about ten years in an architectural firm in Boston, before deciding to go out on his own, specializing in designing unique, luxury waterfront homes, particularly on the ocean. Dave and Eileen live comfortably in their Rye, NH oceanfront home, the third such oceanfront home they have lived in, all obtained by buying an old worn-out home, tearing it down, designing a new luxury home, living in it for a few years, and then selling it for a ridiculous profit.

Eileen is a potter, making gorgeous pieces, mostly as a hobby to give away as gifts. She has been in some craft shows, including the NH Craftsmen's Fair at Mt. Sunapee and the Meredith craft show in August. You often find her pieces displayed in some of the League of NH Craftsmen Fine Craft Galleries throughout the state.

They stop in Dover and pick up their son, Wayne, whose maintenance-free, wavy black hair is cut short. Wayne sits in the front seat with Dave to get more legroom for his 6′ 4″ body and size 13 shoes. Sam always said, "Just think how tall he would be if he didn't have so much turned up for feet."

In Meredith, they pick up groceries for the next few days before heading down Moultonborough Neck and crossing the bridge to Long Island.

"We're almost there," Dave says.

"The ice on the lake seems to be pretty much in now," Wayne says. "A little early this year."

"Maybe enough for some skating and ice fishing, but I wouldn't drive a car on it yet."

Wayne remembers watching jalopy races on the ice when he was a kid, and even today, airplanes land on the Alton Bay ice airport.

When they arrive at the big white farmhouse with green shutters, Sam and Laura are already there and have turned on the water and gotten the downstairs rooms cleaned up. Sam has taken the tractor out of the barn and plowed the driveway all the way down to the lake house on the shore. He is now starting a fire in the large stone fireplace in the living room.

"Welcome to Christmas on the lake," Sam says.

"This is going to be really special," Dave says. "I think the last time we had Christmas here I was in college."

"It will be my first time," Wayne says.

"Sam and I are sleeping in our usual downstairs bedroom," Laura says. "Dave, you and Eileen can have the blue room upstairs with the king-size bed, and Wayne, you can have the green room upstairs. It has a queen-size bed."

Eileen makes soup and sandwiches for everyone and then the three men go out to cut down a Christmas tree. About ten years ago, the three of them planted a dozen balsam firs on the hillside above the farmhouse.

"Look at these Christmas trees," Wayne says. "Can you believe how much they have grown?"

"This 7-foot one is nice and full," Sam says. "It should look good in the living room."

Dave takes the chain saw he brought from the barn and makes quick work of cutting down the tree. They drag it through the snow down to the house, bring it into the living room, and stand it in the corner across the room from the fireplace.

"I found the old ornaments in the attic," Laura says, "and we brought new lights with us as we figured the old ones here weren't likely to work anymore."

They all pitch in and have the tree trimmed in no time.

"Who's all coming?" Wayne asks.

"Your Uncle Joe and Aunt Kate are coming tomorrow," Laura says, "along with your cousins Peggy and Matt. Then on the day after Christmas, Peggy and her dad are driving back to Portsmouth to pick up Peggy's boyfriend, Bill Parker, and Connie Baker, a young nurse who works with Aunt Kate. They had her over for Thanksgiving dinner and everyone enjoyed her and she loves to ski, so we invited her to join us for our ski outing. Her parents live in Texas and she had to work on Thanksgiving. She normally works 12-hour shifts Thursdays through Saturday, but she switched this week to work on Christmas Eve and Christmas day, which will give her a whole week off when she comes here on Wednesday."

"She's single and about your age, Wayne," Sam says, "and a real looker. You never know what Christmas at the lake can lead to."

"To be determined," Wayne says.

The next day, Wayne is in the back yard at the woodpile getting some wood for the fireplace when he hears a car horn beep. The car turns into the driveway and Joe, Kate, Peggy, and Matt all jump out.

"Peggy, I haven't seen you in ages," Wayne says, as he gives her a big hug. Wayne welcomes everyone to the farm and takes them all inside.

"So Peggy," Wayne says, "Grandpa tells me that you are going to UNH."

"Most likely, but I haven't been officially accepted yet. I wanted to go to Dartmouth, but didn't get in. But this way I will be near Uncle Sam, so I guess that is good."

"I also hear you have a boyfriend now."

"Sort of. I'm going down to pick up Bill on Wednesday."

"I understand you're bringing back someone else too."

"Yes, Connie is coming too. She's a nurse who works with mom."

"She's hot," Matt says. "Wait until you see her."

"I don't know about your taste, Matt," Wayne says. "We'll see. Peggy, is Bill going to UNH too?"

"No, he applied for early decision at RPI and just learned a week ago that he was accepted. So I guess he's going to your Alma Mata."

"You're all staying in the lake house," Laura says, "so you can just drive the car down there and unload. It's all open and we've turned on the water and heat."

Peggy loves the brown-stained lake house, tucked in among the tall pines. She is struck by how different everything looks in the winter from when she was here last summer. The sandy beach transformed to deep white snow; the blue lake water transformed to snow-covered ice, stretching for several miles to the base of Gunstock Mountain, its summit kissing a white fluffy cloud drifting by against a deep blue sky.

"Just think," Peggy says, "we're going to be skiing down that mountain in a few days."

"I can't wait," Matt says.

"Matt, can you and Peggy bring the luggage in from the car," Kate says. "Your dad and I will be in the front downstairs bedroom and Peggy, you can have the other downstairs bedroom. Matt, you and Bill will be upstairs. You can pick whichever room you want. I'll make up all the beds."

The sun is getting ready to set across the lake.

"It looks like we may have a good sunset tonight," Joe says. "Peggy, why don't you run up to the farmhouse and tell everyone to come down for the sunset? I will make some hot chocolate for everyone."

"Ok. Hold the sunset until I get back."

The entire family gathers on the porch, watching the spectacular sunset, snapping one photo after another, sipping their hot chocolates, soaking in the entire sky filled with brilliant reds and yellows, listening to the light breeze wiggle the pine trees, and agreeing with Peggy when she says, "It doesn't get any better than this."

The next day is Christmas Eve, bright and sunny. Peggy, Wayne, and Matt decide to walk down to Harilla Landing and back. Kate is busy in the kitchen preparing their traditional Christmas Eve dinner, Alfredo lasagna with sweet Italian sausage. Dinner is served around five o'clock on the old farmhouse dining room table, made by Sam's father from a long, thick, single natural pine plank, easily seating five people along each side plus one at each end, the site of countless memorable meals.

After dinner, Dave and Eileen set up the card table in a corner of the living room and take on Joe and Kate in their favorite card game, contract bridge. Laura, Matt, and Wayne play three-way cribbage on the dining room table. Sam and Peggy settle into the two big easy chairs between two sofas facing each other in front of the fireplace.

"So tell me Peggy," Sam says, "how did you like the movie *The Theory of Everything*?"

"I liked the movie and the story of Stephen Hawking's life, but I'm not sure I like his physics. Bill and I went to Prescott Park after the movie and were looking at the stars and all this about an expanding universe that started with a big bang just doesn't make any sense to me."

"You and a lot of other people."

"But I thought all physicists agree that the universe began with a big bang almost 14 billion years ago."

"Not by a long shot."

"But that is all you hear about in the press. They say that the science is settled."

"Science is never settled," Sam says. "A theory is only as good as the next experiment. Remember Woodbury's Law, and how often a theory in physics turns out to be wrong, or to not apply in certain cases."

"But I'm always hearing politicians say 'The science is settled' and that there is a consensus among the vast majority of scientists."

"They're ignorant and have no idea what they're talking about. Science is not a democracy where the majority rules. The reason that Woodbury's Law is true is that when everyone starts to believe the same thing, then everyone's thinking just reinforces each other's and there is no room left for objective analysis based on empirical evidence."

"But how do you prove that a given theory is true?" Peggy asks.

"That's the whole point. You can't. A scientific theory can never be proved to be *true*. It can only be proved to be *false*. If a particular theory predicts that an experiment will produce a certain result, and you do the experiment and the result doesn't occur, you must throw out the theory."

"But if the theory predicts that an experiment will produce a certain result, and you do the experiment and you get that result, doesn't that prove that the theory is correct?"

"Not at all. There may be any number of other theories that would also predict the same result."

"Well if that happens, then how do you pick which theory is the best one?"

"That's a good question, Peggy. In general, the simplest one, or the one with the fewest assumptions, is preferred. William of Ockham, an English Franciscan friar, who lived around 1300, stated this principle and it is known today as Occam's razor. Some also think that the more elegant theory is to be preferred, but here you have to be careful and not get sucked into your aesthetic feelings."

"Why do people think that the universe is expanding?" Peggy asks.

"The idea that the universe is expanding goes back to the 1920s when Edwin Hubble was using the 100-inch telescope at Mt. Wilson in California to measure the distance to nearby galaxies by measuring their brightness. He assumed that dimmer ones would be further away. He also discovered that the frequency spectrum of the light coming from the dimmer, and therefore he thought further away, galaxies is shifted to lower frequencies relative to the spectrum of the same light you would measure in the lab. Because the light frequency is shifted to the red end of the visible spectrum, it is called the *redshift*."

"If the frequency of the light is shifted to lower frequencies, why does this mean the universe is expanding?"

"It's called the Doppler effect. If a light source is moving away from you, the light is still traveling at the speed of light, so the wavelength – the distance between each wave peak – must get bigger, which means the frequency goes down. Therefore, when Hubble found that light coming from distant galaxies was redshifted, scientists immediately jumped to the conclusion that the universe must be expanding. That idea became the conventional wisdom, to the point where now it is almost taken for granted."

"But why wouldn't that make sense?" Peggy asks.

"It turns out there are contradictory data," Sam says. "Dr. Halton Arp, who worked with Hubble, has probably collected more redshifted data over the years than anyone, and lots of his photographs show quasars that have a very high redshift compared to the galaxy they are physically connected to."

"What is a quasar?"

"Quasars are highly luminous quasi-stellar objects with a broad spectrum of electromagnetic energy, and as I said, there are lots of photographs which show a quasar even in front of a galaxy, so it must be closer to you, but it has a much higher redshift than the galaxy. Astrophysicists insist that they must be very distant objects, much further away than the galaxy to which they are clearly connected by the photographic evidence. Dr. Arp has written books that describe all of this."

"How can the scientists ignore this evidence?" Peggy asks.

"Well that's the sad part of science these days. Initially, they try to ignore the evidence and refuse to publish the results in the scientific journals, which they control. If that doesn't work, they will try to discredit the investigator who provides the evidence. If that doesn't work, they will come up with new explanations by inventing new things that you can't measure such as dark matter, dark energy and the like to try to salvage their pre-conceived theories about an expanding universe. The theory then gets more and more convoluted and complicated, with many additional assumptions, quite contrary to Occam's razor."

"But what basic theory does all this rely on?"

"It is Einstein's theory of general relativity, which the astrophysicists take as gospel. It is really a theory about gravity, but gravity is a very weak force, and the gravitational attraction between two stars, say our sun and the nearest star to our solar system, is negligible."

"But doesn't gravity cause our earth to revolve around the sun, and doesn't the gravitational pull of the moon cause our ocean tides?"

"Yes, but on an astronomical scale, we are very close to our sun compared to the distance from our sun to the nearest star. On a scale where the earth is one foot from the sun, and the size of the sun would be about one tenth of an inch, the distance to the nearest star would be over fifty miles. Moreover, the gravitational force drops off as one over the square of the distance. So gravity can't really be the major force driving the universe."

"Well why do astrophysicists stick to this theory then?" Peggy asks.

"Mainly because it is all they know. They make their living writing and publishing papers about it, reviewing the papers of other like-minded folks, receiving government grants to continue inventing new mechanisms to try to explain things, and it is a comfortable self-perpetuating cycle. Comfortable, that is, until someone tries to challenge them. Then all hell breaks loose."

"Doesn't sound like real science to me."

"Me neither. It really is too bad."

"Are there competing theories to explain what we see in the universe: the sun, stars, and galaxies?" Peggy asks.

"There are. Space probe measurements have shown that low-density plasmas, positive ions and electrons, populate the entire universe. The electric forces between charged particles are tens of orders of magnitude stronger than gravitational forces. Moving charges, or currents, produce magnetic fields. The sun and stars are high-density plasmas. Their behavior can be explained by studying how plasmas are created and maintained by electric and magnetic fields. Plasma experiments have been conducted in the laboratory, which produce behavior analogous to that observed in the sun and galaxies. Did you know that I did my Ph.D. thesis on plasmas and started my book on plasma physics when I was still a graduate student at RPI?"

"No, I didn't. That's cool. So the universe is a big plasma that can be explained without resort to Einstein's general theory of relativity?"

"I think so, and just using classical electromagnetic theory that physicists and electrical engineers have known about for years."

"How would this affect the search for a Theory of Everything?"

"Well the stumbling block on finding a Theory of Everything has been the inability to combine general relativity with quantum mechanics. You know that quantum mechanics is used to describe what goes on when dimensions are very small, like inside an atom, while general relativity supposedly describes big dimensions like the entire universe. However, when you try to combine the two, everything blows up. They both can't be right. And if they both can't be right, most likely neither one is right."

"Does that mean that general relativity might not be necessary if the universe is a plasma, which can be explained by regular electromagnetic theory?"

"I think that is quite likely and, in a way, it is too bad. Einstein developed the general theory of relativity in a purely deductive way without reference to any empirical evidence. The theory is quite elegant using tensor analysis to describe a 4-dimensional space, our normal 3-dimensional space plus time, which becomes curved in the presence of massive bodies. The effects of gravity can then be calculated by assuming that space-time becomes warped by mass and that objects then follow the shortest path, called geodesics. The theory was so beautiful, that scientists began to believe that space really did become warped and when the redshift data suggested an expanding universe, it was only a small step to say that it was the space itself that was expanding, like blowing up a balloon. Once the press got a hold of this picture, and everyone started making money promoting it, there was no turning back."

"I can't believe that this is how science works." Peggy says.

"That's the dirty little secret," Sam says. "String theory is the latest fad in trying to find a Theory of Everything with a theory that can't be tested. But lots of money can be made writing papers and books and getting government grants."

"You said you'd tell me about quantum mechanics sometime."

"Well, it's getting late and Santa will be coming soon, but I'll give you a brief introduction after we check on how the card games are going."

After learning that Joe and Kate are killing Dave and Eileen at bridge, Sam and Peggy grab a deferred piece of apple pie and a cup of tea, and return to their places in front of the fireplace.

"So, what's the story of quantum mechanics?" Peggy asks.

Sam tries to figure out where to begin. "Remember that Maxwell discovered his equations describing electric and magnetic fields in the 1860s. But the electron wasn't actually discovered until 1897 by J. J. Thomson. Now Maxwell's equations predicted that accelerated charges would produce electromagnetic waves and that light was a form of electromagnetic waves. Now you can produce plasma in the lab by putting a low-pressure gas in a tube with electrodes at each end and applying a high voltage across the electrodes of a few thousand volts. The electrons will get stripped from the atoms producing separate positive ions and electrons. The tube will then glow."

"Is that how a neon sign works?"

"Yes. If the gas is hydrogen, then the ion will be a single proton. If you pass the light from this glowing hydrogen plasma through a prism, the different frequencies of the light will become separated and you can take a photograph of them. The remarkable result of the experiment is that instead of getting all colors of the rainbow, you will see only three sharp lines, a red line, a cyan line, and a dark blue line. There are actually a lot of other sharp lines in the hydrogen spectrum that you can't see with your eye because they occur in the infrared and ultraviolet regions of the spectrum."

"When did people first do these experiments?"

"Detailed measurements of these spectra, called spectroscopy, were carried out during the last third of the 1800s. No one understood why only sharp lines appeared, corresponding to specific frequencies. But they came up with clever formulas that predicted where the lines would be. But no one knew why."

"Is that where the Bohr model of the atom comes in?"

"Exactly. Following Thomson's discovery of the electron, Ernest Rutherford did experiments, showing that an atom had a small core, the nucleus, which was much heavier than the surrounding electrons. He suggested that the atom might be something like a tiny solar system with the negatively charged electrons circling around a much heavier positively charged nucleus."

"Does it really work that way?"

"Well there is a big problem with this model. When a particle moves in a circle, it is accelerated toward the center of the circle, the so-called centripetal acceleration. This is what causes the velocity of the particle to change direction as it goes around the circle. And what happens when a charged particle is accelerated?"

"It produces electromagnetic waves."

"Very good. You're paying attention."

"Is this the light we see?"

"No, because if all atoms gave off light, everything would be a light source! And there is a bigger problem. Such electromagnetic waves would carry away energy, causing the electron to spiral into the nucleus."

"So what keeps the electrons circling around the nucleus without falling in and without producing electromagnetic waves?" Peggy asks.

"Well, nobody could figure that out. So Bohr just said it happens that way, but that the electrons are restricted to specific orbits at different fixed distances from the nucleus and the energy of the electron is a function of its distance from the nucleus. He then theorized that when an electron jumps from one fixed orbit to another fixed orbit closer to the nucleus, a pulse of electromagnetic energy would be propagated whose frequency is proportional to the energy difference between the two orbits."

"Are these the photons of light?"

"Yes, Einstein introduced the idea that light could be considered to be a massless particle, called a photon, when he published his explanation of the photoelectric effect in 1905."

"What is the photoelectric effect?"

"When you shine light on certain metals, electrons will be emitted if the frequency of the light exceeds some threshold. Below that frequency threshold, no electrons are emitted no matter how much light you shine on the metal."

"So is light really a particle or a wave?"

"That's the problem. Scientists like to call it the wave-particle duality because sometimes light seems to act like a wave and other times it seems to act like a particle."

"But that doesn't make any sense," Peggy says. "It's got to be one or the other."

"Oh, it gets worse," Sam says. "Particles like electrons sometimes behave like waves!"

"This is too weird. I think physics is all screwed up."

"I have to agree with you on that."

"How will I ever be able to make any sense of all this?"

"You'll just have to discover your Theory of Everything."

"Hey, you guys," Kate says, "Santa is almost here."

"Did you end up killing them?" Sam asks.

"Yes, we had all the good cards tonight."

Matt comes in from the dining room and announces, "I won more cribbage games tonight than Wayne or Aunt Laura.

"Beginner's luck," Wayne says.

"Everyone put your presents under the tree while I fill the stockings," Laura says.

"Then we've all got to get to bed," Sam says. "Big day tomorrow."

Peggy is in bed, listening for Santa, beginning to feel as if maybe she was lucky after all, thankful for her loving, extended family, for this opportunity to spend Christmas at the lake.   Maybe it is best that she did not get into Dartmouth.   Maybe UNH will work out after all.   Maybe being near Uncle Sam will help her discover her Theory of Everything.   Maybe.   But not getting into Dartmouth still hurts.

5

A light snow is falling Christmas morning as Kate, Joe, Matt, and Peggy walk up from the lake house to the farmhouse. Laura already has their traditional Christmas breakfast, sausage and cheese casserole, in the oven, and Sam has started a fire in the fireplace.

"The casserole will be ready in an hour," Laura says. "Help yourself to juice and coffee, and let's open our presents."

The family tradition is that the gifts they exchange with each other should not be store-bought gifts, but rather something the person made or created. Peggy and Matt both like photography and often give special photos as gifts. Peggy also loves poetry and often makes up her own poems.

"Dad, open your present from me."

Joe unwraps the present and opens the box. It is a beautiful framed photo of a sunset over the lake, which Peggy had taken last summer. Superimposed on the sunset is the following poem that Peggy wrote:

Time

Time is the distance from day to day,
From when the sun rises till it goes away.
From the time we were born, to the day that we die,
The time ticks on, and the years roll by.
The past, present, and future, are times that we know,
While they go by fast or sometimes very slow,
But people just sit there, and don't stop to think,
How precious the time is when it's gone with a wink.
For time rushes by us, and the next thing you know,
Is that your time is up, and now you must go.
The times may be good, and sometimes unpleasant,
But the best time of all, is the time called the present.

"That's very thoughtful," Joe says. "I love the poem."

The first present that Peggy opens is from Wayne. It is one of the electronic pens he invented. He calls it a U-Pen.

"Oh, thank you, Wayne. I can't wait to try it. Why is it called a U-Pen?"

"Well, the first big application is to use it as a biometric identification device that will recognize you by your signature. The pen literally becomes part of YOU. Get it. U-Pen. I have been texting too long! I'll tell you all about how it works later."

"I can't wait."

Matt gives Peggy a framed photo that he had taken of her making a jump shot in one of her basketball games. Sam gives Peggy a copy of his new book on *Vectors and Tensors*, telling her that she will definitely find it useful in college, but can start reading it now. Peggy gets a hand-made coffee mug from Eileen and a hand-made cribbage board from Dave. She opens a large present, which is a ski sweater that her mom has knit. Her dad gives her a booklet he has put together giving her genealogy on both sides of her family. He is a direct descendant of Lawrence Leach who settled in Beverly, (then Salem) Massachusetts in 1629. Her mother, Kate, along with Uncle Sam, are descended from John Woodbury, who first came to Cape Ann in 1624 and was one of the original settlers of Salem. Peggy's dad often uses genealogy to motivate his history students, helping them fill in their family trees. Peggy's last present is from Aunt Laura, a painting she made showing the lake looking out from the farmhouse. Along with the painting is a small box of 25 note cards with a print of the painting on the front.

"I know you kids all use email and texting to communicate," Aunt Laura says, "and people don't send written notes much anymore, but you would be surprised at how much people will remember, respect, and like you when you send them a thoughtful written note. I still have notes that your uncle sent to me from before we were married. It's a habit I hope you will acquire. You will never regret it."

"Thank you so much," Peggy says. "I will try to do it. I'm going to send my first note to you thanking you for the painting and note cards. Now can I read some of Uncle Sam's old love letters to you?"

"Ok, the casserole's done," Laura says. "Let's have breakfast."

After breakfast, Peggy, Matt, and Wayne decide to try skating on the ice in front of the lake house. Finding shovels and old skates in the barn, they head down the hill to the lake and push away enough snow to make a pretty good skating rink. Peggy skates doubles with Matt and Wayne, and she and Wayne try to teach Matt to skate backwards. After two hours of skating, they head into the lake house for some hot chocolate. Meanwhile, back at the farmhouse, Eileen and Kate are busy preparing the beef Wellington for Christmas dinner, which is scheduled for four o'clock.

"I look forward to this beef Wellington every Christmas," says Joe as everyone gathers around the dining room table for dinner.

"Me too," Peggy says.

As dinner progresses, the conversation turns to history.

"Joe, in your history classes, do you teach the Great Man theory of history?" Sam asks.

"Well, I do mention that in the 1840s, Thomas Carlyle put forward the theory that history can largely be explained by the impact of heroes or great individuals. I also tell them that about twenty years later Herbert Spencer challenged this theory and argued that society and the current social conditions were more important."

"I think both of these ideas miss the point completely," Sam says. "And the reason they are wrong is because history is written by persons who have studied only social science. It is obvious to anyone with a technical background that the people with the biggest influence on history are the scientists, engineers, and inventors."

"Sounds like another example of Woodbury's Law to me," Peggy says.

"Just think about it for a minute," Sam says. "What bigger influences on the course of history are there than inventions such as Gutenberg's printing press, James Watt's steam engine, Samuel Morse's telegraph, Marconi's wireless telegraph, Henry Ford's model-T automobile and his assembly line, the Wright brother's airplane, or Victor Babits' vidicon tube?"

"Who is Victor Babits?" Joe asks.

"He was my electronics professor at RPI. He had come from Hungary and he had a photographic memory. He had a patent on the vidicon tube that is used as the guts of TV cameras. Scores of such unknown inventors and engineers were responsible for the development of radio and television, which of course, has changed the course of history."

Dave says, "Not to mention how history has been altered by transportation inventions such as railroads, jet airplanes and of course trucks and automobiles."

"Which led to the interstate highway system and the development of the suburbs," Joe adds.

"Of course, one of the biggest inventions has been the computer," Peggy says, "and the development of the internet."

"And the biggest driver of that," Sam says, "is the development of solid state devices, starting with the invention of the transistor at Bell Labs in 1947, followed by the invention of the integrated circuit in the late 50s. The number of transistors you can fit on a single chip has increased from two in the late 50s to over a billion today. It is a remarkable achievement that has changed the course of history probably more than anything else in the last 50 years. It is what allowed us to go to the moon in 1969 and what allows us today to have cell phones, iPads, and samiPhones."

"How can history books ignore all of this as the main driver of historical events?" Matt asks.

"Woodbury's Law," Peggy says.

"But if technological advances are what change history, how do technological advances come about?" Dave asks.

"Well that's a complicated question," Sam says, "and there are many factors. You first need to distinguish between scientists and inventors. They are not always the same person. For example, Samuel Morse, who invented the telegraph, was first a painter who painted some pretty good portraits as well as large mural paintings. His motivation was to make money and become famous in the process. He was not a scientist who really understood the science behind the telegraph. A scientist who did was Joseph Henry, who taught at Princeton and later became the first secretary of the Smithsonian Institution. In fact, he helped Morse out a little, but initially Henry did not think that the telegraph had much future other than a curiosity that he demonstrated in his lectures. Morse did not know, as Henry believed, that it was impossible to send a telegraph message over a wire for a long distance. Therefore, like many inventors, he just plowed ahead and tried lots of different schemes, including inventing a relay that could boost the strength of the signal every mile or so, and thus succeeded in sending telegraph messages across the country. Of course, once he succeeded, Henry challenged Morse's patents, saying he really invented the telegraph. This sort of thing happens all the time."

"Wasn't Marconi the same kind of inventor as Morse?" Wayne asks.

"Yes. At the age of twenty, he studied how Heinrich Hertz generated electromagnetic waves and detected them across a room, and then set up a transmitter on the second floor of his Bologna, Italy home and with a lot of persistence was able to detect the waves a mile away over a hill in his backyard. He then moved to England and kept at it until he was able to transmit and receive wireless signals across the Atlantic Ocean. In this case, it was the British physicist Sir Oliver Lodge who knew the theory of wireless communication and wanted the credit that Marconi was getting, but it was Marconi who just kept doing one experiment after another without giving up with each failure, who set up his own wireless company and eventually succeeded."

"You don't hear about such lone inventors these days," Joe says.

"Except, of course, for Wayne!" Dave says.

"Yes, don't forget me," Wayne says.

"Wayne Woodbury, the next Marconi!" Peggy says.

"You're right, Joe," Sam says. "Most big inventions these days are collaborative efforts that require lots of people and lots of money. In the old days, big companies like AT&T would set up basic research labs like Bell Labs where the transistor was invented. But with the breakup of AT&T, the old Bell Labs went away and most basic research was relegated to university labs mostly funded by government grants. This is not the ideal situation, as the government is in control and will often push research in particular politically correct directions, which may not be the best direction to go to discover the real science."

"Is there a better way to go?" Joe asks.

"Well in the talk where I introduced Woodbury's Law, I suggested that federal funding of university research should be abolished."

"That must have been well received," Kate says.

"It certainly raised some eyebrows. But overall, I think federal funding of university research has been a negative, directing resources to the wrong areas of study. The researchers at universities will work on what they think will be funded, rather than on what they might really want to do based on their best insights and hunches. No one will take a big risk for fear of losing their funding. Therefore, high risk – high payoff research is just not done. We will never know what we may have missed out on. A lot of the big advances have come out of companies motivated to come up with the next big idea that will catapult them ahead of the competition."

"So what's the solution to funding research?" Joe asks. "Does the government have any role?"

"The government does best when it has a single big goal, such as going to the moon, and then lets everyone figure out how to do it. The Manhattan Project to develop the atomic bomb and the big effort to develop radar in World War II are other examples of engineering goals that required a lot of basic research to get the job done. But if there is no big engineering goal, I would like to see basic research done in independent research labs with long-range funding by industry. Let's bring back Bell Labs kind of quality."

"Perhaps when Wayne's company becomes as profitable as Apple," Dave says, "he will set up the Wayne Woodbury Research Labs for basic research."

"I think that is a great idea," Peggy says. "If I ever set up a company that becomes that profitable, I would do it."

"This conversation is getting too much for me," Kate says. "How about another round of bridge?"

"I'd like to stay and hear what kind of company Peggy's thinking of starting," Joe says. "Laura, why don't you take my place at bridge, and you and Kate can take on Dave and Eileen."

"Sounds good, the rest of you can stay here and solve the world's problems."

Peggy, Sam, Joe, Wayne, and Matt get some more coffee and tea and return to the dining room table.

"So Wayne," Peggy says, "tell me how the U-Pen works and what it can do?"

"Well, when I was in graduate school I had taken courses in pattern recognition and artificial intelligence as well as a course in micro-electromechanical systems, or MEMS. When I was transferring some money from my bank account one day, I realized how vulnerable these online banking systems really are. My bank account was really just one hacked password away from being wiped out. People had talked about various biometric devices for identifying someone, such as fingerprint or eye retina scans, and such devices exist, but they are expensive and not convenient for widespread use. So I thought about how I could develop a simple device that could positively identify who was on the other end of a computer line."

"And this led you to invent the U-Pen?" Peggy asks.

"Yes, the pen looks just like a regular pen and writes just like a regular pen. However, it is a very smart pen. I have built in a MEMS circuit that contains microscopic accelerometers, gyros, pressure sensors, and other intelligent sensors such that it knows the exact location of the pen tip and the amount of pressure on the paper at every instant of time. As you write, it keeps track of how fast you move in every direction and exactly how you speed up and slow down. When you write your signature, a special pattern recognition program that I developed, can tell to a very high degree of confidence, if it is really you who is writing your signature. No one else will ever come close to writing your signature as you do. Even if they have a picture of your signature, it will be impossible for them to write it at exactly the varying speed and varying pressure that you use when writing your signature. We have tested the system on thousands of people, and it is foolproof."

"That's pretty cool. So how will banks use it?"

"It is not only good for banks. Now that I have developed it, there are tons of applications. First, all the data associated with what you write is immediately sent wirelessly to any computing device such as your smart phone, iPad, or laptop. It can be displayed there or processed. As an example of its use, every time you sign a credit card receipt, the credit card company will immediately know it is you. Therefore, no one can ever forge your signature. However, it gets better than that. You no longer need a credit card. The waiter in a restaurant simply brings a device to the table that opens up a connection to the credit card company. You just write the amount you want to pay on any piece of paper and sign your name, and the computer can read the number you wrote and identify who you are and charge your account. We have just eliminated all credit card fraud. If you lose your pen, it is useless to anyone else. It has a unique serial number that is identified only with you."

"But if you lose it, do you have to get another one?" Peggy asks.

"Actually, the U-Pen also has GPS tracking in it, so you can always find it with your smart phone if you lose it. When you get close to it, you can tell it to beep and flash a red light."

"What if the battery goes dead?"

"The built-in permanent battery will almost never go dead. It is a specially designed, long-lasting battery and the U-Pen goes into a sleep mode that uses almost no current when the pen has not been moved for several seconds. In addition, every time you move the pen and write something, electromagnetic induction creates a voltage that recharges the battery. Therefore, the battery always stays mostly charged. We also make a nice looking stand where you can place the pen when you go to bed at night. This pen holder will also charge the U-Pen, so it is always almost fully charged."

"Sounds like you have thought of almost everything," Sam says.

"Not by a long shot," Wayne says. "Almost every day I think of another potential application for the U-Pen."

"Like what?" Peggy asks.

"Remember it was transferring money in my bank account that gave me the idea to begin with. I then realized that it is good for any banking transaction. If you go to an ATM machine to get money, you do not have to put a card in the machine anymore and type in a pin number. You can just press a button to get started and sign your name on any piece of paper. The ATM machine will now know who you are, check your bank account, and ask how much money you want. It will no longer be possible for someone to steal your ATM card or watch you enter your pin number."

"Could you use it anytime you need to enter a password on your computer?" Peggy asks.

"Exactly. No more need to remember many different passwords that you are suppose to make strong by including capital letters and numbers. No need to change them periodically. You only need your own unique signature, which no one can forge. I think we can pretty much eliminate identity theft."

"This is huge," Sam says. "A real game changer."

"I know," Wayne says, "but this is only the beginning, Peggy. Grandpa told me about your idea of taking notes in college and he thinks you're onto something, right, Grandpa?"

"I do. As I told Peggy, when I was in college I rewrote all of the lecture notes from my classes, and this is how I learned everything so well. Today, school children are not even taught cursive writing any more. Educators think that students only need to learn how to type on a keyboard. This is a huge mistake. Recent psychological studies, some even involving brain scan imaging, show pretty conclusively that there is a direct and deep connection between writing things by hand, and how the brain processes this information. Numerous studies have shown that children who first learn to write by hand are better readers and learners. I'm afraid that the educational "experts" are shortchanging an entire generation of students."

"I smell another example of Woodbury's Law," Peggy says.

"So do you see the potential of your idea, Peggy?" Sam asks.

"Yes, I'm going to use the U-Pen to re-write all my lecture notes or things

I read in a book. And then I'll write a software program that will convert all of my writing to text and also clean up my hand sketches, so I'll have a nice clean permanent record of all my classes."

"You're definitely on the right track," Sam says. "But the big problem is still the current one-hour lecture format and great big textbooks that present material in one particular order, which may not be the best order for every student. Do you see how you might be able to solve those problems too?"

"I think so. We need to make short five to ten minute audio/video clips like you put out on YouTube for your digital design course. But when the students watch them, we need to have them write something with the U-Pen which reinforces their learning by taking advantage of this handwriting – brain connection."

"Bingo!" Wayne says. "I think we're on the way to revolutionizing education in addition to banking!"

"The first book I wrote on vectors and Cartesian tensors over thirty years ago," Sam says, "was actually called a programmed text. It was made up of small little blocks of text where the reader had to fill in a blank or answer a question in each block. The following block gave the answer. This was in the days of mainframe computers and punched cards, so it was all we had. But the idea was sound."

"But now," Wayne says, "when your little video clip asks a question, you can just write the answer on a piece of paper using my U-Pen and the computer will know right away if your answer is correct."

"And depending if it is right or wrong, can direct you to the proper next clip," Peggy says. "I can see a whole bunch of new possibilities."

"Me too," Wayne says, "things like automatically generated individualized tests and exams for students to take."

"And there can be no cheating," Peggy says. "You can't have someone else take your exam, because the computer will recognize your handwriting and know if it is you."

"I think that may be possible to do," Wayne says.

"This gives me a lot to think about," Peggy says.

The bridge group walks in from the living room.

"Are you guys still at it?" Kate asks.

"You won't believe what we have covered tonight, Mom," Peggy says.

"You will have to fill me in. Now you had better get some sleep. You and your dad have to leave early in the morning to go down and pick up Bill and Connie."

"Oh, I meant to tell you, Kate," Joe says. "I got a call today from our friends, the Wilsons in Meredith, and they would like us to stop by and have lunch with them tomorrow. So I was wondering if Wayne could take my place and drive down to Portsmouth with Peggy in the morning."

"Yes, Wayne, can you?" Peggy asks. "We can talk more about your U-Pen, and then you can meet Connie and get to know her on the drive back."

"I'm not sure what you're getting me into," Wayne says. "I've never met Connie."

"Here, let me show you some photos of her," Peggy says. "I took them at Thanksgiving."

Peggy gets out her smart phone and shows Wayne a photo of Connie sitting at the dining room table, her beautiful face, blonde hair, big smile, and bright blue eyes grabbing Wayne's attention. Peggy shows Wayne a second photo that Matt took of Connie standing next to Peggy.

"She's nearly as tall as you are," Wayne says approvingly.

"Convinced?" Peggy asks.

"Ok, I'll drive you down tomorrow. We can take my dad's minivan."

Peggy is tired after a long, fun day, but can't get her new ideas of using the U-Pen out of her mind. She keeps thinking about what kind of great app she and Bill could put together. She can't wait to see Bill tomorrow and bring him up to date on everything. She can't wait to have Wayne meet Connie. Tomorrow will be fun.

6

Wayne and Peggy are on the road by eight o'clock. All during the trip, Peggy and Wayne go over the previous night's discussion, speculating on future applications of the U-Pen. Peggy asks Wayne how he was able to get money to start the company and what was involved in getting the company up and running. Wayne tells her how he and three roommates at MIT had always wanted to start their own company. Therefore, when he came up with his U-Pen idea, they put together a working prototype while in graduate school. Their big break came when he read that credit card fraud costs the credit card companies over eight billion dollars a year. They figured that credit card companies would pay big bucks if they could make that loss go away. They put together a slick video that illustrated the problem in sharp detail, outlined their solution to the problem, and showed how the credit card company's profits would soar. The video ended with instructions on how to contact them for more details. Wayne tells Peggy that they sent copies of the videos to all the major credit card companies and sat back and waited.

"Did you hear from any of them?" Peggy asks.

"We heard from them all! We flew out to meet with all of them and gave them a detailed proposal. We figured that if we could get ten million dollars from one of them, we could design and build a small, automated manufacturing plant that could produce 1000 pens per hour. With down time for maintenance, this plant should be able to produce about four million pens per year. We found an old, empty manufacturing plant in Rochester, one that we could fix up and use. We told them that the first credit card company that gave us the ten million dollars would be the company we would work with exclusively for the first year. We would work with them to set up a pilot program of 25,000 customers in one section of the country and this would give them a year's head start on other credit card companies in saving money. Our calculations showed that the savings in fraud cases would more than pay for itself that first year."

"Did any of them take you up on it?"

"Did they? They all wanted to be the first and bid up our ten million dollars to fifty million dollars. So we got fifty million dollars and have built our first manufacturing plant in Rochester. The pilot program is underway and it looks to be on target for them to save fifty million dollars in fraud in the first nine months."

After picking up Bill in Portsmouth, they drive to Connie's apartment in Dover with the help of the car's GPS navigation system. Peggy and Wayne walk up to the front door and ring the doorbell. Connie opens the door and Wayne's first impression is that Connie is more attractive in person than in Peggy's photos.

"Connie," Peggy says, "this is my cousin, Wayne."

"It's really nice to meet you," Connie says holding out her hand.

Wayne is already glad he came as he grasps her hand.

"It's nice to meet you too. Let me help you with your luggage and skis."

Peggy gets in the back seat with Bill while Wayne holds the front passenger door for Connie. As they drive out of Dover and head back to the lake, Peggy tells Bill about how she and Uncle Sam talked about *The Theory of Everything* on Christmas Eve and how Uncle Sam told her that not all scientists believe that the universe is expanding. She tries to remember what he told her about the redshift data and about Occam's razor, and about how scientific theories can never be proved to be true, only false. She tells Bill that Uncle Sam thinks Einstein's theory of general relativity may not describe physical reality after all, and how the behavior of the sun and galaxies might be described in terms of the low-density plasma that exists throughout the universe.

"It sounds like I missed a lot," Bill says.

"Oh, there's even more."

Peggy goes on to tell Bill about Uncle Sam's skepticism of quantum mechanics and the wave-particle duality of light and electrons.

"I can't wait to talk to your Uncle Sam about all of this," Bill says.

Meanwhile in the front seat, Wayne asks Connie where she grew up. She tells him that she was born in Syracuse, New York and lived there until the second grade, when her family moved to Pittsfield, Massachusetts, where she graduated from high school. She raced on the high school ski team and gave skiing lessons to children on nearby Berkshire ski slopes. Her family would often ski at Mt. Snow in Vermont on weekends. Wayne asks her where she went after high school and Connie says that she enrolled in the Fitchburg State College School of Nursing in Fitchburg, Massachusetts. After her first year, her father, who worked for a cyber security firm, was transferred to Austin, Texas, where her mother and father now live. Connie tells Wayne that labor and delivery was her favorite rotation, so when she graduated last June, she looked around for openings in that specialty and that is how she ended up in Portsmouth working with Peggy's mom. Wayne looks at her. *What a stroke of luck for me.*

In the back seat, Peggy moves on to Christmas day and tells Bill what she got for Christmas including the U-Pen that Wayne had given her.

"Hey, Wayne," Peggy says, "tell Bill and Connie about the U-Pen and how you came to invent it."

"Well, it's sort of a long story. Let me start at the beginning."

Wayne tells them that he was born in Beverly, Massachusetts, where his folks lived at the time, and he went to school in Beverly through the eighth grade. Then his folks moved to Rye, NH where he attended high school. When he graduated from high school, he went to RPI, just like his dad and grandfather, majoring in electrical engineering. He then decided to go to MIT for graduate school. His first term there, he met three other guys who have become his best friends. At the beginning of his second term at MIT, the four of them rented a house in Cambridge and roomed together for the next four years.

Wayne says that toward the end of that first year, a speaker from Japan came and gave a talk at MIT about a new semiconductor process that had been developed in Japan and was about to be put into production. It used a completely different technology involving amorphous semiconductors rather than the traditional silicon-based crystalline semiconductors. In addition, it would support asynchronous digital design rather than the usual synchronous design that uses a high-frequency, power-hungry clock. What's more, very tiny, high-density chips could be manufactured on big rolls of substrate, which would hold about a million chips. Once a chip has been designed, the cost to produce this roll of a million chips would be about $100,000, so the cost of a single chip would be about 10 cents.

Wayne says this was a turning point. He and his roommates went back to their house and talked through the night about the implications of this new technology. They had previously talked about possibly starting a company of their own some day, but they had no idea of anything that might give them an edge. To take advantage of this new technology, they would need to design a high-volume product that would sell at least a million units. Moreover, they would have to use their digital design skills to design something very powerful, yet simple and elegant. In addition, it had to be something very useful that people would buy. It seemed like an impossible combination. However, while they were all in the electrical engineering department, they were each doing research in different areas: Wayne in artificial intelligence, and the other three in computer systems and architecture, devices and materials, and signal processing. One of the others had already gotten an MBA at Harvard. Over the next few months, they kept batting around various ideas for a mass-produced product they might build.

Wayne then tells about the day he is transferring money in his bank account and gets the idea of the U-Pen. He goes on to tell Connie and Bill how it works and what it does. Connie thinks, *This guy is amazing.*

After Wayne finishes his U-Pen odyssey, Peggy tells Bill and Connie about how she thinks she can use the U-Pen to help her study in college and create hyperlinked, multimedia modules from her lecture notes. She tells Bill that this might be their big chance to write a great app. They talk about the importance of the hand-brain connection and how writing by hand is becoming a lost art. Peggy tells Bill and Connie about the note cards that her Aunt Laura gave her for Christmas and how she encouraged her to get in the habit of writing notes by hand and not just texting all the time.

They arrive at the farmhouse in time for leftover beef Wellington sandwiches for lunch. After Peggy introduces Bill and Connie to those who had not met them before, Kate shows Connie where her room is upstairs. Bill will be staying in the lake house.

Bill gets a small package out of his coat pocket, and as everyone is sitting down for lunch, hands Peggy a small wrapped box. "Here, Merry Christmas."

Peggy unwraps and opens the small box. It is a single pearl pendant on a silver chain. Peggy takes it out of the box and puts it around her neck. She looks at Bill and says, "You remembered, thank you," and kisses him on the cheek.

"Remembered what?" Matt asks.

"None of your business. It's our secret."

"How touching!"

Peggy goes and gets a small flat Christmas present and hands it to Bill. "This is for you. Merry Christmas."

Bill opens it and sees that it is a 5" x 7" picture frame you can set on a table. When he turns it over, he sees it is a photograph – their class photo from kindergarten. Bill and Peggy smile at each other.

"Bill has a new example of Woodbury's Law," Peggy announces.

Everyone turns to listen. Bill looks embarrassed.

"You're not going to tell them, are you?"

"Of course, I am. Bill says that it's conventional wisdom that people who have known each other since kindergarten never end up marrying each other."

"Does that mean that Bill is going to marry you?" Matt asks.

"Bill told me that one day he will."

Everyone laughs except Bill, who feels like crawling under the table.

"Can't you keep any secrets?" Bill asks.

"I can keep the pearl secret."

"I think I know that secret," her mom says.

After lunch, Wayne drives Bill, Peggy, and Connie down to the lake house to unload Bill's luggage. They all stand on the porch looking out over the lake.

"What a gorgeous view," Connie says.

"That's Gunstock Mountain across the lake," Peggy says. "That's where we will be skiing tomorrow."

"Wow, I can't wait," Bill says.

They go inside and Peggy gets out her U-Pen.

"Wayne, can you show me how to use this?"

"Sure, but right now it's programmed to just recognize your signature. Why don't you and Bill see if you can interface it to your samiPhone?"

"That would be fun," Bill says. "Is there documentation?"

Wayne shows them how to download a document that describes the signals coming from the U-Pen when you write with it. The exact location of the pen point and the pressure of the tip on the writing surface are sent out wirelessly using encrypted signals and a proprietary communication protocol. With this information available, Bill sits down to write a program on the samiPhone that will display on the samiPhone's screen everything that Peggy writes with the U-Pen.

"I'll let you two figure this out," Wayne says. "Connie and I are going for a walk."

Wayne and Connie go up to the road and walk until the road ends at the lake at Harilla Landing. They stand on the dock and Wayne points to the island across the ice.

"That's Little Bear Island out there and to the right is Cow Island. There is a small gap between the two islands called 'The Hole in the Wall.' It is just big enough to get through with a boat. When I was a kid, we would kayak from here and go around Little Bear Island. Sometimes, we would even kayak around Whortleberry Island, which is a big island on the other side of Little Bear. You can just see part of it if you look to the left of Little Bear."

"This is so beautiful here," Connie says. "I can't believe your grandfather grew up here in the farmhouse."

"I know. I love it here. I used to spend the whole summer here when I was growing up. When I was in high school, I'd get summer jobs around here including working at the marina just over the bridge and as a life guard at the town beach just this side of the bridge."

Wayne and Connie talk for a long time. They then head back toward the farmhouse, taking a shortcut through the woods down to the lakeshore south of the farmhouse, from where they can follow a path along the lake back to the lake house. They stop under a tall pine tree. The sun is about to set and they look across the lake to Gunstock Mountain. Wayne puts his arm around Connie's shoulder, she putting her arm around his back.

"You know what's strange?" Wayne asks.

"What?"

"We've known each other for only a few hours, and yet I feel like I've known you all my life."

"I know what you mean. I feel the same."

"I'm really glad that Kate invited you for Thanksgiving dinner."

"Me too."

They turn and look into each other's eyes. As their lips meet, Connie wonders, *What is happening to me?*

Connie and Wayne walk into the lake house just as the sun disappears below the distant mountains. Peggy is sitting at the table by the picture window and is writing on a piece of paper with the U-Pen. The samiPhone that Bill has programmed is on the table. Wayne goes over and takes a look. Whatever Peggy writes on the piece of paper immediately shows up on the samiPhone screen. It is as if she is writing directly on the samiPhone screen.

"You did it," Wayne says. "Nice job."

"This is fun," Bill says. "Can we convert her cursive writing into typed text on the screen?"

"It should be fairly easy," Wayne says. "In part of my Ph.D. thesis, I developed a new theory I called Multidimensional Connectivity and I used this theory to develop an algorithm that converts cursive writing into printed text. The algorithm is built into the U-Pen, so if you enable that feature, when Peggy writes a word in cursive, the algorithm generates an ASCII code for each character, and transmits it wirelessly. So all you need to do is send the enabling code to the U-Pen, read in the ASCII codes for all the characters, and display them on the screen."

"That sounds pretty straightforward," Bill says. "I'll work on it later."

"Time to go up to the farmhouse for dinner," Peggy says.

At dinner, Peggy and Bill tell about the progress they have made in getting the U-Pen to interface with the samiPhone. Sam is impressed. "You two make a good team. You should think about making a good app that uses the U-Pen on any smart phone or tablet."

Peggy says, "Actually, we've talked about making some app that we could sell to help put me through college."

"I think you may be on the right track," Sam says.

The conversation then turns to skiing and the need to get a good night's sleep for the big day on the slopes tomorrow.

"I think my skiing days are over," Sam says. "Laura and I are going to stay here tomorrow while all you young folks hit the ski trails. I've got some reading and writing to do and Laura is going to set up her easel down by the lake and paint Gunstock Mountain."

"Ok," Dave says. "We leave in the morning at eight-thirty sharp."

Before turning in, Peggy and Bill bundle up and walk through the snow down to the beach. They hold each other tight, shivering in the cold, looking up at the bright stars against the black sky. It is quiet – very quiet. Peggy wonders what the future will hold.

7

Peggy and Bill are riding up the Panorama chair lift to the summit of Gunstock Mountain. A light snow fell overnight, leaving about an inch of fresh powder on the slopes. The bright sun makes it feel warmer than the 35-degree temperature. They talk about the success they had yesterday getting the U-Pen to write on the samiPhone; they talk about writing an app for smart phones or tablets, an app that will use the U-Pen; they kick around lots of ideas.

When they step off the chair at the top of the mountain, Wayne and Connie are waiting for them.

"Can you believe this view!" Connie exclaims.

"That's Long Island way over there," Peggy says pointing. "If you've got good eyes, you can see the lake house."

"Shall we all go straight down Hot-Shot?" Wayne asks pointing to the black-diamond trail.

Peggy demurs. "Bill and I are going to start on Upper Gunsmoke. It's blue-diamond and will give us a longer run."

"Why don't we go with them," Connie says to Wayne. "It will get us warmed up, and then I'll race you down Hot-Shot."

She's a competitor too, Wayne thinks.

The four agree to meet for lunch at noon in the food court of the main lodge. Then Peggy skis off with Bill, while Connie skis off with Wayne.

At lunch, they meet up with the rest of the family.

"So where did you guys ski?" Peggy asks.

"We all went up the Pistol-Triple Chair to begin with and got warmed up skiing down Pistol," Kate says.

"Then we took the Panorama all the way to the top," Joe says.

"But then we took the nice long leisurely route down Flintstock and the Flats," Eileen says. "You know, we aren't as young as we used to be."

"Matt, did you ski with mom and dad?" Peggy asks.

"I did to begin with, and then went off on my own. I met this nice chick who wanted to ski with me."

"I'm sure," Peggy says sarcastically.

"The five of us may leave around mid-afternoon," Kate says. "You four can stay as long as you want, and we'll see you back at the farmhouse."

"Ok," Peggy says. "We'll probably leave around four-thirty."

"I'm exhausted!" Peggy says as they drive out of the Gunstock parking lot and head home.

"That was great fun," Connie says. "It is the first time I've skied in some time. I didn't get a chance to get out at all last year."

"You sure didn't forget how to ski," Wayne says.

"Did she race you down Hot-Shot?" Peggy asks.

"No," Wayne says. "We skied down Hot-Shot together, but I told her I didn't want her to get hurt, so it probably wasn't a good idea to race."

"Oh yeah," Connie says poking Wayne in the side, "when I beat you down Gunpowder and Shotgun on our first run, I think you didn't want to be embarrassed going down Hot-Shot."

"I could have passed you any time I wanted," Wayne says.

"Wayne, I think you've met your match," Peggy says.

After turning on Rt. 25 in Meredith, they pass the movie theater.

"Look," Peggy says, "*The Theory of Everything* is playing. Have you seen it, Wayne?"

"No."

"Me neither," Connie says.

"Oh, you've got to see it," Peggy says. "Why don't we all go tomorrow night? I'd love to see it again, wouldn't you, Bill?"

"Sure."

"We can just pick up something to eat in Meredith after skiing and then go to the movies."

"Sounds good to me," Wayne says.

When they reach the farmhouse, Aunt Laura has already prepared hot chili and homemade corn bread, and everyone quickly gathers around the dining room table for dinner.

"I can't believe all the skiing we did today," Peggy says.

"It was so much fun," Connie says.

"Oh, guess what, Uncle Sam," Peggy says. "*The Theory of Everything* is playing in Meredith. Wayne and Connie haven't seen it yet, so Bill and I are going to see it again tomorrow night with them. We're going to go directly from skiing after grabbing something to eat in Meredith."

"Then we probably don't have to get to Gunstock tomorrow as early as we did today," Joe says.

Kate agrees. "If we get there by ten, we should all be able to get enough skiing in."

"I think tomorrow may be the last day of skiing for some of us old folks," Dave says. Eileen, Joe, and Kate nod in agreement.

"I think all of us may take a break from skiing on Saturday," Wayne says. "But Connie and I talked about skiing Mt. Cranmore in North Conway on Sunday. Do you and Bill want to come with us?"

"Yes, definitely," Peggy says. "Right, Bill?"

"Sounds like fun. I've never skied Mt. Cranmore."

"Then you must come," Wayne says.

The next day, the skiing conditions at Gunstock are perfect, snow having been made overnight, and the trails groomed in the morning. On every trip up the chairlift, Peggy and Bill keep going over different ideas for a great app that will use the U-Pen. When they leave in the afternoon, Peggy, Bill, Wayne, and Connie had skied every open trail at Gunstock over the past two days.

After stopping for pizza at Mill Falls in Meredith, they get to the movie theater for the seven o'clock running of *The Theory of Everything*. They get back to the farmhouse around 9:30 and find Uncle Sam, by himself, reading in front of the fireplace.

"Where is everyone?" Peggy asks.

"They're all down at the lake house playing cards. Tell me, Wayne, how did you like the movie?"

They all join Uncle Sam in front of the fireplace – Wayne and Connie on one sofa, Peggy and Bill on the other.

"I liked it a lot. But Peggy tells me you think that Hawking's quest for a Theory of Everything went down the wrong path and that the whole general relativity stuff, the expanding universe, the big bang, black holes, and everything is on the wrong track."

"I do think it is quite likely."

"Peggy says she wants to discover a Theory of Everything," Bill says. "Do you think that is remotely possible?"

"Anything is possible," Sam says.

"I would like to *know* the Theory of Everything," Peggy says, "but if the smartest people in the world haven't been able to figure it out in the last hundred years, how could I possibly learn everything they know before even starting to find some Theory of Everything?"

"That's the whole point," Sam says. "You don't have to learn everything they know, particularly if what they know isn't true. Then you certainly don't want to learn it."

"But then how do I know what to learn and where to start?"

"Remember how Woodbury's Law comes about. Take quantum mechanics as an example. Some experimental result cannot be explained. A theorist needs to pick some approach to solve the riddle. It is like coming to a fork in the road. The theorist chooses one of the two paths to take and writes a paper about his or her results. These results lead to another fork in the road, and another choice is made. Other people follow the same paths, writing more and more papers, until the paths get worn."

"I think I get it," Peggy says. "It's Robert Frost's poem, *The Road Not Taken*."

"Exactly," Sam says. "If you go back to the very first fork in the road that confronted the theorist, what do you find?"

"The one he or she took is all worn down, and it looks as if no one ever went down the other road."

"And what does that mean for your quest for a Theory of Everything?"

"It means that Robert Frost had the answer, and I should take the one less traveled by."

"You've got it," Sam says. "Just think, if the wrong path was taken in that very first fork in the road, then all the rest of the forks for the next hundred years don't matter. There's no need to learn all of those mistakes, which were all a result of taking the wrong path at the very beginning."

"So I just need to go back to the beginning," Peggy says, "and ask the very basic question of why a particular path was taken, and then perhaps take the one less traveled by."

"That's it," Sam says. "So when you take physics courses in college, never accept anything at face value. Always go back to the original source. If you read what the people who developed the theories say in their own words, you will appreciate that not everything was obvious to them at the beginning. They had to make guesses and they stumbled around a lot. If you read the correspondences they had with one another, you will see that they argued a lot and they often did not agree on the meaning of various theories."

"But if someone comes along with a better theory, won't everyone then agree that it is better?"

"Not by a long shot. Once you have spent years going down a particular series of paths, you are psychologically not prepared to abandon all of that work. That is why someone who has been working on it for decades will never discover a Theory of Everything. If he or she were on the right path, it would have been discovered by now."

"You mean it has to be discovered by someone like me, who doesn't know much and doesn't have years of work invested in a wrong approach?"

"That's right, Peggy," Sam says. "But if you discover a Theory of Everything, don't expect that many scientists will believe you right away. I've already told you how many astrophysicists resist believing empirical data staring them right in the face."

Peggy ponders that. "Then I'll just have to figure out a way to convince them, which they can't ignore."

8

It's New Year's Eve and Laura is preparing cheese fondue for dinner. On Saturday, everyone had hung out at the farm, Bill and Peggy spending most of the day in the lake house getting the samiPhone to display text from Peggy's writing with the U-Pen, Wayne and Connie exploring more of Long Island, walking up to the bridge and down little side roads. No one who has watched Connie and Wayne together the last several days doubts that they will have an ongoing relationship. On Sunday, the ski trip to Mt. Cranmore was a success, with more good weather and excellent ski conditions. Connie was blown away with the views of the White Mountains and Tuckerman Ravine.

"Ok," Laura says, "the fondue pots are on the table and hot. Let's get started with dinner."

Sam sets his samiPhone to signal when the New Year arrives at midnight, as everyone starts dunking their fondue forks filled with various vegetables and breads into the fondue pots.

"Uncle Sam," Peggy asks, "did you see that Bill has programmed the samiPhone to convert my cursive writing into displayed typed text on the screen?"

"I did. Bill showed it to me this morning. That's very impressive."

"Actually," Bill says, "the hard part was done by Wayne's algorithm that is built into the U-Pen."

"Even so," Sam says, "getting all the communications set up and working isn't exactly trivial. Bill did a really good job."

Peggy looks at Sam. "Bill and I have been thinking about your idea of writing an app for smart phones or tablets that uses the U-Pen."

"So have you come up with any ideas?"

"Well, I want to get something working that will be useful for me to use in college. You told me how, when you were in college, copying your lecture notes by hand very carefully was very helpful in learning the material. You also said that you only really learned something when you had to teach it. There are also the short video clips you made for your digital design class, the ones you put on YouTube that students can view before coming to class. So putting all this together, I'd like to make something where, after each class, I could rewrite the notes using my U-Pen and easily turn the results into two or three short video clips that I could later review when studying for exams."

"I like that idea a lot," Sam says. "Using the U-Pen with something like an Android Tablet or an iPad could open up lots of potential applications."

"That's a good direction," Wayne says. "Why don't you see if you can write some kind of app for the Android Tablet or iPad?"

"What does it take to do that?" Peggy asks.

"Well apps for the Android Tablet are generally written in Java," Sam says, "which both of you know. Apps for the iPad are usually written using Apple's own language, Objective C. I would start with the Android Tablet. It is an easier process to get those apps up and running."

"Ok," Wayne says, "I have a couple of MacBook Pro notebook computers back at the office that you two can have to start working on. You can keep them and take them to college with you. You will each need one anyway, and you might as well have a good one. They are both loaded with the maximum amount of RAM and flash storage as well as the best applications. We will add a virtual machine running Windows so you can program easily in Java. I'll give each of you an Android Tablet that you can use to test out the fantastic app you develop."

Peggy is thrilled. "That would be great!"

"Wow, this is going to be fun," Bill says.

"Just come up with a cool app that will sell a lot of U-Pens," Wayne says.

"I think you're really on to something now," Sam says. "I can see lots of other applications other than just studying course material."

"Me too," Bill says. "Instead of texting clumsily with your thumbs, you can just write what you want to say on a piece of paper, or in a notebook, and tap *send*, and you'll have a permanent written record of what you sent."

"The written record is more important than you think," Sam says. "People don't realize that digital data is not permanent. A number of years ago the university built a new building and we buried a time capsule to be opened in fifty years. The question was what to put in it to represent our current age. It quickly became apparent that we could not put anything containing digital data in the time capsule, because no one would be able to read it in fifty years. In those days, we stored digital data on 3.5-inch floppy disks. Today, I have no computer that still reads those floppy disks. When cleaning my office at the university, I have thrown out stacks of old punched cards, 8-inch floppy disks, 5.25-inch floppy disks, and 3.5-inch floppy disks. I had hundreds of them that contained programs I had written and I couldn't read any of them. There won't be any equipment in fifty years to read the CD ROMs and USB thumb drives we use today to store data. Unless you print out all the photos you have taken with your smart phone, your grandchildren and great-grandchildren will never be able to see them. They will all have just disappeared into the air."

"That's a pretty frightening prospect," Kate says.

"I told you that writing notes to people is important," Laura says.

"Yeah Bill," Matt says, "when you're at RPI you can write all your love letters to Peggy using the U-Pen instead of regular email, so you'll have a permanent record that you can bundle up and give her when you get married."

"Matt!" Peggy snaps.

"You know, Matt, that is a good point," Wayne says. "While digital emails are not permanent in the long run, they do stay around for years, as corrupt government officials and Hollywood executives have discovered to their dismay. So we could have our U-Pen texting/email system automatically destroy permanently the digital version of the message once it has been sent on the sending end and then read on the receiving end."

"People might buy your system just for that feature," Sam says. "Many are realizing only now that everything they put on Facebook or Twitter never goes away. I think people's desire for some privacy is going to grow in coming years."

"That reminds me of one of my favorite poems by Omar Khayyam," Joe says. "It ought to be on the top of everyone's Facebook page. It goes like this."

> "The Moving Finger writes; and, having writ,
> Moves on: nor all your Piety nor Wit
> Shall lure it back to cancel half a Line,
> Nor all your Tears wash out a Word of it."

"That's right," Kate says. "You can't un-ring the bell."

"Getting back to Bill and Peggy's love letters," Laura says, as everyone laughs. "It's not a bad thing to just drop them in the mail even after you've written them with the U-Pen. You can keep you're digital version for a while or even print it out so you'll have a 'carbon copy' of what you wrote, but reading an email is not the same as the thrill of getting a sentimental letter in the mail that you can put away in a shoe box."

"And I bet you have many such shoe boxes in the attic, right Aunt Laura?" Peggy asks.

Laura just smiles.

"Well, that fondue was delicious," Sam says. "Why don't we all go into the living room and wait for the New Year to arrive? We can continue solving the world's problems in there. But before we do that, Laura is going to unveil the painting she has been working on all week."

They all go into the living room where Laura's easel is sitting in the corner with a sheet draped over the painting. Everyone gathers around in anticipation as Sam and Laura lift the sheet from the painting.

"Wow," Peggy says. "Look at that gorgeous painting of Gunstock Mountain. I can't believe we were skiing on that mountain as you were painting this."

"And there's Welch Island in the foreground," Dave says. "Mom, I think this is one of your best paintings. I love it."

"Tomorrow, we'll hang it on the wall between the two front windows," Sam says.

Dave puts more wood in the fireplace and Joe and Wayne arrange the chairs and sofas in a big semi-circle in front of the fireplace so everyone can get in on the conversation.

"I read recently that many elementary schools today don't teach cursive writing anymore," Eileen says. "Is that really true?"

"Oh yes," Sam says. "I'm beginning to see students coming to the university who can't read or write cursive. It's a horrible development."

"I'm glad I learned cursive," Peggy says.

"The idea that typing on a keyboard is going to eliminate the need to write by hand is very shortsighted and educationally wrong," Sam says. "And teaching them just to print robs them of an important connection between their brain and hand and between thinking and writing. Having to lift up your finger between each letter in a word disrupts your continuous thought process."

"And just like floppy disks, who is to say that keyboards are going to be around forever as the ideal input device," Wayne says. "They have largely been replaced by touch screens where you just point at things."

"They're going to be replaced by the U-Pen," Peggy announces.

"I've been thinking," Bill says, "that we need to make the U-Pen interface such that it is easy to add photos and video clips to the image on the screen. That is, the U-Pen needs to have a kind of mouse-mode where you can grab things, resize them, move them around, that sort of thing."

"When you retract the ballpoint pen cartridge by pressing the button at the top of the U-Pen," Wayne says, "the pressure-sensitive tip that remains can be used as a non-writing stylus, which could form the basis for a mouse."

"You are going to be busy, Bill," Sam says.

"I've been thinking about how I can use your U-Pen in my history classes," Joe says. "First of all, I can see how it would be great for giving exams in any kind of class. Questions can come up on the screen – not necessarily the same question at the same time for each student – and when the student writes the answer, the system not only knows if the answer is correct, but can also identify the student by the handwriting. Cheating can all but be eliminated, and if the answer is incorrect, the system could provide immediate feedback on the correct path to take. Exam taking could be a real learning experience."

"Yeah, I would say we have pretty much revolutionized the entire educational system," Peggy says.

"We've had so much fun this week," Wayne says, "skiing and everything, I think we should all spend Christmas and New Year's here every year that Peggy is in college."

"That's fine with me," Sam says.

"Are Connie and Bill invited too?" Matt asks.

"Yes, of course," Wayne and Peggy say in unison.

"And I've got another idea," Dave says. "Everyone is invited to our place on the ocean for next Thanksgiving. We have plenty of room for everyone, and Peggy and Bill can demonstrate their U-Pen applications and bring us up to date on RPI and UNH. Bill, you can bring your parents, and Connie, if your parents can come from Texas they are invited too. As I said, we have plenty of room."

"Wow, what a year this is going to be," Peggy says.

"Peggy," Sam says, "my electromagnetics class meets at seven-thirty on Monday and Wednesday nights next term. I will be starting Special Relativity on the second day of the class. If you can come for those two classes, you should get a good introduction to Special Relativity."

"I'll be there," Peggy says. "Our basketball games are only on Tuesdays and Thursdays, so that won't be a problem. By the way, you promised to come to one of my basketball games."

"Don't worry, I will."

At fifteen seconds before midnight, Sam's samiPhone connects itself to the wireless speaker in the living room. At exactly midnight, Sam's favorite rendition of Auld Lang Syne – all five verses – fills the farmhouse. Matt looks around. Aunt Laura is kissing Uncle Sam; Aunt Eileen is kissing Uncle Dave; his mom is kissing his dad; Peggy is kissing Bill; Connie is kissing Wayne. When the music stops, Matt says, "Isn't anyone going to kiss me?"

Connie crosses the room, takes Matt in her arms, and kisses him on the lips.

"Happy New Year, Matt," she says.

Matt nearly faints.

9

Peggy gets her first points of the game – a jump shot from 15 feet – as Sam smiles from his third row seat in the bleachers behind the PHS bench. He has not seen Peggy since she attended his second lecture on the Special Theory of Relativity on Monday night. He will talk to her after the game and find out what she thought.

Portsmouth is playing Concord tonight and the first thing that Sam recognizes is that at each starting position, the Concord girl is taller than the corresponding Portsmouth girl is. *Concord has some really tall girls, this could be a long night.* Nonetheless, Portsmouth jumps out to a quick 10 – 2 lead, and Sam immediately sees their strategy. Rather than run down the court after a Portsmouth basket and set up for a half-court defense – the conventional wisdom – Portsmouth has run a full-court press since the opening whistle. They never give Concord a chance to capitalize on their height advantage, and make them fight just to get the ball inbounds. There have already been three turnovers in Portsmouth's favor. *Speed could beat height tonight. Woodbury's law working again!*

By half time, Portsmouth is ahead 28 – 24. Peggy has 6 points and gives Sam the thumbs up as she heads to the locker room with her team. In the second half, Portsmouth does not let up, keeping the full-court press on for the entire game. They keep pulling ahead of a dejected Concord team and when the final whistle sounds, the scoreboard shows Portsmouth 61 – Concord 52. Peggy has scored 12 points, her season average. The PHS center and the other forward are their one-two scoring punch with Peggy counted on for extra rebounds.

"Hi, Uncle Sam," Peggy says coming over to his seat on the bleachers. "How did you like the game?"

"I see your coach knows Woodbury's Law and was able to turn the tables on Concord."

"That is what I told her when she said we were going to play full-court press in every game this season for the entire game. All we do in practice is run."

"You played a great game. I'm glad I came and got to see you play."

"Thanks. It means a lot to me."

"Did you understand any of the Special Relativity material in my class on Monday?"

"Actually, it makes a lot more sense now. Those graphical diagrams make all the difference. I'm going to get Bill to help me implement them on the Android Tablet using the U-Pen."

"I will be very interested in seeing it."

"I've got to run and take a shower. Thanks again for coming."

"I wouldn't miss it, Peggy."

Peggy smiles and heads off to the locker room.

A week later, Peggy calls Uncle Sam and tells him that the principal at the high school asked her if she would call him and invite him to be the commencement speaker at Peggy's upcoming graduation. She gives him the date.

"You'd be great," Peggy says. "Please do it."

"Let me think about it," Sam says. "I'll call you tomorrow."

The next day, Sam calls Peggy and accepts. She also receives her official acceptance letter from UNH with the promise of a full-tuition scholarship. Peggy now knows what college she will be attending in the fall.

The Portsmouth Girls Basketball team ends the season with only one loss and they win the quarterfinals playoff game on their home court in the Division II statewide tournament. It's Thursday night in mid-March and the team runs onto the floor as 2000 fans are screaming in the field house at Southern NH University in Hooksett. On hand to watch Peggy in the semifinals game are her parents, Matt, and Uncle Sam. Portsmouth is playing Lebanon, who has also lost only one game this season.

Portsmouth sticks to its season-long strategy of running a full-court press for the entire game. Lebanon has scouted them well, and they execute several tactics to break the press. Some succeed and lead to easy baskets. At half time, the score is Lebanon 28 – Portsmouth 25. In the locker room at half time, the Portsmouth coach reminds everyone on the team how they got here. They are in better shape than the Lebanon players. Just keep pressing until the final whistle. Lebanon players will not be able to keep up. They will tire and turn over the ball. Just stick to the strategy.

Peggy intercepts a pass on the first play of the second half and throws it down the court to a teammate for an easy layup. The Portsmouth players continue to press without letting up. They take the lead midway through the second half and the lead goes back and forth several times before the final whistle blows. When it does, Portsmouth has eked out the victory 56-54. Based on their scouting, Lebanon double-teamed the PHS center and other forward. This left Peggy open more than usual, and as a result, she was the high-scorer on her team for the first time this year with 20 points.

"I'm not sure I can take another one like this," Sam says.

"This means they play the winner of Hanover and Pembroke in the finals on Saturday," Joe says.

The final match-up is against Pembroke at four o'clock on Saturday in the same field house where they beat Lebanon. Joe, Kate, Matt, and Uncle Sam drive over from Portsmouth in the early afternoon. Wayne picks up Connie as she gets out of work at 3:00 and they make it to the field house just before the game starts.

Pembroke also scouted Portsmouth well and not only double-teams the PHS high scorers, but they also adopt the same full-press all-the-time strategy. This causes PHS to struggle, and the lead goes back and forth many times. With five minutes to go, the PHS center fouls out. Just as in the semi-final game, Peggy takes advantage of the Pembroke defense focusing on the PHS center and other forward, and ends the game as the PHS high-scorer with a season high of 24 points. However, that is not quite enough, and Portsmouth loses to Pembroke 66 – 59. Nevertheless, Peggy is the only PHS player named to the All-Tournament Team. Her picture appears in the Sunday Union-Leader.

Peggy and her whole family, including Uncle Sam and Aunt Laura as well as Matt and Connie, are in the high school gym, which has been converted into a lavish banquet hall. The Girls Basketball Booster Club has organized an awards banquet in recognition of their making it to the Division II finals. They have raised funds from local merchants to put on this banquet. All the players, their families and friends fill the gym. A local caterer has provided a chicken dinner with all of the fixings.

Seated at the head table are the high school principal, their coach, the mayor and other city dignitaries, and the guest speaker, Donna Johnson, the head coach of the varsity women's basketball team at UNH.

After dinner, each player is called to the front and presented with a Maroon and White jacket and a big letter P. Their coach then introduces Donna Johnson, who will make a special presentation before giving her talk.

Donna Johnson walks around in front of the head table. "Will Peggy Leach please come forward."

Peggy walks to the front and stands next to Donna Johnson, who picks up a trophy from the table.

"Peggy, it is my pleasure to present you with this trophy for being named the starting forward on the All-Tournament Team. You were the high scorer and leading rebounder on your team in both the semi-final and final game of the tournament. You richly deserve this honor. Congratulations."

Peggy accepts the trophy from Donna Johnson. "Thank you very much."

A photographer snaps a photo of a smiling Peggy holding the trophy in her left hand while shaking hands with Donna Johnson. As Peggy returns to her seat, her parents beam with pride and join in the applause.

Donna Johnson begins to speak. She talks about women's basketball at UNH and about the many life lessons one learns from playing team sports. She then looks around the gym and reminds the players of all the effort and hard work that goes into putting together a banquet like this. She thanks the members of the Booster Club who are there, and she asks the players if they know why these people would go to all of this trouble for them. She says it reminds her of one of her favorite poems written by Will Allen Dromgoole called *The Bridge Builder.* She says that an excerpt from the poem is on a plaque on the Vilas Bridge in Bellows Falls, Vermont near the site of the first bridge to span the Connecticut River to New Hampshire. She then recites the entire poem from memory:

> An old man going a lone highway,
> Came at the evening, cold and gray,
> To a chasm, vast, and deep and wide,
> Through which was flowing a sullen tide.
>
> The old man crossed in the twilight dim;
> The sullen stream had no fear for him;
> But he turned, when safe on the other side,
> And built a bridge to span the tide.
>
> "Old man," said a fellow pilgrim, near,
> "You are wasting strength with building here;
> Your journey will end with the ending day;
> You never again will pass this way;
> You've crossed the chasm, deep and wide -
> Why build you this bridge at the evening tide?"
>
> The builder lifted his old gray head:
> "Good friend, in the path I have come," he said,
> "There followeth after me today,
> A youth, whose feet must pass this way.
>
> This chasm, that has been naught to me,
> To that fair-haired youth may a pitfall be.
> He, too, must cross in the twilight dim;
> Good friend, I am building this bridge for him."

When Peggy gets home, she looks up the poem, *The Bridge Builder,* online and commits it to memory. She senses that Donna Johnson was talking directly to her when she recited the poem. Peggy knows she is going to make a difference. Someday.

10

Peggy stands at the first row, aisle seat as her classmates continue to march into the auditorium and fill in the rows behind her. The high school band is at the back of the stage playing Pomp and Circumstance. The teachers and the platform party follow the students down the center aisle and walk up the steps to their chairs on the stage. At the very end of the procession, are the principal and Uncle Sam. As he passes her, Uncle Sam winks at Peggy, and then mounts the steps to the stage, Peggy admiring the bright Cherry and White colors on the back of Uncle Sam's hood. These are the colors of RPI, where he received his Ph.D. degree. The dark blue velvet trim on his gown, including the three stripes on each arm, is the Doctor of Philosophy color. As one of the top-ten graduating seniors, Peggy was selected to give the senior salutation and to introduce Uncle Sam as the graduation speaker. Peggy is hoping that when the band stops playing, people will not be able to hear her heart pounding. She just wants to get this over.

After some introductory remarks and reading the list of the top-ten graduating seniors, the principal introduces Peggy. Uncle Sam smiles at her as she steps behind the lectern. When she looks out over the audience in the packed auditorium, she realizes that all of those eyes are on her. She remembers that Uncle Sam had told her to picture everyone in the audience in their underwear. She chuckles to herself. *I will show them who is the only one fully dressed.*

She places her remarks on the lectern and begins to read in a strong clear voice. She talks about their years at PHS, the friends they have made, and how they have all grown and matured. She thanks the administrators, teachers, and coaches. Then she introduces Uncle Sam. She gives a brief biographical sketch and then tells her classmates how lucky she is to have been so close to her uncle her entire life.

The audience applauds as Peggy goes back to her seat in the front row and Sam steps to the lectern. He looks down at Peggy and thanks her for her flattering comments. Then he looks at the graduating seniors and tells them that when Peggy said how lucky she is, he looked around at all of them and thought of how lucky they all are.

"The reason you are all lucky," Sam says, "is that you are all ignorant!"

Peggy almost chokes. *What is he doing? Was this a big mistake inviting my unpredictable uncle?*

"You are not dumb," Sam says, "just ignorant. There is a lot you know, but there is a lot more that you don't know. There are things that you know you don't know, but there are a lot more things that you don't know you don't know."

Uncle Sam never takes his eyes off the students, and Peggy realizes that he has no written speech and no notes. *Where is this going?*

"And that is why you are so lucky," Sam says. "There are many things that people think they know, that turn out not to be so. And the fact that you don't know these things is a big advantage for you. It means that there is a lot you won't have to unlearn."

Peggy smiles to herself. She thinks she smells Woodbury's Law coming. Sam never mentions Woodbury's Law by name, but he stresses the importance of not taking things at face value, of not following the crowd, of following your own instincts. At one point, he recites Robert Frost's poem *The Road Not Taken* from memory. He reminds them that sometimes the path less traveled by will reveal unexpected treasures.

Sam looks at the students in the front row and says, "Those of you in the front row who are falling asleep and daydreaming, don't let me disturb you. Because now I want to talk to you about dreams."

He quotes Douglas Everett who wrote:

> There are some people who live in a Dream World,
> And there are some who face Reality.
> And then there are those who turn one into the Other.

Sam tells the students that it is their job to turn their dreams into reality. He tells them that dreams alone are not enough. You need a plan.

Quoting Zig Ziglar, Sam says, "If you aim at nothing, you will hit it every time."

Sam goes on to quote Mark Twain:

> Twenty years from now you will be more disappointed by
> the things that you didn't do than by the ones you did do.
> So throw off the bowlines. Sail away from the safe harbor.
> Catch the trade winds in your sails. Explore. Dream.
> Discover.

Finally, Sam starts to wrap up – never having taken his eyes off the students.

"Both John and Bobby Kennedy would often paraphrase the Serpent in

George Bernard Shaw's play *Back to Methuselah*. Particularly Bobby Kennedy would often end his speeches with the quote:

> 'Some people see things as they are and say why?
> I dream things that never were and say, why not?'

"I ask each of you to leave here today and go dream things that never were, and to say, why not? Congratulations and sweet dreams."

Sam takes his seat to roaring applause, a big smile growing on Peggy's face. The graduates line up on each side of the stage for the handing out of diplomas. When Peggy's name is called, Sam stands up and presents Peggy with her diploma and a big hug.

That night Peggy takes out one of the note cards that Aunt Laura had given her for Christmas and writes a thank you note to Uncle Sam. She then goes to bed, falls asleep, and dreams of things that never were.

The next morning Peggy is excited. She did dream of things that never were. Picking up her U-Pen, Peggy writes down how the app she and Bill have been working on can be modified to turn it into a super-successful app. She is sure this is an idea that will change everything. She can't wait to tell Bill.

11

The sign outside the building in the Pease International Tradeport in Newington reads

The U-Pen Company
Engineering Division

The Tradeport is next to the Portsmouth International Airport and the entire complex was formerly the Pease Air Force Base, part of the Strategic Air Command, which closed in 1991. Since then, it has been transformed into a world-class industrial park with state-of-the-art facilities and amenities. The U-Pens are manufactured in the Rochester facility, but a year ago, Wayne leased this building in the Tradeport and moved all engineering operations here. It is a much better working environment for the engineers and technical staff, and a closer commute for most of them.

Peggy and Bill enter the building at 7:50 a.m., walk down the hall, and enter a room with the sign *Special Projects* on the door. Wayne told them that they could use this room to work on their U-Pen app. They have been working here for a week, starting right after the high school graduation. Each morning, Bill picks up Peggy in his Ford Taurus, and they make the eight-minute drive to Newington together. Today they are meeting with Wayne and Uncle Sam to bring them up to date on what they have been doing and to fill them in on their new big idea.

Wayne and Sam enter the room at eight o'clock sharp. The four sit down at the table in the center of the room.

"So tell me, how are things going?" Wayne asks.

Bill tells Wayne and Sam how they have written an app for the Android Tablet that behaves like the samiPhone program he wrote over Christmas. Peggy demonstrates how anything she writes on paper is displayed on the tablet, and how her cursive writing is converted to printed text.

"We've come up with a great idea, which will sell lots of U-Pens," Peggy says.

"I'm all ears," Wayne says.

"Well, Bill and I both took Calculus last term in high school and we started doing our homework problems together. When we weren't together, we would FaceTime on our MacBooks and ask each other questions. Then Bill said, 'Why not use our U-Pens and our Android Tablets so we can show each other how to do the problem'. This worked great."

"Then I wrote a program that would capture each problem-solving session in a short video clip," Bill says, "which we could review for the test. It really was helpful."

"So, here's the big idea," Peggy says. "This summer, Bill and I will write an app for the Android Tablet that will allow anyone in the world to log on and record on a video clip their solution to a particular calculus problem, or a homework problem in any other class. All of these solutions will be stored on a server that the app accesses. Users will be able to communicate and interact in unique ways. For example, when you click on a particular homework problem, it will list on the right all users worldwide who are currently working on the same homework problem. You can join a videoconference with others who are working on that particular problem. You can join the conversation in real time by raising your hand – clicking a raised hand – and getting in the queue to talk. No one could talk for more than, say, a minute if someone else is waiting to speak. A timer would show you how much time you have left to speak. People will not only be able to see you, but in a separate window, they can see what you are writing on a piece of paper with the U-Pen. And, if you wanted, they could get an electronic version of what you write."

"This has real possibilities," Sam says.

"Yes," Bill says, "within a short period of time the solutions, in the form of video clips where a real person is going through the solution step by step, for all homework problems in every textbook will be online in our app."

"This could have real value," Wayne says. "How are you going to market it?"

"Bill and I have talked about starting a company to market it," Peggy says, "but we have no idea how to do that. When I mentioned it to my dad, he said it takes a lot of money to start a company, money I don't have, and money I would need for college if I did have it. So he was not too encouraging. What do you two think?"

Sam responds. "I think your dad should be a little more open-minded. Done right, this app could make money that would help with your college expenses."

"It shouldn't take that much money to get started," Wayne says, "certainly not the fifty million dollars I had to raise to build a complete factory. You have everything you need to write the app, so you can probably bootstrap the company from sales revenues."

"Heck," Sam says, "I'll invest in your company by providing whatever you need in terms of a server to get started."

"I'd go for it," Wayne says. "Have you thought of a name for the app?"

"Not really," Peggy says.

"You could call the app Peggy," Sam says.

"No," Bill says, "let's call it The Pearl."

"How about 'Pearls of Wisdom'," Peggy says.

"That's it!" Sam says. "Perfect."

"And we can call the videoconference feature PearlTiming," Bill says.

"That's perfect," Peggy says. "Let's PearlTime."

"Now that you've got a name for the app," Sam says, "what about a name for the company?"

"It ought to have the word Pearl in it," Bill says, "but needs to be different from other Pearl companies."

Everyone tosses around various names with 'Pearl' in it.

"How about something like Pearlton Industries," Wayne says. "I just Googled it and there isn't one."

"It's probably a good choice," Sam says, "as I think you'll end up with lots of divisions before you're done."

"I can't believe we're talking about starting a company," Peggy says. "What do we have to do?"

"It's not that hard," Wayne says. "I can help you with those details. But first you need to figure out exactly how the Pearls of Wisdom app would work in terms of marketing and getting revenue."

"We've been thinking about it," Bill says. "We'll start with the calculus and physics classes that Peggy and I are taking at UNH and RPI in the fall and everyone in those classes will be able to use it. Perhaps we can give each of them a U-Pen and a copy of the app. This will help us test it out."

"I got the idea for funding in a dream I had after graduation," Peggy says. "To get the Pearls of Wisdom app, you would buy a U-Pen and this would give you a year's subscription to Pearls of Wisdom. We would then have an annual subscription of, say $20, to keep getting the latest version with new homework assignments that are continually being added. To provide incentives to make good homework solutions, we would put aside, say, half of our revenues for distribution to the contributors. At the end of each term, this money would be distributed through PayPal to the contributors based on the number of 'views' their video clips get. It is a way for good students to earn a little extra cash by helping other students learn. Sort of like Uber, but this is crowd-learning."

"I like it," Wayne says.

"If Pearlton Industries were to buy U-Pens from you in bulk," Peggy asks, "how much would each one cost?"

"It would probably be best to sell your own version and give it your own name, maybe a PearlPen, with your own logo on it. We could produce those pens for about $10 each."

"So if we sold them for $50 each," Peggy says, "that should give you a good profit and provide us with some start-up money to get going."

"Actually," Bill says, "I checked the statistics and something like a half a million science and engineering degrees are awarded each year in the United States. About 63% of those who start such a degree program graduate, so it looks like about 800,000 students might take freshman physics and calculus each year just in the United States, which has less than 15% of college enrollment worldwide."

Sam did a quick calculation. "If even half of the 800,000 U.S. students taking freshman calculus and physics each year bought a PearlPen for $50, that would be $50 x 400,000 or 20 million dollars. Seems like enough to get started!"

"And a new batch of 800,000 freshmen appear every year ready to buy a new PearlPen," Peggy says, "and the $20 annual subscription could bring in over 20 million dollars each year including all engineering and science students."

"And remember," Sam says, "you haven't counted the 85% of all college students who are in other countries, or the several million students attending community colleges, many of whom take calculus and physics. I would say there is plenty of growth potential. Let's get together tomorrow and see if there is anything we are missing. We can also work out the details of setting up the company."

"I can have our lawyer draw up everything we need," Wayne says, "and then Peggy and Bill can have their company by the end of the summer."

"Sounds perfect," Sam says.

"I still can't believe it," Peggy says.

The next day, Peggy and Bill meet with Sam, Wayne, and the lawyer. They agree that Peggy will be president and own 45% of the company. Bill will be vice-president and own 45% of the company. Wayne will have a 5% ownership and the day-to-day operations of Pearlton Industries will be run out of The U-Pen Company facility in Newington. Sam agrees to put in some startup money for the server and other expenses and will own 5% of the company and be Chairman of the Board of Directors. Peggy, Wayne, and Bill will also be on the board. Pearlton Industries will buy bulk PearlPens from The U-Pen Company.

After the lawyer leaves, Peggy, Bill, Wayne, and Sam continue to discuss the implications of producing the Pearls of Wisdom app.

"I've been thinking more about your Pearls of Wisdom app," Sam says, "and some of the problems you might run into."

"Like what?" Peggy asks.

"Professors in most math, science, and engineering courses in college will assign homework problems. Some will not collect the homework and just tell the students that they are responsible for knowing the material on the exams."

"Then our app should help students learn the material," Bill says.

"I agree," Sam says, "but many professors collect the homework and grade it. Some encourage students to work together, but require each student to do his or her own work. Just copying someone else's solution is not acceptable and is considered cheating by some professors. I know professors who have referred students who turn in identical homework assignments to a university conduct committee who can hand out punishments including expulsion."

Wayne asks, "Do you think that some professors might accuse Peggy of contributing to cheating by making this app available to all students?"

"I wouldn't put it past some who I know," Sam says.

"That's not fair," Peggy says. "This is such a good app that will help lots of students learn the material better."

"I agree," Bill says. "What can we do to get around this?"

"I think you need to get the faculty to accept the app as a positive," Sam says.

"How do we do that?" Peggy asks.

"I'm not exactly sure," Sam says, "but you need to convince them that it is a benefit for them, something that will make their life easier."

"I have an idea," Wayne says. "The professor could require the student to hand in the homework problem done with a U-Pen. In fact, they could collect the electronic version which could verify that it was actually written by the same person whose signature is at the top of the page."

"That's brilliant," Sam says. "The electronic version could even include the audio of the student explaining each step of the solution. There's no doubt that the students would learn more and the professor would know it is the student's own work."

"That's a great idea," Peggy says. "How can we get the professors to use the system?"

"Do you think you can get the app finished by the end of July?" Sam asks.

"We should be able to get the Android Tablet version working by then," Bill says.

"If that's the case, then I'll talk with Prof. Kelly, who I'm sure is teaching Physics-I in the fall. She is a friend of mine, and I will tell her that I am associated with a company who has a new app called the Pearls of Wisdom, which uses a unique input device called a PearlPen. I'll explain the opportunity to use this to improve student learning and to allow unique homework submissions, which include a foolproof method of recording the student actually doing the assignment."

"We need her to adopt the method," Wayne says. "We can offer her free PearlPens and apps for each student in the class, as a sort of beta test of the system."

"That might work," Sam says. "I'll also talk with Prof. Rodriguez, who is teaching freshman calculus in the fall."

"Bill could also give free PearlPens and the app to other students in his physics and calculus courses at RPI," Peggy says. "They could help get lots of homework solutions made."

"This will be a good way to get it off the ground," Wayne says.

"Do you think this will work?" Peggy asks.

"We'll see," Sam says.

"Let's revisit the funding mechanism," Wayne says. "In the fall we will give away PearlPens and the app to the students in the freshman physics and calculus courses at UNH. But other students will find out about it – students in other sections or even their friends at other universities. So how do we get other students to buy a PearlPen?"

"We need to encourage them to use the app," Peggy says. "Why not make a basic introductory version of the app free to get them hooked. Something they could just download and view without being able to add content with a PearlPen."

"That's a good idea," Sam says. "I would restrict its capability by limiting the number of homework solutions that they can view to so many per month."

"That would be easy to do," Bill says. "We should probably limit it to a fairly small number; say ten per month, something less than the number of homework problems they really need to solve."

"The app should then give clear instructions on how to order the upgraded complete version of the app and the PearlPen to go with it," Wayne says.

"And also the app needs to tell them clearly, by means of a video clip, how they can make money by uploading their solutions to homework problems," Peggy says.

"We'll call it *Learn and Earn*," Bill says.

That's brilliant," Sam says. "Now you need to get the Android Tablet app finished by the end of July."

"We're on it right now," Bill says.

"By the way," Sam says, "you're all invited up to the lake for the 4th of July long weekend. We're going to the fireworks in Wolfeboro in Dave's boat."

"I can't wait," Peggy says. "We'll need a break."

That night Peggy can't sleep. She can't believe she is going to be the president of her own company, a company that's going to produce an app that university students will use, an app that might actually make money, money that might help pay for college, even though that college isn't Dartmouth. *Why didn't I get into Dartmouth?*

12

It is sunny and 80 degrees on the afternoon of Friday, July 4th and all of the activity is around the lake house. Sam and Wayne have challenged Joe and Dave to a game of doubles horseshoes, Sam throwing against Dave, Wayne throwing against Joe. Sam and Dave have been playing horseshoes against each other since Dave was a teenager. Sam taught Dave how to throw so that the horseshoe remains flat in the air, making one and a half rotations before landing open at the stake. Wayne and Joe both throw the horseshoes end over end. The current score is 10 to 6, in favor of Sam and Wayne.

Laura and Kate are in the house fixing potato salad for the cookout. Peggy and Bill are out kayaking. Eileen and Connie are sitting on the beach watching Matt swim laps in front of the house.

Connie and Wayne have been dating regularly since New Year's Eve. Connie's work schedule has changed and she now works the 12-hour shift from 6:00 a.m. to 6:00 p.m. Monday, Tuesday, and Wednesday. So she was able to come up yesterday with Wayne.

Kate comes out to the horseshoe pit and asks, "Who is winning?"

"Sam and Wayne beat us in the first game 21-15 and are ahead in this game 15-10," Joe says.

"We need the grill started when you finish that game."

"I'll do it," Dave says.

Peggy and Bill pull the kayaks up on the beach and go for a quick swim while Dave and Wayne cook hot dogs and hamburgers on the grill.

"Come get your hot dogs and cheeseburgers," Wayne yells as they load up the platters and put them on the porch table with the potato salad, baked beans, and drinks. Filling up their plates, they all find a place to sit.

"Your Uncle Dave and I are so excited about your new company," Eileen says to Peggy and Bill.

"I think they bit off more than they can chew," Joe says.

"Dad, you're supposed to be excited about it too," Peggy says. "This app is going to be great."

"Yes," Connie says, "Wayne tells me that he may have to build a new factory to keep up with all the U-Pen sales."

"PearlPens, please!" Bill says.

"Well," Joe says, "I still think you should concentrate on your studies when you're in college, not diverting your attention by starting some company."

Peggy is frustrated and ignores her dad's comment. "Aunt Laura, you're such a good artist, I'd love it if you could design a logo for our company. Maybe it could look like a pearl, somehow including the letters P and I for Pearlton Industries. Would you be able to do that?"

"I would be happy to come up with something. It would be a fun project."

"The fireworks in Wolfeboro are at nine-thirty tonight," Dave says, "so we'll leave here around eight-thirty and enjoy the sunset on the way down the lake."

Dave stops his 28-foot boat in the large middle part of the lake called the broads. It is about ten miles from the lake house to Wolfeboro bay and the lake is about four miles wide where Dave is drifting off the western end of the two-mile long Rattlesnake Island, shaped like a reptile. He is not far from the deepest point on the lake – 187 feet. Peggy takes some good sunset photos looking back up the lake. Proceeding into Wolfeboro bay, Dave drops anchor close to the public beach where they will have a great view of the fireworks. As it gets darker and darker, the red, green and white running lights of the more than 200 boats in the bay provide an eerie mood. At 9:30, the first fireworks are set off, exploding in bright, colorful, and different shapes directly overhead, a new red heart shape added this year, the pyrotechnic display continuing for nearly half an hour. The final continuous volleys of fireworks are particularly spectacular. When the fireworks are over, Dave pulls up the anchor and proceeds at headway speed through the maze of boats, past the flashing blue light of the Marine Patrol boat, and out of Wolfeboro bay. He swings around Parker Island and heads up the center of the broads under a moonless sky full of bright stars.

Dave slows down the boat to headway speed, as slow as he can go and still steer. The lights in the windows of cottages along the distant shore make it a challenge to find the blinking buoys that will mark their route home. The bright stars sparkle from horizon to horizon, blending in with the silvery Milky Way directly overhead.

"A great night for star gazing," Dave says.

Bill can't believe how much brighter the stars are here on the lake than at Prescott Park where the lights from Portsmouth interfere.

"There is the big dipper," Peggy says, "and I can follow the side of its bowl to the North Star."

"How far away is the big dipper?" Matt asks.

"Your Uncle Dave is the amateur astronomer," Sam says. "Maybe he knows."

"Just because you gave me my first telescope for my 10th birthday, doesn't make me an expert."

"But you've built bigger and bigger ones ever since. So can you answer Matt's question?"

"Actually, I do know quite a bit about the big dipper. Of the seven stars in the big dipper, the closest one to the Earth is the dimmest one, the one connecting the handle to the bowl of the dipper. Its name is Megrez and it is somewhat over 58 light-years from Earth. This means that the light you see coming from that star left the star on its way to the Earth before I was born."

"That is hard to believe," Peggy says.

"The one farthest away from the Earth is the last one in the bowl, the one pointing to the North Star. Its name is Dubhe and it is 123 light-years from Earth."

"The third one down the handle looks like the brightest of the seven stars," Joe says.

"That's right. Its name is Alioth and it is 81 light-years away."

"How far away is the North Star?" Matt asks.

"It is much farther away than any of the stars in the big dipper. It is about 434 light-years away."

Joe does a quick calculation. "That means the light you are seeing right now from the North Star left the star almost forty years before the Pilgrims landed at Plymouth in the Mayflower."

"That *is* hard to believe," Matt says.

Wayne raises a question. "Suppose you were on the star Megrez 58 years ago just as the light we see was starting to come to earth. At that instant of time, light from the North Star will not reach Megrez for another 376 years. Since nothing can travel faster than the speed of light, how can Megrez possibly know that it should be feeling a force of gravity due to the North Star? Or from any other star for that matter?"

"That is the old 'action at a distance' problem," Sam says. "Everyone knows that Newton's law of gravity, while predicting lots of things correctly, can't be the final word on how gravity works."

"Doesn't Einstein's general theory of relativity come to the rescue?" Dave asks.

Peggy pipes in, "Uncle Sam doesn't think so, do you?"

"You're right, I have my doubts. I guess we will have to wait for your Theory of Everything to figure things out."

"How many stars can we see in the sky?" Matt asks.

Dave continues his recollections of astronomical facts. "If you can look at the sky all year long from both the northern and southern hemispheres, you could probably see almost 9,000 stars. With good binoculars, that number might increase to about 200,000, and could go to around fifteen million with a good telescope."

"Isn't the Milky Way the galaxy we are in?" Kate asks.

"Yes, it is a big spiral galaxy about 120,000 light-years across, and we are about 27,000 light-years from its core."

"That sounds big," Matt says. "How many stars are in the Milky Way?"

"A huge number – probably 400 billion."

"How many galaxies are there?" Peggy asks.

"Another huge number – at least 170 billion, coming in different sizes and shapes."

"It is hard to comprehend the size of the universe," Joe says.

"Not only its size," Sam says, "but what it is actually made up of. What we see with our eyes is only visible light. However, these are just electromagnetic waves in a very narrow part of the entire electromagnetic spectrum. Infrared telescopes give a different picture of what is out there, and the new ALMA radio telescope array in Chili shows a whole different picture of what the universe looks like if your eyes could perceive millimeter and sub-millimeter radio waves."

Peggy is intrigued. "Suppose our eyes could see all wavelengths of the electromagnetic spectrum, from very low frequencies all the way to gamma rays. What do you think the universe would look like then?"

"Very hard to say," Sam says. "Unlike anything anyone has ever seen."

"Maybe that's all the universe really is," Peggy suggests, "just electromagnetic waves of all different frequencies."

"Is that going to be your Theory of Everything?" Bill asks.

"I don't know, but it would be a simple idea."

"At least it is a place to start," Sam says.

Their slow headway speed home has brought the boat within 200 feet of the lake house dock. Dave turns off the running lights, making the star-filled sky even more dramatic. All quietly sit in the boat, looking up in wonder at their small window into the vast universe, feeling very small indeed. After several minutes, Dave turns on his docking lights and pulls the boat slowly up to the dock, the wailing sounds of two nearby loons welcoming them home.

"That was an interesting ride," Connie says. "It is the first time I've been out on this big a lake in this size boat at night."

"It won't be the last time," Wayne says. "By the way, Connie and I won't be here for dinner tomorrow night as we are going to have dinner on the cruise ship Mount Washington."

The following afternoon, Peggy, Bill, Wayne, and Sam are floating in the lake about 200 feet off shore. They are sitting on individual water hammocks, making them appear to be sitting upright with their head and shoulders out of the water.

"So Bill, have you got the U-Pen working as a mouse?" Sam asks.

"Yes, I use the velocity data from the U-Pen to calculate the position of the cursor on the screen," Bill says. "Tapping the U-Pen on the paper twice represents a click."

"How do you distinguish a left click from a right click?" Sam asks.

"If you're right handed, when you are writing, the U-Pen slopes up toward the right. The accelerometers in the pen can detect this slope. If you double-tap the point in this position, it is a left click. Think of the pen tip pointing to the left. To make a right-click, just turn the U-Pen so the pen tip points to the right and double click. Voila!"

"Not a bad idea," Wayne says.

"What about dragging?" Sam asks.

"The U-Pen measures the pressure of the pen tip on the paper," Bill says. "If you double click the tip, that's like pressing the left key. Now if you press the tip into the paper beyond some threshold pressure, it is like holding down the key."

"Does it work well?" Sam asks.

"Works like a charm," Bill says. "The U-Pen gives a very fine control of the cursor location."

"On another subject, Peggy," Sam asks, "have you taken a closer look at my Special Relativity notes?"

"I have, and I want to see if I can make a number of short videos this summer that will cover relativistic kinematics. If Bill and I can make those graphical diagrams dynamic so I can move the lines around, it should be easy to solve various relativistic kinematics problems."

"You're exactly right. I'll loan you a couple of physics textbooks that have lots of relativity problems in them, and you can see if you can solve them using your interactive graphical system."

"That will be great. I can then make short videos showing how to solve the problem."

"I'll then give them to my students to help them learn the material."

"I've been thinking of majoring in physics rather than engineering. I really like this special relativity stuff and want to be able to take more physics courses than the engineering students do. After all, I've got to figure out what's going on if I want to discover my Theory of Everything."

"I think that's a good choice for you. Physics graduates can always do engineering if they need to make a living."

That night as Peggy lay in bed, she could picture Uncle Sam's students using her videos to study relativity. *This could be big,* she thinks.

The next morning, Kate and Eileen are preparing the Sunday morning brunch – eggs, pancakes, fruit, coffee and juice. Some folks slept in this morning and it is after ten o'clock when everyone gathers around the table on the lake house porch.

"So Wayne, how was the moonlight cruise last night?" Peggy asks.

"It was great. Connie has something to show everyone."

Connie stands up and holds out her left hand displaying a large, sparkling diamond ring.

"Wayne and I are engaged," Connie says smiling.

Everyone yells with excitement.

"I call that a successful cruise," Sam says.

"When's the wedding?" Matt asks.

"Sometime next summer," Wayne says.

"How exciting!" Kate says.

Everyone gets up and congratulates Wayne, hugs Connie, and examines her ring.

"Will that make you my aunt, Connie?" Matt asks.

"Actually," Joe says, "Wayne is your second cousin, so I guess Connie will be your second cousin-in-law. So, she'll still just be Connie to you."

"I'm really glad you will be part of the family," Matt says.

"We all are!" Peggy says.

Over the next few weeks, Bill, with some important help from Peggy, gets the Pearls of Wisdom app up and running on the Android Tablet. Peggy has tested it by making eight short video clips explaining special relativity using the graphical method from Sam's notes. She then makes some additional video clips, each one solving a particular problem in relativity using the graphical method. She sends them all to Sam, who makes them available to his graduate students. Their reaction is overwhelmingly positive. His students ask where the clips came from. Sam smiles and tells them they came from a secret source. He did not have the heart to tell them that a recent high school graduate made them.

Laura has designed the logo for Pearlton Industries. It is an artistic sphere that looks like a beautiful pink pearl. The light reflecting from the surface of the pearl looks like a P and an I. The overall effect makes for a very attractive logo.

The Pearls of Wisdom app is maintained on a server hosted by The U-Pen Company. Wayne has an employee named Harry, who is a graduate of UNH and was recommended by Sam. He is an excellent programmer and maintains The U-Pen Company website among other duties, but has been looking to do more programming. Wayne agrees to share him with Peggy and Bill and have him maintain the Pearlton Industries website and help with upgrades of the Pearls of Wisdom app. He also programs in Objective C and works with Bill in August on converting the Pearls of Wisdom app for the

Apple iPad.

Toward the end of August, Sam reports that Prof. Kelly has accepted the offer of free PearlPens and Pearls of Wisdom apps to try out in her fall Physics-I class. However, because he does not collect or grade homework, Prof. Rodriguez was not interested in the app.

Peggy and Bill have been working together every day all summer long, and have spent most weekends at the lake. However, tomorrow they will both head off to college – Peggy to UNH and Bill to RPI. They have both been dreading the imminent separation, but have been reluctant to talk about it until now. They have spent the last few days packing, meeting with some of their high school friends, and trying to get mentally prepared to go away to college.

Tonight they have dinner in one of their favorite restaurants, right on the waterfront in downtown Portsmouth, and then go to Prescott Park where they talk about their relationship and future. They have come here often over the summer and always sit on the same bench – the one they first sat on the day after Thanksgiving.

"I can't believe that I'm going to be in Durham tomorrow night and you'll be in Troy," Peggy says.

"Me neither," Bill says.

"What's going to happen to us?"

"I don't know. You'll probably go and fall in love with some Wildcat."

"No I won't! You'll probably fall for some RPI or Russell Sage chick."

"Peggy, you know I love you."

"I know, and I love you too."

"We'll make it work."

"It's only three months until we'll be together at Thanksgiving at Uncle Dave's."

"And we can PearlTime every day, so I'll see you every day."

"But I won't be able to put my arms around you and kiss you, like this."

13

Durham is a typical college town, not much of a downtown, dominated by the University of New Hampshire campus, a campus with older red brick buildings interspersed with newer buildings sporting more glass, the center of campus recognized by the iconic clock tower of Thompson Hall; under its arches have passed generations of UNH students on their way to classes or meetings with a future spouse. Peggy is taking it all in, sitting in the back seat of their car next to Matt.

"Well, here we are at UNH," Joe says.

Kate is sitting in the passenger seat next to Joe. "Your home for the next four years."

"Are you nervous?" Matt asks.

"No, just excited."

They approach Handler Hall, Peggy's dorm, which is across the street from the new Kingsbury Hall where Sam has his office. Joe finds a spot to pull in among the cars being unloaded by other anxious freshmen.

Peggy's double room is on the third floor. Her roommate is not there yet, so Peggy selects the lower bunk bed. The room is new and clean, and they share a bath with the adjoining room.

"This room should be pretty comfortable," Kate says.

Joe and Matt bring her trunk up from the car, and Peggy and Kate bring the rest of her belongings. It does not take long to unpack and settle in.

"We'll take the empty trunk back with us," Joe says. "There's no room to store it here."

Just then, her roommate walks in with her parents.

"Hi, I'm Natalie Walker. You must be Peggy."

"Yes, we've met by email. Nice to meet you in person."

Natalie introduces her parents to Peggy, Joe, Kate, and Matt.

"So Peggy tells me you're from Keene," Joe says.

"Yes."

"And you're also studying physics?"

"I'm in engineering, but I think Peggy and I have similar schedules."

"It looks like you both are going to be busy this term."

"We will," Peggy says. "I can't wait to get started."

"We'd better let Natalie get unpacked," Joe says. "Why don't we see if your Uncle Sam is in his office? Perhaps we can pick up some lunch with him."

Walking across the street to Kingsbury Hall, Matt points to a strange-looking sculpture made from steel I-beams bolted and welded together in a tree-like fashion. "What is that?"

"I think they call that modern art," Kate says.

Joe shakes his head. "How much do you suppose they spent on that?"

"Now dad," Peggy says, "I like it. It screams engineering and the intricate form is sort of interesting."

Peggy hands her samiPhone to her dad. "Here, take a picture of Matt and me standing in front of it."

Peggy puts her arm on Matt's shoulder and smiles as Joe snaps the photo. He hands Peggy her samiPhone. "It is a conversation piece. I'll give you that."

They enter Kingsbury Hall and quickly find Sam's second-floor office. Sam sits behind his desk, piled high with papers and books, as is the table behind him in front of the window. The office is small, four file cabinets leaving little room for the two other chairs in the room, a small whiteboard filled with equations, floor to ceiling bookshelves occupying all remaining wall space.

"Not enough room for everyone to sit in here," Sam says. "You'd think by now I'd have a larger office."

"Any place to eat around here?" Joe asks.

"Let's go to the Philbrook Dining Hall," Sam says. "It's right next door, and Peggy will find this convenient to her dorm."

After saying goodbye to Peggy, her parents and brother head back to Portsmouth. It is a quiet ride home with only the music from the radio breaking the silence. When they get home, Joe brings Peggy's empty trunk into the house.

"It's not going to be the same without Peggy here," Kate says.

"I know," Joe says.

"I'm going to miss her," Matt says.

Peggy likes Natalie right away; they talk into the night about their boyfriends and families. The girls will be in the same calculus and physics classes. Book buying is on tomorrow's agenda, for Monday classes begin.

After buying her books the next day, Peggy PearlTimes with Bill.

"How is my pearl?" Bill asks.

They talk a long time. Bill is also taking Calculus and Physics, using the same books in these classes as Peggy. They agree to PearlTime often when doing homework in these two classes. Peggy tells Bill about her roommate, Natalie, and Bill tells Peggy about his roommate, Jason. Peggy tells Bill she is going to start making video clips from her lecture notes. They agree to PearlTime again after their first physics class.

"How did your physics class go?" Bill asks as he PearlTimes with Peggy.

"It was good. I have a woman professor, Prof. Kelly, who outlined the course and then talked about SI units. She went over the basic units of length, mass, and time - the meter, kilogram, and second, but the definitions of them are a little weird."

"I know, these definitions have changed over the years."

"Did you know that they have to add a leap second every few years so that the new definition based on an atomic clock keeps in sync with the rotation of the earth?"

"Yes, and this screws up lots of computer programs and GPS systems, and lots of people want to stop adding these leap seconds, but it is very controversial."

"After that," Peggy says, "she handed out PearlPens and told us how we were to do our homework problems using the Pearls of Wisdom app. She told us how we could install a free copy on our tablets. I couldn't help laughing to myself."

"That's funny."

"Prof. Kelly said that she thinks that the Pearls of Wisdom app will allow us to do more homework problems. She demonstrated solving a problem using the PearlPen and showed us how to record a copy and upload our solution to the class website. She then said, somewhat jokingly, that the only thing the Pearls of Wisdom app was missing was a feature that would automatically grade each homework assignment and keep a grade book for her."

"I can add that feature!" Bill says. "It shouldn't be too hard."

"Let's do it, and then everyone can download an update."

"Ok, I will. You'll need to tell me how your professor reacts when she sees that her wish mysteriously came true!"

"I can't wait to see her expression."

Prof. Rodriguez is teaching Peggy's calculus class and hands out a course summary. The handout includes a list of suggested homework problems from the textbook. He tells the class that he will not collect or grade the homework problems, but they are responsible for knowing how to solve them, as similar problems will be on the exams.

After her first calculus class, Peggy goes to the gym and joins a pick-up basketball game, meeting three other girls who are majoring in engineering and one who is majoring in physics. She joins the Ski and Board Club – looking forward to skiing in the winter – and finds a couple of friends with whom she can run cross-country.

Peggy has brought extra boxes of PearlPens with her and sends emails to those students in her calculus class who are not in the physics class, telling them that other students in the class will be doing homework problems using the Pearls of Wisdom app. She offers these students a free PearlPen and a free download of the app, which they can get by stopping by her dorm room. Bill does the same for all students in his calculus and physics classes.

Two girls stop by Peggy's dorm room to pick up a PearlPen.

"How did you get these?" one of the girls asks.

"I have an in with the head of the company," Peggy says.

"Hi Uncle Sam," Peggy says as she knocks on his open office door. "Are you busy?"

"No, come on in. How are things going?"

"So far, so good. What do you know about Prof. Rodriguez? He says he doesn't collect any of our calculus homework problems, we just have to know how to do them."

"That's typical of lots of math professors. They don't get the number of teaching assistants that we do in engineering to help with homework grading, so they just don't bother to collect homework."

"I would think that lot's of students just wouldn't do the homework then."

Sam smiles. "You're right. That's why calculus weeds out lots of students that might otherwise succeed as engineering or science majors."

"Perhaps my app will help them!"

"Perhaps."

Over the next two weeks, Bill writes the update for the Pearls of Wisdom app. A professor can now enter a course name and number and upload a class list. Students in the class can log on with their PearlPen and submit a completed homework video clip. The app can compare the answer with known correct submissions, and record a grade in the class grade book, which the professor can download any time. Bill sends an email to all students and professors who have a PearlPen and reminds them to download the new update.

Peggy is sitting in her physics classroom when Prof. Kelly enters the room.

"Have you all seen the new update to the Pearls of Wisdom app?" she asks. "This is really spooky. Just what I told you a couple of weeks ago would be a big improvement, all of a sudden appears. As a physicist, I'm skeptical of extra-sensory perception, but now I'm having second thoughts."

Peggy smiles to herself.

Peggy and Bill are PearlTiming again.

"We started going over vectors today in physics," Bill says.

"What did you cover in vectors?" Peggy asks.

"Basic addition and subtraction of vectors and coordinate systems. Did you make any video clips?"

"Yes, the book Uncle Sam gave me for Christmas was very helpful. I introduced the index notation for Cartesian coordinate systems. Uncle Sam told me that most of my courses that use vector analysis won't use the notation of Cartesian tensors, and that this is a mistake. He covers it all in his book, so I'm going to include it as I go along. He says it will really pay off in the end. Here, I'll show you the video clips I made."

Bill likes the video clips and tells Peggy that they make the material much clearer and easier to understand than what the professor had covered in class or what was in their textbook. He will show them to his roommate and get his reaction.

"I show each one to Natalie when I complete it, and she has the same reaction," Peggy says.

"I think you have a real knack for explaining something in a way that makes it easy to understand," Bill says.

"I have to understand it completely myself first. Uncle Sam was right. You only really understand it when you have to explain it to someone else."

It is Saturday noon of Family Weekend, a UNH tradition, and Kate, Joe, and Matt have just completed a tour, with Peggy, of some of the engineering and science labs. The sunny day with white puffy clouds against a deep blue sky makes it a perfect day for the football game later this afternoon, but right now everyone is enjoying lunch at a picnic table set up outside Peggy's dorm.

"I really enjoyed the concert last night," Kate says.

"Me too," Matt says. "I think it would be fun to play in an orchestra like that."

"Keep practicing your trumpet," Joe says, "and maybe you'll be able to play in a college orchestra someday."

"Wait until you see the marching band at the football game today," Peggy says. "I'll bet you'll really want to do that."

"So Peggy, how's this company of yours doing?" Joe asks. "Have you made any money yet?"

"Dad, we're just getting started. It will take some time before we start to get some revenue."

"Well, you're not going to make any money if you keep giving everything away for free. I hope your cousin and uncle haven't taken you down a dead end path."

Peggy shakes her head. *Dad just doesn't get it.* "Let's change the subject."

Peggy and Bill do their homework every night on Pearls of Wisdom and post their solutions. Peggy also posts each video clip of her lecture notes as she completes it. She calls these Pearl video clips to distinguish them from the homework video clips.

"You've been busy," Bill says.

"This is really fun," Peggy says. "It's hard to explain, but every time I complete one of the videos and I like it, I get a big rush. I think doing these actually releases endorphins. I feel as good as when I run a long distance."

"And I'm not even there!"

"I wish you were."

By the time of the first exams in calculus and physics, hundreds of solved homework problems have shown up on the Pearls of Wisdom app from students at RPI and UNH. Peggy has posted a dozen or more Pearl video clips for each course. The Pearls of Wisdom app provides a rating system where after someone views a video clip completely, he or she must rate the clip from one to five stars. These ratings, along with the number of views, are used to determine how much money a particular contributor earns at the end of each term.

Prof. Rodriguez is handing back the first exam. He hands Peggy her exam, which has 100% written on the top, and says, "Peggy, please stop by my office this afternoon during my office hours."

Peggy wonders what this is all about. She goes to his office and knocks on the door.

"Come in, Peggy," he says.

Peggy sees that his Android Tablet has the Pearls of Wisdom app open and is displaying one of her calculus Pearl videos.

"Did you make this video?" he asks.

"Yes," Peggy says, "why?"

Prof. Rodriguez tells her how another student in the class had shown him the videos and told him how useful they had been in understanding the material. He says he recalled talking with Sam Woodbury about this app, but did not think it was anything useful for his class. However, after the student showed him the video, he asked Sam to give him a PearlPen and access to the app. When he ran the app, he saw that all students in his class were doing homework together using the app.

"The student told me that you gave her a PearlPen," he says.

"Yes, I did."

"Where did you get the PearlPens?"

"My cousin makes the PearlPens and my company buys them from him."

"Your company?"

"Yes, I'm president of Pearlton Industries. We produce the Pearls of Wisdom app, which works with the PearlPen.

"How did Prof. Woodbury get the PearlPens?"

"He's my uncle."

"He is? Who wrote the app?"

"My boyfriend and I did."

"Really! Does your boyfriend go to UNH?"

"No, he's a freshman at RPI, majoring in computer science."

Prof. Rodriguez pauses to let this sink in. He tells Peggy that the class average on the exam was eight points higher than in previous terms and he did not know what to attribute it to, but now that he has seen the Pearls of Wisdom app, he is convinced that it is Peggy's videos and all the homework examples that made the difference.

"I was skeptical that posting homework solutions would help students," he says. "I assumed that students would just copy the answers and not learn anything, but I guess the exam results proved me wrong."

"The key is the PearlPen," Peggy says. "Students have to go through each step on paper and explain each step as they go along. The students can then post these homework videos and others rate them. Contributors get paid based on the rating and the number of 'views'. So students are motivated to produce good homework video clips."

Peggy tells him how Prof. Kelly is using the app as an integral part of her physics course and how the app automatically grades the homework assignments.

"This certainly is an interesting app," he says.

"We've put a lot of thought into it," Peggy says.

"Good luck with it."

Peggy stops by Uncle Sam's office.

"At lunch I ran into Prof. Kelly," Sam says.

"Did she say anything about the Pearls of Wisdom app?" Peggy asks.

"Yes, she says the students seem to be doing even more homework problems than she assigns, and she told me about an update to the app, which automatically grades her homework assignments. Where did that come from?"

"Oh, it was great. One day she wished out loud that the app would have that feature, so I had Bill put it in, and she really freaked out when it just showed up one day."

"I love it," Sam says. "Anything that makes a professor's life easier, they will lap up. I have looked at some of your Pearl video clips and I like them. What are you working on now?"

"More vector stuff. We've covered vector multiplication, dot products and cross products, and I like the description in your book the best, so I want to make video clips of that."

"You should include the index notation version."

"Oh, I will. Those are the most fun. I can't believe that the dot product is just repeated indices that automatically get summed from 1 to 3."

"Did you know that when Einstein discovered the summation convention for repeated indices, he thought it was his most important mathematical discovery!"

"That is cool. Another cool one is that epsilon symbol used in the cross product. That identity using two of those symbols is so easy to remember and makes proving any vector identity almost trivial."

"That is why you need to make some good videos showing how easy it is to prove those vector identities. It is almost never included in any undergraduate course, which is a shame."

"Well, I've got to run to class," Peggy says.

"Keep me up-to-date."

Peggy cannot believe that the Thanksgiving break is next week. She feels good about her first term at college; she has kept busy and done well in her classes; she has met some new friends; she likes popping in on Uncle Sam. But she wonders what a first term at Dartmouth would have been like.

14

On the day before Thanksgiving, Peggy goes home for the first time since moving into the dorm. Bill calls her as soon as he gets home from RPI, comes over, and they drive to Prescott Park, both agreeing that this beats PearlTiming. Bill will join them for Thanksgiving dinner at Uncle Dave's tomorrow, his parents spending Thanksgiving with Bill's older brother, John, in New Jersey.

Peggy and Bill stand in Uncle Dave's sunroom looking out over the ocean.

"What a spectacular view," Peggy says.

"It sure is. Look at how the horizon bends down at each end. I guess the earth really is round!"

Sam, Wayne and Connie walk into the sunroom and they all sit down to enjoy the view.

"So Peggy, how is the Pearls of Wisdom app working in your calculus and physics courses?" Wayne asks.

"It is working well. We have video clips posted for a lot of the homework problems in our calculus and physics textbooks. Everyone, including our professors, likes it."

"The idea of being able to do a given homework problem with other students at other universities is really useful," Bill says.

"How many people have downloaded the free basic version of the app?" Sam asks.

"As of yesterday," Bill says, "there have been just over twelve hundred free downloads. A lot of these were other students at RPI and UNH who heard about it by word of mouth."

"Have any of these upgraded to the full version with a PearlPen?" Sam asks.

"About 300, I think," Wayne says.

"Peggy," Sam says, "I suggest that you and Bill update the *Learn and Earn* video that is on the app and turn it into a separate marketing video. You can put it on the Pearlton Industries website, on your Facebook pages, email it to everyone who has already downloaded the app and ask them to pass it on, stuff like that. With finals coming up before Christmas, students might want access to lots of solved homework problems before then. Perhaps we can move some more PearlPens before Christmas."

"That's a good idea," Peggy says.

"I thought of a new application for the PearlPen," Connie says. "At the hospital, we have a childcare center where expectant mothers can drop off their younger children while they are having an appointment or attending Lamaze classes. I sometimes stop in to see the kids. These young pre-school kids are all tapping the screen of tablets playing video games of one kind or another. Based on all the conversations that we have had about the links between writing and learning and the potential of the PearlPen, I think these pre-school kids would learn a lot more by using the PearlPen to write things, which might then show up on a tablet."

"I think you are absolutely right," Sam says. "For example, when I was a kid we used to have these dot-to-dot books where you would draw lines from one numbered dot to the next in sequence to form some figure. It was lots of fun and I think moving the pencil from dot to dot certainly helped you to count and reason. The direct link between the hand, writing with a pen, and the brain is, I think, very important for learning."

"Peggy, you've got a whole new division of Pearlton Industries devoted to pre-school children," Wayne says.

"And Connie can head it up!" Peggy says.

Kate walks into the sunroom and announces that Thanksgiving dinner is ready.

"It's really great to have everyone here for Thanksgiving this year," Dave says as he passes the platter of turkey.

"You should see all of the course video clips that Peggy has posted on the Pearls of Wisdom app," Sam says.

"I can't believe that as a freshman you've written all of these video clips," Connie says.

"It turns out that it is best to do this as soon as you learn the material," Sam says. "I wrote my first book on plasma physics while I was in graduate school learning the material. I knew exactly what it took to understand some derivation and so I put all of that in the book. Textbook authors who have known the material for years often forget how some concepts are difficult to grasp. So young authors are often the best. My plasma physics book was used as the text in many plasma physics courses around the country. Just another example of Woodbury's Law."

Peggy says, "I also adopted Uncle Sam's idea of researching the lives of the scientists, such as Isaac Newton, whose laws we study. When you realize that they are just normal human beings with flaws and doubts about their own work, it takes a lot of the mystery out of how these laws of physics came about."

"And how they're still screwed up," Bill says. "But Peggy's going to fix that, when she discovers her Theory of Everything."

"Have you made progress on finding your Theory of Everything yet?" Joe asks.

"Don't laugh," Peggy says. "I'm taking only Physics-I this term, and I don't think cylinders rolling down inclined planes is on the right track."

"You'll get into electric and magnetic fields next term," Sam says, "and that should point you in a better direction."

As everyone is finishing dessert, Wayne stands up and says, "I have an important announcement to make. Connie and I have set the date for our wedding. It's going to be the third Saturday of next August. And dad has agreed to have the wedding and reception right here in the back yard overlooking the ocean."

The dining room explodes in applause.

"Last month," Wayne continues, "Connie and I flew down to Texas where I met her folks for the first time. They are great people and will be here for the wedding."

"Did Wayne pass the test?" Matt asks.

"With flying colors," Connie says. "I so much feel a part of this family ever since Kate invited me to Thanksgiving dinner a year ago. Peggy, you have become such a good friend and I admire you so, I would be very happy if you would be a bridesmaid in my wedding. Would you, please?"

Peggy's eyes become the size of silver dollars.

"This is a surprise! Of course, I would love to. I've known from the beginning that you and Wayne are meant for each other."

Wayne smiles. "Even though I haven't known her since kindergarten?"

That night Peggy and Bill drive back to Portsmouth and go to Prescott Park. They talk seriously about their future and the future of Pearlton Industries.

"Bill, do you think we can really pull this off?" Peggy asks. "Get the Pearls of Wisdom app to really take off and be used in courses all across the country?"

"I know, it's a little scary when you think about it, isn't it?"

"My dad will say, 'I told you so,' if we fail."

"We just can't fail." Bill sounds serious. "We just have to keep focused and work hard."

"Uncle Sam has a good idea about making a new *Learn and Earn* marketing video that can get into the social media bloodstream."

"I'll start working on it tomorrow and get it out there by the time we go back to school next week."

"We do make a good team," Peggy whispers into Bill's ear. "And I do love you."

Two weeks later Peggy is PearlTiming with Bill as they study for their final exam in physics. Peggy is explaining one of the homework problems that she had posted on the Pearls of Wisdom app. Suddenly, both of their tablets go blank. Peggy can no longer see or hear Bill. Nor can she bring back up the Pearls of Wisdom app.

Peggy calls Bill on her cell phone. "What happened?"

"I don't know," Bill says. "Everything just stopped working."

"Let me call Harry over at the U-Pen Company and see if anything is wrong with the server. I'll call you back."

Peggy places a call to Harry and learns that the server has crashed. Harry says that the number of persons accessing the database has spiked in the past two days, and the volume of video streaming just overwhelmed the server.

"Can you fix it?" Peggy asks.

"The current server configuration isn't capable of handling that kind of volume," Harry says.

"What can we do?"

"You need more server capability."

Peggy thanks Harry and places a call to Uncle Sam. She fills him in on what has happened. Sam suggests that Bill disable the videoconferencing feature in an attempt to get the Pearls of Wisdom up and running again. He asks Peggy to stop by his office in the morning and they will try to figure out a permanent solution.

Peggy then calls Bill back and brings him up to date on the bad news. Bill agrees to disable the videoconferencing feature and to work with Harry to try getting the app back up on a limited basis.

The next day Peggy meets with Sam to consider their options. Sam suggests that they look into moving the app onto a cloud server, managed by professionals, allowing for seamless growth if app sales really take off. Peggy says that she needs to get through finals before she can spend a lot of time on this.

Complaints about not having the Pearls of Wisdom app available for studying for finals begin to show up on social media. Bill is unsuccessful in getting it back running in a stable mode. Peggy schedules an emergency meeting with Bill, Sam, and Wayne as soon as Bill gets back to Portsmouth after his finals. Running this company is not as easy as she thought it was going to be.

15

A light snow is falling outside the farmhouse on Christmas afternoon and the snow-covered trees look like something out of a picture book. Peggy's family drove up two days ago, and Bill will arrive later this afternoon after spending Christmas morning with his family in Portsmouth, and stay through New Year's Day. At the emergency meeting with Bill, Sam, and Wayne, Peggy approved a plan to move the Pearls of Wisdom app to a well-established cloud server where the entire operation will be managed around the clock. It should be in full operation before the end of the year. Peggy was assured that this would avoid any further embarrassing crashes. If sales continue to pick up next term, they will easily be able to afford the rental fees for this cloud server.

"It was only a year ago today that we all gathered around this table for Christmas dinner," Sam says. "A lot has happened during this past year."

"It sure has," Peggy says.

"You're telling me," Connie says.

"So, Peggy, I hear you had some problems with the Pearls of Wisdom app," Dave says.

"Yes, but they are all fixed now and we will be much better off with the new system."

"I was afraid that this company would take a lot of time away from your studies," Joe says.

"Now, Joe," Kate says, "I think it is great what Peggy and Bill are doing. They're learning a lot about the real world, and all education doesn't necessarily take place in the classroom."

"Thanks, mom. You know, dad, I can walk and chew gum at the same time."

Wayne decides to change the subject. "Peggy, how are you integrating your video clips into the Pearls of Wisdom app?"

"The next version of the app will include complete courses that are separated into topics and sub-sections with the table of contents on the left so you can jump to any section with the PearlPen. Then once in a section, you'll be able to read about the background for each topic and then click on hyperlinks that take you to one of the short videos, including biographical sketches for all of the scientists mentioned in the course as well as related homework videos"

"That makes sense," Wayne says.

"We will use the same method for anyone to contribute a 5-minute 'lecture' or Pearl video on any topic," Peggy says. "They will get paid based on ratings and viewings just like the homework videos. We may even attract professors to contribute 5-minute Pearl video clips. Pearls of Wisdom will keep the best Pearl clip for a particular topic and the best contribution for a given homework assignment."

"This is a major update from an app that just focuses on homework solutions," Sam says. "It could replace all textbooks in the future."

"I think you should consider including this feature in a 'premium membership' with a higher annual subscription fee," Wayne says.

"I agree," Bill says. "I would make the premium membership at least $40 per year, twice the regular subscription for the homework only version."

"That sounds good to me," Peggy says. "I think we need to make another video, one that might go viral to help market the Pearls of Wisdom app."

"Now that it won't crash again," Wayne says.

Everyone at the table brainstorms various ideas. Finally, Bill suggests that he could put together a clever video that shows a bookshelf full of textbooks. One by one, each book flies off the shelf and disappears inside a tablet. Then the commentator could say something like "Why spend thousands of dollars on textbooks that are difficult to read?" The Pearls of Wisdom app would then appear and reveal the Pearls of Wisdom Courses with all of the hyperlinked Pearl and homework videos and a tag line like "Don't get left behind: The Pearls of Wisdom and PearlPen – Keys to Success." All agree that Bill should do this and get it on YouTube and their Facebook page as soon as possible.

"How can you motivate more people to want to learn calculus and physics?" Joe asks.

"I'll tell you what I tell my students," Sam says. "I always hear the same complaint. My students will say, 'Why do I need to learn calculus? My father is an engineer and he tells me he has never used calculus since he graduated.'"

"What do you tell them?" Wayne asks.

"I tell them that they don't take calculus because they may need to use it to make a living. They take it to become educated and to learn to solve problems. They will need to solve problems all their life, and most people do a lousy job of it. I cannot believe all of the supposedly smart people on television – politicians, news commentators, journalists and such – who brag about hating math and never being good at it. Why would you announce to the world that you are stupid? No wonder they don't know what they are doing."

"That is pretty harsh, Grandpa," Wayne says.

"It is true," Sam says.

"You are right, Uncle Sam," Peggy says. "I am going to motivate students to use the Pearls of Wisdom by making calculus and physics fun to learn, and that is not by watering it down, but by making it complete and rigorous so they don't get discouraged by not understanding it. If I don't understand something in a physics book, it is usually because the author has forgotten to tell me something important, and without that something, the rest doesn't make any sense. I often need to consult several different physics books that I get from the library before I find the best explanation of a particular topic."

"You're absolutely right, Peggy," Sam says. "When students finish a Pearls of Wisdom course, they will have a great feeling of satisfaction."

"The endorphins will have been released!" Bill says.

"Well that beef Wellington certainly released my endorphins," Sam says. "Why don't we all go into the living room and sit around the fireplace?"

"I'll bring in coffee and dessert," Kate says.

Dave and Joe arrange the sofas and chairs around the fireplace and everyone settles in with dessert, coffee or tea.

"So Connie," Peggy says, "Wayne tells me you have been using the PearlPens at the childcare center at the hospital."

"Yes, we have talked about how important writing is to the learning process, particularly in young people. So I started taking a PearlPen into the childcare center at the hospital and I showed the first and second graders how to write their names in cursive. Then I made up a sheet that showed how each upper and lower case printed letter is written in cursive. Then everyone practiced writing in cursive the names of everyone else in the room. They loved it, and before long everyone knew everyone else's name and they didn't forget it."

"Now that's what I need to do to remember names," Bill says.

Connie continues, "I have a friend who teaches first grade in Portsmouth and when I told her what I was doing, she thought it was a great idea and was very enthusiastic. She thinks that the nationwide trend to de-emphasize cursive writing is a big mistake, just like we do."

"A PearlPen in every first grade in the country," Wayne says. "I like the sound of that!"

"We need a strategy to make it happen," Sam says.

"I've got it," Bill says. "We donate a PearlPen to every first and second grader in the Portsmouth Elementary School. I'll write a program for the tablets they use, which will display on the screen, one by one, a photo of a student with his or her full name printed below it. Also on the screen will be the printed letter to cursive conversion guide. We will provide a pad of ruled paper for cursive writing. The students will go through each student in the class, writing their full name in cursive. They will keep doing this until they can write the names without the printed name displayed on the screen. Heck, I won't even need to use my samiPhone facial recognition program to remember names anymore!"

"You know," Sam says, "I think Connie and you are on to something. If it turns out that first and second graders in Portsmouth can learn the names of everyone in their classes quickly by writing in cursive, we could get the local TV station to do a piece that demonstrates this. It would be impressive and get lots of attention. We could then give talks in Rotary Clubs around the state and get local businesses to buy the PearlPens and donate them to their local schools. Once all first and second graders in New Hampshire know all of their classmate's full names by sight, we'll get 60 Minutes to do a piece and pretty soon every first and second grader in the country will need a PearlPen."

"I just checked the statistics online," Bill says. "There are over 3.7 million first graders in the U.S. and over 35 million students in grades K-8, and over 50 million students in grades K-12.

"Now my head is spinning," Peggy says.

"Actually, I think it gets better than that," Wayne says. "At the Rotary Clubs, you demonstrate it by taking each person's picture on your smart phone and asking their name. When they tell you their name, you write it in cursive on any piece of paper. Then, when you're done, you go around the room saying everyone's name."

"You have a lot of faith in cursive learning," Sam says.

"You can always use my samiPhone facial recognition program as a backup," Bill says.

"Actually," Peggy says, "I have no doubt that writing someone's name on a piece of paper when you meet them will help to remember the name and associate it with a face, particularly if you just took their picture."

"I think we should introduce a new protocol for meeting new people at business meetings and conventions," Connie says. "*Excuse me, can I take your photo, and how do you spell your name?* As I write it on a piece of paper."

"You know that isn't a bad idea," Sam says. "A simple app for your smart phone where you simply take a photo of a new person you meet and when you repeat their name the app displays the name. If the spelling is wrong, you verify the correct spelling with the person. The person should actually be flattered that you are interested in their name. Then you just click save and the photo and name are stored in the app."

"I've got it," Bill says. "Later you go through the photos and names and write them in cursive on a piece of paper, which helps to remember them. The app will then cycle through all photos without the names shown and you can either write the name in cursive or just say the name, and the app will tell you if you are correct. You can keep doing this until you get all names correct."

"I should have had this all the years I was teaching," Sam says. "I always had a hard time remembering every student's name in my classes. In fact, I started the practice of taking a head photo of every student in my class on the first day of class and then made a class list with the student's photo next to the name. This helped me remember who was who when grading exams, but I still had trouble during class remembering everyone's name. I think if I had actually written out everyone's name in cursive as I was looking at their photo this would help a great deal."

"I'll put together the app right away," Bill says, "and we can see how it works."

"I'm thinking," Peggy says, "that rather than trying to push it into first and second grade classes and fighting with the teachers unions and school administrators, maybe we should just market the app to parents to help their young children learn. In fact, the photos could be anything, not just faces, which the child is learning to spell."

"I agree," Wayne says. "Let's begin with the face recognition – cursive writing app, and we can market this to grownups like me. What shall we call the app?"

"How about *Name that Face*," Connie says.

"That will be our code name for now," Peggy says. "I think our market has now expanded from college students, to elementary school students, to all businessmen, heck to everyone!"

The next day Bill starts programming the new *Name that Face* app. Sam joins Peggy who is sitting in the lake house living room looking out over the frozen snow-covered lake.

"What are you thinking about, Peggy?"

"I was thinking about the computer course I just took at UNH where the professor actually used the flipping method of teaching. She had a whole bunch of videos clips that we would watch on our own before coming to class, and then in class we put that knowledge to work actually writing programs."

"And did it work out well?"

"Very well. I'm trying to figure out how to get good course content in the form of video clips into our app so that professors would use them and switch to the flipping method of teaching."

"I was thinking the same thing last night," Sam says, "and I've got an idea that I think I will try in my electromagnetics class this coming term."

"What's the idea?"

"Well, you know how I start that class with Special Relativity – you sat in on the first two lectures last year – and then I go on and derive Maxwell's equations from Special Relativity and Coulomb's Law."

"I know, it's all in the book that you wrote."

"That's right, but the derivation is fairly long and a little tricky, so I go through it in detail on the whiteboard. The students only learn it by actually following me through all of the steps and writing it down themselves."

"But some have trouble keeping up with you and just race to get it down on paper as you're talking and then really need to recopy it after class so they can think of every step as they go along."

"Exactly," Sam says. "I wish I had a series of video clips of me going through the derivation, which they could watch before class, and follow along by writing it down themselves at their own pace. Then I could use the class time to talk about the implications of the derivation and have the students work out problems."

"But it is a lot of work to put together all of those video clips."

"That is my new idea. I am going to do it in class this term. Instead of standing at the whiteboard and doing the derivation, I will sit at the front desk and do the derivation on a piece of paper using my PearlPen. Everything I write will be projected on the big screen in the front of the room. They can ask questions as I go along and I will answer them. Everything gets recorded using the app, and afterward I can edit it into smaller chunks that are easier to follow. Now I have my video clips that I can use the next time I teach the class using the flipping method."

"And they will be available on the Pearls of Wisdom app for other professors around the country, and world, to use!"

"I am definitely going to do it for the whole course. Anything that I would normally do on the whiteboard, derivations, solving problems and the like, I'll do on paper using the PearlPen and then post the video clips for the students to review."

"You also wrote the book you use in that course," Peggy says. "How do we get everything else that is in the book into the Pearls of Wisdom app?"

"You had the right idea before. We need to start calling them a Pearl Course, because it will not be the usual book that is just read online. What I will do is turn my electromagnetics book into an Electromagnetics Pearl Course, which will have a table of contents with chapters, sections and sub-sections. These will all be hyperlinked, so if you click on a particular chapter, it will take you there and you will start reading about that topic. However, when you come to a derivation or an example problem, you click on a link that takes you to the video clip, where you can follow along at your own pace, backing up and replaying it if you need to. You will then be taken back to the link where you can continue reading or jump to some other chapter or section from the table of contents link on the left. It now becomes a dynamic book."

"I like it. Do you think other professors will make Pearl Courses?"

"They should," Sam says, "because I think this approach is inevitable. The advantages are just too compelling. Authors will get the equivalent of royalties depending on how many classes 'adopt' their Pearl Course based on the number of 'views' and ratings. The other advantage is that they do not have to produce all of the Pearl video clips used in their course. Their course can link to any video clip in the app including ones in other courses, and other courses can link to video clips in their course. The author of a particular video clip gets paid on the number of 'views' so the more courses that link to it the better."

"It seems like a good approach to me," Peggy says.

"I would have three main headings in your Pearls of Wisdom app: Pearl Courses, Pearl Topics Videos, and Pearl Homework Videos. The Pearl Courses, like my Electromagnetics Course can link to any of the two types of videos. But a student could just search for a particular topic and find all Pearl Topic Videos for that particular topic."

"This is going to be great. Can I sit in at the beginning of your electromagnetics course and watch you derive Maxwell's equations from Special Relativity and Coulomb's Law? I really want to see that derivation and also see how using the PearlPen in class works out."

"Absolutely. I will be interested to see how much of it you can follow. It is mostly just a lot of Cartesian tensor manipulations."

"Great. This has been very helpful. I'll get Bill to update the app right away."

The next day, Peggy and Bill take a break and go skiing with Wayne and Connie at Gunstock. Peggy needed the break to air her brain, a brain overflowing with ideas on how to make the Pearls of Wisdom better. She is looking forward to starting the spring term at UNH, where she is beginning to feel at home.

16

The entire family is having dessert at the farmhouse dining room table after finishing their traditional New Year's Eve fondue dinner.

"Uncle Sam is going to teach his Electromagnetics course this term using the PearlPen," Peggy says. "And I'm going to sit in during the first part of the course."

They fill in the rest of the family on Sam's idea of creating Pearl videos directly in the classroom while teaching the class.

"I've got a version of the *Name that Face* app ready to test," Bill says. "Joe and I have a game to play with it tonight."

"Yes," Joe says. "I'm beginning to warm up to these apps of yours. You are all going to learn the 44 presidents of the United States. Bill and I have downloaded photos of all 44 presidents with their dates in office and party affiliation. Your goal tonight is to use the PearlPen to learn to recognize all 44 presidents by their photo, or number, and to learn their dates in office and party affiliation."

They all move into the living room and Joe hands out a sheet to everyone with the following list of presidents.

1 George Washington (1789-97)
2 John Adams, 1797-1801 (Federalist)
3 Thomas Jefferson, 1801-9 (Democratic-Republican)
4 James Madison, 1809-17 (Democratic-Republican)
5 James Monroe, 1817-25 (Democratic-Republican)
6 John Quincy Adams, 1825-29 (Democratic-Republican)
7 Andrew Jackson, 1829-37 (Democrat)
8 Martin Van Buren, 1837-41 (Democrat)
9 William Henry Harrison, 1841 (Whig)
10 John Tyler, 1841-45 (Whig)
11 James Knox Polk, 1845-49 (Democrat)
12 Zachary Taylor, 1849-50 (Whig)
13 Millard Fillmore, 1850-53 (Whig)
14 Franklin Pierce, 1853-57 (Democrat)
15 James Buchanan, 1857-61 (Democrat)

16 Abraham Lincoln, 1861-65 (Republican)
17 Andrew Johnson, 1865-69 (Democrat/National Union)
18 Ulysses Simpson Grant, 1869-77 (Republican)
19 Rutherford Birchard Hayes, 1877-81 (Republican)
20 James Abram Garfield, 1881 (Republican)
21 Chester Alan Arthur, 1881-85 (Republican)
22 Grover Cleveland, 1885-89 (Democrat)
23 Benjamin Harrison, 1889-93 (Republican)
24 Grover Cleveland, 1893-97 (Democrat)
25 William McKinley, 1897-1901 (Republican)
26 Theodore Roosevelt, 1901-9 (Republican)
27 William Howard Taft, 1909-13 (Republican)
28 Woodrow Wilson, 1913-21 (Democrat)
29 Warren Gamaliel Harding, 1921-23 (Republican)
30 Calvin Coolidge, 1923-29 (Republican)
31 Herbert Clark Hoover, 1929-33 (Republican)
32 Franklin Delano Roosevelt, 1933-45 (Democrat)
33 Harry S Truman, 1945-53 (Democrat)
34 Dwight David Eisenhower, 1953-61 (Republican)
35 John Fitzgerald Kennedy, 1961-63 (Democrat)
36 Lyndon Baines Johnson, 1963-69 (Democrat)
37 Richard Milhous Nixon, 1969-74 (Republican)
38 Gerald Rudolph Ford Jr , 1974-77 (Republican)
39 James Earl Carter, 1977-81 (Democrat)
40 Ronald Wilson Reagan, 1981-89 (Republican)
41 George Herbert Walker Bush, 1989-1993 (Republican)
42 William Jefferson Clinton, 1993-2001(Democrat)
43 George W. Bush, 2001-2009 (Republican)
44 Barack Obama, 2009-2017 (Democrat)

"The photos will come up in a random order," Bill says, "displaying the name and other information. You then write the number, name, dates, and affiliations with your PearlPen on a piece of paper. The app will then go through the photos in random order without the name and you can just say the name. The app will tell you if you are right."

"After everyone thinks they have learned them all," Joe says, "we'll break up into two teams, men vs. women, and I will bring up one face at a time. We will alternate between teams in guessing the name, number, dates in office, and party affiliation. If any guess is wrong, the other team gets a chance to answer. A point for each guess, so four points per photo."

"This sounds like fun," Peggy says.

"After one round we will have a second round that is harder," Joe says. "Instead of seeing the photo, I will just ask the number, like 'Who was the 19th president of the United States?' and you have to give the name, dates, and party affiliation – total of 3 points"

"Now that isn't fair," Eileen says.

"That will separate the men from the boys," Sam says, "let's play *Name that President.*"

Everyone finds a table to work on in the dining room, kitchen, or living room and starts writing names and dates in cursive using the PearlPen. After some have gone through all of the photos, you start hearing president's names being spoken. Soon it sounds like a rowdy reunion of past presidents. After several cycles through all of the presidents, a few brave souls are expressing guarded optimism.

"Ok," Joe says, "enough playing around. Time for the men to take on the women in 'Do You Know Your Presidents?'. Women go first."

Joe brings up the first random photo. The women correctly guess William Howard Taft, the 27th president who served as a Republican from 1909-13 for all four points. The next is a photo of Franklin Pierce. The men correctly guess the name and the fact that he served from 1853-57 and was a Democrat, but thought he was the 15th president instead of the 14th, so they get only 3 points.

"You should have known that," Joe says. "He is the only president from New Hampshire!"

The game continues with the score going back and forth. When they get to the second round, Matt knows that the 14th president is Franklin Pierce. At the end of the second round, the women are ahead 168 to 140.

"It looks like women can read faces better than men," Eileen says.

"Particularly, if all the faces are men!" Dave says.

"This really is a good app," Joe says. "I think I will start using it in my history classes."

Just then, the sound of Auld Lang Syne interrupts the conversation.

17

It is the first day of spring classes. Peggy knocks on the office door of Prof. Kelly, who she has not seen since taking the Physics-I final exam last term.

"Come on in, Peggy," Prof. Kelly says. "What can I do for you?"

"I want to talk with you about the Pearls of Wisdom app that we used in class last term."

"Did you find it useful for doing the homework problems?"

"I did, but I want to ask you if you know that my boyfriend and I are the ones who wrote the app?"

"You're kidding."

"No, I didn't really keep it a secret, but I didn't want to have you treat me any differently in the class, so I didn't mention it to you last term."

"But the app was recommended to me by Prof. Woodbury."

"He's my uncle."

Peggy goes on to explain the history of the PearlPen and the establishment of Pearlton Industries. She explains how Prof. Kelly's wish for the homework-grading feature mysteriously showed up on the app. Peggy tells her that she is the one that has created most of the Pearl topic videos for the Physics-I class based on her class notes and the textbook.

"I hope you're not mad at me for not telling you sooner," Peggy says.

"No, I'm not mad, but that explains a lot."

Peggy tells Prof. Kelly how her goal is to have the Pearls of Wisdom app contain hundreds of topic video clips for all courses that professors can use to teach their courses using the flipping method where students view the video clips before coming to class. She explains how Uncle Sam is going to produce video clips while teaching his electromagnetics class this term by sitting in the front of the room and doing derivations and solving problems using the PearlPen and a piece of paper.

"You could do this in Physics-I," Peggy suggests, "and then you could flip the course next term."

"You know, that is not a bad idea," Prof. Kelly says. "I know that Prof. McDonald uses video clips for this purpose in her computer classes and I've wanted to do the same, but didn't have any video clips. Using your uncle's method together with the ones you made last term, perhaps I could try it next term."

"That would be great," Peggy says. "If you have any suggestions on how the app can be improved, please tell me."

"I'll let you know how things go."

Uncle Sam is sitting at the small table in the front of the Parents Association Lecture Hall in Kingsbury Hall, deriving Maxwell's equations from Coulomb's Law and Special Relativity by writing on a piece of paper with the PearlPen. Peggy is sitting in the back of the class. This is the second week she has come to his class. Uncle Sam first had his students watch Peggy's videos on relativistic kinematics. Last week, he went over relativistic dynamics and made video clips with the PearlPen, just as he is doing today. Today, he started by going over Coulomb's law and then showed how the magnetic field and the Lorentz force fall out of the derivation. He has just derived the last of Maxwell's four equations.

Peggy is surprised that she could follow all of the steps in the Cartesian tensor manipulations. Making those video clips of Cartesian tensors last term really helped. Peggy notices that the form of Coulomb's law is almost exactly the same as Newton's law of gravitation that she learned about in Physics-I last term. *Why will the same derivation that Uncle Sam just did for Coulomb's law not also work for Newton's law of gravitation?* She will have to ask Uncle Sam.

The next day, Peggy stops by Uncle Sam's office. Uncle Sam is talking to a good-looking, tall guy with wavy blond hair.

"Come on in, Peggy. Ryan is doing a senior project with me. This is my niece, Peggy."

Ryan stands up. "Hi, I'm Ryan Richardson."

Peggy shakes his hand. "Nice to meet you. I'm Peggy. Don't let me interrupt you."

"No, sit down," Sam says. "I've been showing Ryan the Pearls of Wisdom app and telling him how I made the video clips of the Maxwell equations derivation using the PearlPen. I told him how you and Bill wrote the app."

"I'm impressed," Ryan says.

"Ryan is graduating at the end of this term," Sam says, "and has applied to Dartmouth's graduate school. He wants to study plasma physics and they have a good program."

"I wanted to go to Dartmouth," Peggy says, "but didn't get in."

"I won't know for a few weeks whether or not I get accepted," Ryan says.

"Why do you want to study plasma physics?" Peggy asks.

"Well, I'm taking a space plasma physics course this term and find it very interesting so far. I have done a lot of reading about the subject and think it may be an overlooked area ripe for research. And I've talked to your uncle about plasma physics."

"You know he wrote a book about it a hundred years ago," Peggy says.

"I know. He let me borrow a copy."

"You also know he thinks the universe is filled with plasma and is not expanding."

"Yes, we've talked about that too."

"So, you've got the full indoctrination."

"I'm still here," Sam says.

"I've got a class coming up," Ryan says, "so I have to run. It was very nice to meet you, Peggy."

"Nice to meet you, too. Good luck on getting into Dartmouth."

"Thanks."

After Ryan leaves, Sam asks Peggy how she liked the derivation of Maxwell's equations.

"I liked it a lot, and I can't believe that I could follow it."

"If you know Cartesian tensors, the derivation is really straightforward. Just a little long."

"I noticed that the equation for Coulomb's law has exactly the same form as Newton's law of gravitation that we covered in Physics-I last term. Why won't the same derivation that you did for Coulomb's law also work for Newton's law of gravitation?"

Sam thinks for a minute. "You know, you are absolutely right. As far as I know, no one has ever done that."

"But doesn't that mean that gravitational fields must satisfy Maxwell's equations?" Peggy asks.

"It would look that way," Sam replies. "But you know what that means?"

"What?"

"It means that there is not just one gravitational field – the one that everyone knows about, which is analogous to the electric field. There would have to be a second gravitational field, analogous to the magnetic field, which is created by moving bodies and which exerts a force only on other moving bodies."

"How come no one knows about this second gravitational field?"

"Its effect is likely to be very small, but it might very well explain some gravitational anomalies, such as the perihelion precession of the planet Mercury, which was only explained by Einstein's general theory of relativity."

"You mean if this explained Mercury's precession, we wouldn't need Einstein's general theory of relativity?"

"Well, it would certainly be a simpler explanation. Let me do some quick calculations and see what I come up with."

"Doesn't that mean there should be gravitational waves just like electromagnetic waves?" Peggy asks.

"Absolutely. Einstein's theory predicts such gravitational waves, but in his theory, they are waves of the metric that describes his curved space-time. In your case, they would just be transverse waves of the two gravitational fields exactly analogous to electromagnetic waves. When scientists claimed to have actually detected such gravitational waves, it caused a lot of excitement. Perhaps they were actually detecting your gravitational waves. Wouldn't that be something."

"Maybe I'm on my way to my Theory of Everything!" Peggy says.

"This could very well be a big step in combining gravity and electrodynamics, which has always been one of the big hang-ups. Then you'll just have to tie in quantum mechanics, and you'll be home free!"

"I'm going to have to wait until next year to start taking courses in that area."

"Stop by next week and I'll let you know what I come up with on the new gravitational field."

"I will. Thanks a lot, Uncle Sam."

That night, Peggy calls Bill and tells him all about her new theory of gravitation. She is not sure that he really understands how important this might be, inasmuch as he is not familiar with Uncle Sam's electromagnetics course. Bill tells Peggy about the Astronomy class he is taking. He says it is very interesting and they are learning all about the expanding universe. Peggy tries to warn him not to get too caught up in all the hype, but Bill seems to be all in to the astronomical conventional wisdom.

The next day Peggy is sitting by herself in the Philbrook Dining Hall having lunch.

"Hi, Peggy."

Peggy looks up and sees Ryan holding his lunch tray.

"Can I join you for lunch?"

"Sure," Peggy says.

"I'm glad I ran into you yesterday," Ryan says. "You're uncle has told me a lot about you."

"He has? I hope it's not all bad."

"Not at all. He really thinks a lot of you, you know."

"Well, the feeling is mutual. So, what are you doing for your senior project with him?"

"I'm trying to find some numerical solutions to Maxwell's equations using FPGAs."

"Yeah, he is really into Maxwell's equations."

Peggy tells Ryan about how she sat in on Uncle Sam's class when he derived Maxwell's equations from Coulomb's law and special relativity, and how she thinks that Maxwell's equations should apply to gravity. Ryan is impressed. He tells Peggy about the research in plasma physics that he hopes to do at Dartmouth next year. They talk about how plasma theory might play a bigger role than gravitational theory in explaining the universe. Peggy tells Ryan more about the Pearls of Wisdom app and how she started Pearlton Industries. She brings up the Pearls of Wisdom app on her tablet and shows him some of the video clips that she has made. They long since have finished lunch.

"Say, Peggy. I have an extra ticket to the hockey game on Saturday. Would you like to come with me?"

"I don't know. I haven't been to a hockey game yet."

"Then you will love it. How about I pick you up at six o'clock?"

"Ok, I am in Handler Hall. Here is my cell phone number."

18

"That was an exciting hockey game," Peggy says, "with UNH winning 3-2 in overtime. I could get addicted to hockey."

"We'll have to go to the next game together," Ryan says.

They are in the Philbrook Dining Hall, having walked here after the game for some ice cream. Peggy tells Ryan about how her cousin, Wayne, invented the U-Pen and how they came up with their marketing strategy to pay those who contribute video clips for the Pearls of Wisdom app. She tells Ryan how disappointed she was when she didn't get into Dartmouth.

"You've done so much in the last year since you were denied admission," Ryan says, "that I bet if you applied to transfer to Dartmouth and showed them your Pearls of Wisdom app with all of the video clips that you have made for it, there is an excellent chance you would get admitted."

"Do you really think so?"

"Absolutely. There's still time to apply for admission this fall, so I would do it right away."

"Maybe I will. I'll talk to Uncle Sam about it."

The following week Peggy stops by Uncle Sam's office.

"Any luck with my new theory of gravitation?" Peggy asks.

"Actually, in talking with Prof. Kelly about it, she told me that Heaviside wrote a paper in 1893 where he suggested an analogy between electric fields and gravitational fields. I looked up the paper and, believe it or not, he suggested that gravity should, by analogy, obey Maxwell-like equations identical to the equations you derived from Newton's law of gravitation and special relativity."

"You mean people already know about these gravitational equations?"

"It seems that once Einstein developed his general theory of relativity, Heaviside's idea was mostly forgotten until relatively recently, where it has been revived and called gravito-electromagnetism. It turns out that you can sort of get to them as a linear approximation to Einstein's field equation. But I think your derivation from Newton's law of gravitation and special relativity shows exactly where they come from."

"Were you able to see if these equations explain the precession of

Mercury?"

"I did a few quick calculations, and it looks as if the resulting forces are going to be too small to explain the discrepancy in Mercury's precession. We'll have to take a closer look at it."

"I'd like you to show me how you did those calculations."

"I will when we have some time. By the way, Ryan told me that you went to the hockey game with him on Saturday night."

"Yes, it was an exciting game."

"Anything you want to tell me?"

"About what? Ryan? He's just a friend who's interested in what I'm doing."

"Just a friend?"

"Yes, he thinks that my accomplishments in the past year should help my chances of being able to transfer to Dartmouth."

"Are you still interested in transferring to Dartmouth?"

"I am. I just have this feeling that I would get more out of their physics program in the smaller environment."

"Well, if you apply to transfer, I would be happy to write a letter of recommendation for you."

"Thanks. I'm going to start the application process this week."

Peggy PearlTimes with Bill and tells him that she has started to fill out the application to transfer to Dartmouth. Bill asks if she thinks she has a chance of being admitted. Peggy says that Ryan, one of Uncle Sam's students, thinks that her work on the Pearls of Wisdom app should help her chances a lot. Peggy goes on to tell Bill more about her new theory of gravitation based on Maxwell's equations.

"I went to my first hockey game last week," Peggy says.

"Who went with you?" Bill asks.

"Ryan."

"How long has Ryan been at UNH?"

"He's a senior and will graduate at the end of this term."

"What's he going to do next year?"

"He's applied to graduate school at Dartmouth."

In mid-March, Ryan learns that he has been accepted into the graduate school at Dartmouth and has received a teaching assistantship in the physics department. Peggy will not learn if her transfer application has been approved until early May. She refuses to get her hopes up, not wanting to be devastated again. *On the other hand, what would it be like? I would at least know Ryan. No, stop thinking about it.*

19

On the day of her first final exam, Peggy learns that her application to transfer to Dartmouth has been approved. She jumps with joy and immediately calls Uncle Sam, Bill, and her dad. Uncle Sam is happy for her. Bill is less enthusiastic. Her dad is worried and wants to come over to UNH and talk about it. He says that he and Peggy's mom will stop by this evening.

Peggy, Joe, and Kate are sitting at a corner table in the Philbrook Dining Hall having a light supper.

"I'm so happy I got accepted to Dartmouth," Peggy says. "I can't wait to start there in the fall."

"Now just slow down," Joe says. "It is going to cost us a lot more for you to go to Dartmouth. You've got a full tuition scholarship here at UNH, you've made lots of friends, Uncle Sam is here, your company seems to be perking along, why would you want to transfer?"

"I've always had my heart set on going to Dartmouth. I just have this feeling that my chances of making a difference, of doing something big, will be much better at Dartmouth than here. They are giving me some financial aid to make it possible. Please, let me accept this opportunity to transfer."

"I looked at the financial aid package they offered," Joe says. "It assumes that your parents, your mom and I, dip into our savings to help pay for your college. We have been putting away this savings for a trip to Europe for our 25th wedding anniversary, which will be the year after you graduate. If we use it all up for you to go to Dartmouth, then we won't be able to take our first European trip."

"Dad, our app is beginning to bring in some revenue. I'm sure sales will grow in the next couple of years, and I'll be able to use those funds for college. I promise to pay you back all the money that you will have to spend on my college initially. Please, dad."

Kate has been listening patiently. "Peggy may be right, Joe. This is her only chance to go to Dartmouth. If we don't make it to Europe on our 25th anniversary, we can go on our 30th."

"Kate, I always promised you that I would take you to Europe on our 25th wedding anniversary, and I don't want to go back on my word."

Peggy is beginning to panic. "Dad, I promise you. I will pay you back. You will be able to go to Europe. I promise. Please let me do this."

"If Peggy is so determined to go," Kate says, "I think she should go. We will be able to work things out."

"Well, I guess I have been outvoted," Joe says. "If you are so determined to go, then go."

"Oh, thank you dad." Peggy reaches over and hugs her dad. "I promise you will not regret this."

When Bill gets home after his last final exam, he and Peggy go to Prescott Park and find their favorite bench.

"So, Peggy, I can't believe you're really going to Dartmouth."

"I know, isn't that great?"

"Oh, it will be great being up there in Hanover all by yourself with Ryan."

"What are you talking about? I am not following Ryan to Dartmouth."

"It sure looks that way. Wasn't it his idea for you to transfer there?"

"Well, he knew that I applied there and didn't get in, and when he saw our Pearls of Wisdom app, he thought that might help me transfer in."

"Pretty convenient."

"Don't be jealous. I do not have any romantic feelings for Ryan. He is just someone who was doing a project for Uncle Sam."

"And taking you to hockey games?"

"Well, who did you take to hockey games at RPI?"

Bill smiles, "I will never tell."

"Well, stop worrying about Ryan then."

"Let's change the subject."

They talk about how well the new cloud server for the Pearls of Wisdom is working and how subscriptions have just passed the 12,000 mark. Video clips for solutions to all of the problems in their physics and calculus textbooks are now on the app.

Wayne and Connie are at the farmhouse when Peggy and Bill arrive for the 4th of July weekend. Dave and Eileen are there as well as Sam and Laura. Two of Connie's friends from nursing school are also there. One will be Connie's maid of honor in her wedding and the other will be a bridesmaid. Eileen is an accomplished seamstress and is making Connie's wedding gown in addition to all of the bridesmaid's gowns. She will use this weekend to take the final measurements and fittings for the gowns.

Peggy finds Sam reading on the porch of the lake house.

"Hi, Uncle Sam."

"I brought this copy of my *Introduction to Electrical Engineering* book for you. You'll recognize lots of topics you covered last term, but maybe with a little different take."

"What topics should I definitely turn into Pearl video clips?"

"You can use the introductory chapter, which gives a broad historical look at what led to the discoveries of the theory of electrodynamics. Students should be able to click on hyperlinks to dig deeper into any topic or person."

"Any other special topic?"

"You should definitely go through the derivation of how the currents and voltages in any electrical network can be solved by inspection using nodal or loop analysis. Any time you can find general solutions to a whole set of problems, it means you can solve lots of problems more quickly."

"Can you turn all of your digital logic video clips that you have on YouTube into Pearl video clips?" Peggy asks.

"Yes, I'll do that right away."

"On another topic," Peggy says, "I've been thinking more about my gravitational theory of Maxwell's equations."

"The more I think about it," Sam says, "the more I think you're onto something."

"The only difference between the two is that mass replaces charge and the different constant of proportionality makes gravitational forces very much weaker than electromagnetic forces."

"You're absolutely right."

"So do you think that charge and mass are really the same thing at some basic level?"

"You would think so," Sam says. "But traditionally, there have been two different types of mass. The first is inertial mass – the mass that shows up in Newton's second law of motion; that is, the acceleration of an object is equal to the force acting on the object divided by its mass. The second type of mass is the gravitational mass that shows up in Newton's law of gravitation. One of Einstein's basic postulates is that these two masses are identical, and all experiments seem to show that to be true. So physicists tend to think that charge and mass are two completely different properties of matter."

"But we have just proved that charges and masses both satisfy the exact same set of four Maxwell equations. This cannot be just a coincidence. There must be just a single set of equations that describes both. So charge and mass must be related to some single, common property."

"You make a great case, Peggy, which I can't argue with."

On the night of the 4th, they all climb into Dave's boat for the cruise down the lake to the fireworks in Wolfeboro. Connie tells her two friends that this will be a boat ride to remember. After dropping anchor in Wolfeboro Bay, waiting for the fireworks to begin, Dave looks up at the cloudy sky.

"It doesn't look as if we will have any stars out for the ride home this year."

"Darn it," Matt says. "I wanted another astronomy lesson from you, like last year."

Wayne says, "Let's find out from Peggy if she has made any progress on discovering her Theory of Everything."

"Actually, I have made progress. I have a new theory of gravity that I think may answer the question you raised last year about how the stars in the big dipper can know about the gravity they should feel from the North Star when it takes light from the North Star hundreds of years to get to them."

"So what is the answer?" Wayne asks.

"I realized that Uncle Sam's derivation of Maxwell's equations from Coulomb's law and special relativity must also work for Newton's law of gravitation. Therefore, there must be a second gravitational field, analogous to the magnetic field, and the two gravitational fields will satisfy equations identical to Maxwell's equations. This means there will be gravitational waves, similar to electromagnetic waves, which also travel at the speed of light."

"Does this second gravitational field produce any force on bodies?" Wayne asks.

"Yes, just like a magnetic field, it is generated by moving bodies and exerts a force only on other moving bodies."

"Why haven't people observed this force?"

"They very well may have and not recognized it. I think it may explain some of the observed gravitational anomalies in the universe."

"BOOM." The first fireworks volley explodes overhead.

Peggy and Bill spend most weekends during the summer at the lake visiting with Sam and Wayne and reviewing the sales of PearlPens. They all visit the manufacturing plant in Rochester where the PearlPens roll off the assembly line and are automatically packaged into different boxes depending on the number of pens ordered with the mailing address already printed on the box. Peggy and Bill hire two more full-time employees, one to assist with the day-to-day orders and a second computer programmer to help maintain and update the company website and the Pearls of Wisdom app.

Bill brings up the topic of Connie's upcoming wedding, reminding Peggy of his prediction of their future wedding. He confides to Peggy that he is afraid he is going to lose her when she goes to Dartmouth. Peggy tries to reassure him, but realizes that Bill is worried. She tells him that if it is meant to be, everything will work out in the end. Peggy wonders, *Is it meant to be?*

20

Peggy and Bill drive across the bridge from Portsmouth to New Castle and park next to *Wentworth by the Sea*, where Wayne and Connie are holding their rehearsal dinner tonight. Tomorrow, Connie will become Mrs. Wayne Woodbury. Peggy and Bill enter the Board Room on the upper level where Connie and Wayne are already greeting friends and relatives from out of town. Connie introduces her parents to Peggy and Bill. When Connie's dad, Rodney, learns that Bill is majoring in computer science, they get into a spirited conversation about cyber security. Peggy learns that Connie's mom, Sally, is an author who has written five novels – all murder mysteries. *Another Agatha Christie*, Peggy thinks.

After a scrumptious surf and turf dinner, Connie's dad gets up to speak. He talks about Connie growing up in Pittsfield, Massachusetts and her love of skiing and of children. In addition to teaching children how to ski, he tells how Connie would volunteer after school to help special-needs kids to read. He recalls the phone call they received from Connie on New Year's day two years ago telling them of a wonderful guy she had just met. He says that Connie told them, "I think this is the one!"

"We told Connie not to rush into anything, and I guess she took our advice because it took her six months to get engaged!"

When Connie's dad finishes speaking, Dave gets up to say a few words about Connie and Wayne. He thanks Kate for inviting Connie to Thanksgiving dinner two years ago and tells how Connie immediately fit into the family as if she had always belonged. He tells how Wayne confided to him when they were skiing at Gunstock during that first Christmas ski week that he thought he was falling in love with Connie. He concludes by proposing a toast to Connie and Wayne, saying that everyone in Wayne's extended family has fallen in love with Connie.

Dave stands on the back porch looking out over the ocean, relieved that the sun is shining and there is not a cloud in the sky. To his left, workers are arranging chairs on the lawn overlooking the ocean for the four o'clock wedding this afternoon. To his right, a large tent has been set up, containing large round tables for the dinner later tonight. A second tent for the wedding itself proved unnecessary when he saw the weather this morning. An outside bar, tables for hors-d'oeuvres, and high round standing tables complete the center back lawn. Connie and her bridesmaids, including Peggy, as well as her folks, stayed here last night and are inside making last minute preparations. Wayne and his groomsmen spent the night at a local hotel and will be arriving around three o'clock. Dave expects about 150 guests and has hired two young men to provide valet parking on the grass in the front yard. A large arch, decked in flowers, leads the guests directly along the side of the house to the seating area in the backyard. He thinks he has thought of everything and smiles.

Kate, Joe, and Matt arrive around 2:30 and shortly afterward Sam and Laura arrive along with Bill and his parents. At three o'clock, a limousine drops off Wayne and his groomsmen. Wayne and his best man go into Dave's study where the minister from their local church is waiting. The ushers head out to the backyard and take up their positions next to the guest seating area, where a string quartet is playing background music. Cars filled with guests move slowly up the long driveway.

At 3:50, the minister, Wayne and the best man make their way to the front of the rows of filled seats. The music stops. Eileen and Dave are ushered to their front row seats on the right. Then Connie's mom, Sally, is ushered to her front row seat on the left. A hush comes over the assembled guests. The string quartet starts playing Pachelbel's Canon in D. Peggy comes out the side door of the house and leads the procession down the center aisle, followed by the other bridesmaid and the maid of honor, taking their positions to the right of the minister. The music stops. Wayne smiles as he sees Connie in the doorway. Everyone rises as the string quartet plays the Bridal Chorus by Richard Wagner. Connie is radiant as she comes down the aisle on her dad's arm, Eileen and Kate wiping a tear from their eyes. The ceremony is perfect. As they are pronounced man and wife, Peggy thinks what an idyllic setting this is. Wayne kisses his new bride and the string quartet strikes up Mendelssohn's Wedding March. Peggy brings up the rear of the recessional on the arm of one of the ushers.

Peggy joins the rest of the wedding party in the receiving line as the guests file through. Matt is one of the first through the line and makes sure he kisses the bride. After everyone gets through the receiving line and the group photos are taken, Peggy is able to catch up with Bill. During the reception, they talk with friends and relatives they have not seen in some time. At dinner, Peggy and Bill sit with Uncle Sam, Aunt Laura, Kate, Joe, and Bill's parents. Everyone agrees this has been a perfect wedding.

"When I get married I want to have my wedding right here," Peggy says smiling.

"I hope you do, too, Bill" Sam says.

Dancing continues under the tent well into the night.

Finally, Wayne and Connie go inside to change. The family gathers at the front door to wish them well as they climb into the limousine that will take them into Boston. They will stay there tonight and then catch a plane tomorrow for a two-week honeymoon in St. Moritz in the Swiss Alps.

As Peggy watches them drive away, she wonders when she will go on a honeymoon, and with whom.

21

Bill brings the last of Peggy's belongings up to her second-floor single dorm room in the McLaughlin Cluster at Dartmouth. He drove Peggy here from Portsmouth this morning and will continue on to RPI this afternoon where his fall classes begin tomorrow. Peggy still has two weeks before her classes begin, as Dartmouth's terms are 10-week quarters instead of the two semesters at RPI and UNH. This means that Peggy will finish this fall quarter before Thanksgiving and then have a winter term starting in January and a spring term starting at the end of March.

Peggy is going to use these extra two weeks to get settled at Dartmouth and try to make some new friends. On the drive up, Bill and Peggy tried to figure out how she might get the Pearls of Wisdom app used in some of her courses this term. She plans to make video clips from her notes in the quantum mechanics and differential equations courses she will be taking this term. Perhaps, before classes begin, she will simply go to the professors teaching these two courses and give them the Pearls of Wisdom pitch. After all, she thinks that her work on that app was a big factor in getting her transfer application approved.

Bill helps Peggy unpack, and then they walk down to the Collis Café in the Student Center for lunch. They talk about how they are going to miss each other for the next three months.

"I guess Ryan is the only person you know here right now," Bill says.

Peggy looks annoyed. "Don't worry about Ryan. I'll probably never see him anyway."

After lunch, Bill walks Peggy back to her dorm, kisses her goodbye, and heads south toward RPI.

Peggy sits on the bed in her dorm room and realizes that she doesn't know anyone on campus – except possibly Ryan, if he is here yet. She begins to feel all alone. *Did I really want to come here? Would I be happier staying at UNH? I did make many friends there. I do not even have a roommate here.*

Peggy takes out her cell phone and sends a text message to Ryan. "R u on campus?"

Peggy decides to take a walk and explore the campus. She leaves her dorm and heads south on College Street. As she passes the Fairchild Physical Sciences Center, she makes a mental note to visit the library on the third floor tomorrow, when she will also look up Prof. Olsen in Wilder Hall, who will be teaching her quantum mechanics course. *Will I be able to interest him in the Pearls of Wisdom app?* Peggy passes the Rollins Chapel on her left and finds an empty bench on The Green where she sits down for a rest.

The warm sun feels good as she watches other students pass by. Several small groups of students are sitting on the grass chatting. To take her mind off her loneliness, Peggy starts to think about her new theory of gravitation based on Maxwell's equations. For the past several months, Peggy keeps coming back to it. *It has to be true. It is based only on Newton's law of gravitation and special relativity. When you try to make Newton's law of gravitation relativistically invariant, you get equations that are identical to Maxwell's equations. But if they look just like Maxwell's equations, maybe they are Maxwell's equations. Maybe gravitational fields are really just electric and magnetic fields. So maybe charge and mass are really just the same thing. But why does charge have two different signs, positive and negative, while mass always seems to be positive? Could mass be negative in some parts of the universe? Maybe I should take an introductory astronomy course next term, as Bill did, to see what kinds of unexplained phenomena they observe. Maybe my theory will explain some of it.*

Peggy snaps to when her cell phone beeps indicating a text message. It is from Ryan. "Where r u?"

Peggy texts back. "I am on a bench on the Green."

Ryan replies. "Do not move. I will b right there."

"Hi kid," Ryan says as he gives Peggy a hug.

"You're the only one I know on this whole campus," Peggy says.

"When did you get here?"

"Just this morning. Bill drove me up from Portsmouth, and then continued on to RPI."

"So Bill is still in the picture?"

"Bill is always in the picture. We are business partners, you know."

"Just business partners?"

"No, not just business partners."

"Well, Bill is not here, so what do you want to do?"

"Tell me when you got here and what you've been doing."

Ryan tells Peggy that he has been here a week and has a desk in the corner of the plasma physics lab in Wilder Hall. As a teaching assistant, he has been assigned to be a lab instructor in the Physics-I course and help with grading the homework in that class.

"Can you get them to use the Pearls of Wisdom app in Physics-I?" Peggy asks. "Lots of homework solutions are already there. It won't take students long to find them."

"I know," Ryan says. "I'll talk to Prof. Jackson, who is teaching the course and show him how the app could really help him."

"Thanks. I'm going to talk to my quantum mechanics professor tomorrow about it."

"Why don't we walk back to Wilder Hall? I'll show you my lab."

"Ok."

Peggy PearlTimes with Bill that night. They talk about how they miss each other already.

"Have you met anybody yet?" Bill asks.

"Just Ryan."

Three weeks into her quantum mechanics course, Peggy realizes that her uncle is right about the subject being weird. Because Prof. Olsen really is reluctant to delve deeply into the philosophical foundations of quantum theory, Peggy understands why Uncle Sam refers to it as a "shut up and calculate" course.

Prof. Olsen was intrigued when Peggy approached him before the course began and showed him the Pearls of Wisdom app. He said that he assigns homework problems and then calls on one of the students in the class to go over the solution on the board. This way, all students need to be prepared. Peggy convinced him that the Pearls of Wisdom app would encourage all students to make video clips of their solutions. Prof. Olsen told Peggy he would try it and see what happens. So far, it seems to be working out well in this class.

Prof. Jackson told Ryan that he was agnostic on the use of the Pearls of Wisdom app in Physics-I, but if it helped the students, he was fine with its use.

After class, Prof. Olsen tells Peggy that several of his colleagues have asked him about the Pearls of Wisdom app. He suggests that it might be useful if Peggy could give a short seminar on the Pearls of Wisdom app. It might be useful and informative for both students and faculty. Would she be agreeable to that? Peggy agrees as she immediately sees that this could be good publicity. Prof. Olsen says that he will find a suitable room and schedule it as soon as possible.

The Dartmouth receiver runs back the opening kickoff of the second half for a touchdown that gives Dartmouth the lead, 21-17.

"This is almost as exciting as hockey," Peggy says to Ryan, as they settle back into their seats in the last row of the stands.

Ryan suggests, "Let's make this the first of many football games you attend here at Dartmouth."

"I'm finding that with all of my classes and work on the Pearls of Wisdom app, it doesn't leave much time for a social life."

"We'll need to change that. You really need to start meeting more students."

"I'd like to, but I always seem to be running out of time."

"Prof. Jackson is having a backyard barbeque at his home next Friday afternoon for all of the TAs in the physics department. He told us that we could each bring a guest. Would you like to come with me? It would give you a chance to meet some more students."

"I don't know. Are they all going to be graduate students?"

"Some of the guests will probably be undergraduate students, like you. In fact, some of the lab assistants are actually upper-class undergraduates. You will have fun. Come with me."

"Ok, I guess."

A Dartmouth cornerback intercepts a long pass and runs it back for another touchdown.

Both students and professors have filled the Cook Auditorium, where Peggy is about to give her seminar on the Pearls of Wisdom app. Prof. Olsen steps behind the lectern at the front of the room and spends a few minutes describing how students in his quantum mechanics class use the Pearls of Wisdom app to make video clips of their homework assignments, and how he then has one student go over the solution in class. He then introduces Peggy.

Peggy brings the Pearls of Wisdom app up on the screen and describes how the PearlPen works. She clicks on a homework video clip, which shows someone solving the problem. A list of those currently working on the problem is displayed on the right. She clicks on one of the names and a male student at MIT appears on the screen writing with his PearlPen. Peggy asks him to say Hi to students and faculty at Dartmouth as she flips her tablet camera to show him the audience. He looks surprised. She tells him who she is and that he is welcome to stay and watch the rest of her presentation.

Peggy then clicks on one of the Pearl Video Clips and compares it to the Homework Video Clips. She explains how both types of video clips get made and how students, or even professors, can make money by producing these clips. She then opens up the floor for questions.

A professor stands up and is handed a wireless microphone. "I think this is horrible. You are just posting the solutions to all homework problems. How are students going to learn if they can just copy the answers?"

"First of all," Peggy says, "they can't just copy the answer as if it were printed in a book. They have to watch someone else actually solving the problem and at the same time follow each step by writing the solution on a piece of paper using the PearlPen. So they actually learn how to solve the problem just as if you were explaining it to a student on the blackboard."

Another professor asks, "It seems as if it doesn't make any sense to assign homework problems anymore, which get graded and become part of the student's grade. What incentive will a student have to try solving a homework problem before looking at the answer?"

"The incentive is that they can make money! If they solve the problem and make a homework video clip using their PearlPen, which clearly describes the solution, they can upload it to the Pearls of Wisdom app. Other students will watch their video clip and rate it on a scale of 1 to 5 stars. Even if someone else has solved the same problem, the app will, over time, automatically keep only the highest rated solutions. Students from all universities will compete with each other to provide the clearest solutions to homework problems. This can only increase the overall learning level nationwide."

The microphone is handed to a female student. "How much money can a student earn by posting solutions to homework problems?"

"Since we're still in the early stages of using the Pearls of Wisdom, it is hard to know for sure, but let me give you some figures. Half of the $20 annual subscription for the Pearls of Wisdom is set aside to pay contributors. We currently have 20,000 subscribers so, at this point, $200,000 will be paid out at the end of this term. Right now, there are over 600 homework solutions on the site produced by about 400 different people. If the funds are distributed evenly, which they will not be, that would be $500 per person. However, the most watched and highest rated videos will pay the most, so some will make a lot more money than others will. I hope that gives you some idea. However, right now, we have only 20,000 subscribers, but there are at least 800,000 students taking freshman calculus and physics every year just in this country. So I think there is a lot of potential for good students, or even faculty, to earn lots of extra cash. My recommendation would be to get started."

The questions continue at a lively pace until the hour is up and the questions have to be cut off. Students and faculty crowd around Peggy after the lecture outside the hall and continue to ask questions. Ryan has recorded the entire lecture and tonight Peggy will post it on the Pearlton Industries' website, on her Facebook page, and on YouTube.

Ryan tries to rescue Peggy from further questions. "Let me take you out to dinner tonight to celebrate your great performance."

"Great, I'd like that."

While relaxing at a corner table in the rear of the restaurant, Peggy and Ryan go over the excitement of the past few hours.

"You did a great job with your talk," Ryan says.

"I'm glad it's over, but I'm glad I did it."

"You can't say you are unknown on this campus anymore."

"I guess that's good. And I did meet a couple of nice students at Prof. Jackson's barbeque."

"Perhaps you'll get some professors to contribute Pearl video clips for various topics."

"You should put together an introductory physics course for the app," Peggy says. "If it takes off, you could make some extra money."

"I do have some ideas on how to introduce the material by focusing of the basic fundamentals so the students get a feel for what physics is really all about."

"You know I think physics is all screwed up, and I'm going to discover a Theory of Everything."

"I know!" Ryan says. "Well, there are things in physics that are hard to reconcile."

"Remember, Uncle Sam thinks that the universe is one big plasma, and that plasma physics would give a better explanation of what we observe in the universe than general relativity and gravity. You're studying plasma physics, what do you think?"

"I've read a book that makes that very case," Ryan says, "and it is a strong case. However, my research is about plasmas we produce on earth, not the whole universe."

"Why don't you apply it to the whole universe?" Peggy asks. "Maybe you could overturn all of current astronomy."

"That is something you do after you get your Ph.D. Half of the physics faculty members are doing work in astronomy using general relativity and all the conventional methods. I don't think they would be too happy if I told them that they are all wrong."

"That's the problem," Peggy says. "Uncle Sam introduced Woodbury's Law which says that conventional wisdom is wrong most of the time. I believe it. He also said that the person who will discover a Theory of Everything would have to be someone who has not spent an entire career going down the wrong path. Those people are too committed to what they are doing, and will not change. So the longer you wait to see if the universe is really made up of plasma, the more likely it is that you will never follow that path, and you will just buy into the expanding universe, big bang myth."

"Myth!" Ryan says. "You really are a radical, aren't you?"

"No, I just don't like to take everything at face value. You have to admit that quantum mechanics is weird, and the professors do not want to talk about what quantum theory means. It is just 'shut up and calculate'."

"I know what you mean. Scientists have been arguing about the meaning of quantum theory for over a hundred years."

"I agree with Einstein," Peggy says. "I don't think God plays dice."

"What else are you taking this term?" Ryan asks.

"I'm taking an electromagnetics course, and my Uncle Sam's video clips on the Pearls of Wisdom app are really helpful, even though this is an introductory course that doesn't go into that much detail."

"I saw them on the app. Brings back memories of when I took that class from your uncle."

"Going through the derivation of Maxwell's equations from Coulomb's Law and Special Relativity gives a good insight into how moving charges give rise to a magnetic field."

"But only in the stationary frame of reference. In the frame of reference moving with the charge, it changes into an electric field."

"I think electrostatics and magneto-statics are both myths, that are not really possible," Peggy says.

"Don't you think charges can be at rest?" Ryan asks.

"At rest with respect to what? We know from Maxwell's equations that an electric field is associated with a changing magnetic field, and a magnetic field is associated with a changing electric field."

"That's right. That back and forth between electric and magnetic fields is what is involved with electromagnetic waves, including light."

"Maybe that is all there is," Peggy says.

"But what about particles?" Ryan asks.

"I don't know, it's a mystery. Einstein once said that in a final theory, he thought there would be only fields, and no particles."

"I guess we are not going to solve all of the mysteries of the universe tonight."

"I have to get back and get some studying done tonight. Thanks a lot for dinner."

Peggy sits in her dorm room thinking about her first term at Dartmouth. *I really like it here; I've made a lot of friends since my talk in Cook Auditorium; that was really wild; Prof. Olsen is sort of cool, and has been a big help; I do miss Bill, but I enjoy being with Ryan; it will be good to get home for Thanksgiving.*

22

At the end of the fall term, Peggy and Bill again go to Uncle Dave's for Thanksgiving with the whole family. On the large screen in the media room, Connie and Wayne show videos of the wedding and honeymoon in the Swiss Alps.

Peggy and Sam then move to a couch in the sunroom. The number of Pearls of Wisdom subscribers is up to nearly 35,000 and Peggy's Dartmouth lecture video is already attracting lots of views on YouTube.

"It looks like you have made good progress in converting my *Vectors and Tensors* book to video clips," Sam says to Peggy.

"Yes, I've got just about everything in the first six chapters done."

"Good, you need to do the next two chapters on vector operations in cylindrical and spherical coordinates. These are used for many practical problems in engineering and physics, but most books just give the equations and the students do not know where they came from. Always better to have derived everything for yourself."

"I'll work on that next."

"You can skip the material on generalized tensors for now. You should include this at some point, but it can wait. Its main use is for describing general relativity, and you know my feelings about that."

"Ok," Peggy says, "but I do want to understand it sometime."

"But you should include the material on quaternions," Sam says. "They are important and not found in many textbooks."

"Why not? And why are they important?"

"Quaternions were discovered by Hamilton in 1843 when he was trying to extend the idea of complex numbers in a 2-dimensional plane to 3 dimensions by adding a second imaginary axis. That did not work, but he found that if he added a third imaginary axis in addition to the real axis, he ended up with a 4-dimensional hypercomplex number, which he called a *quaternion*. Hamilton was one of the most accomplished mathematicians at the time that he discovered quaternions. He believed that quaternions were destined to become the best way to carry out vector analysis of physical systems and spent the last 22 years of his life working on them."

"Why didn't they become popular?" Peggy asks.

"There are many reasons. It is important to note that Hamilton's quaternions preceded the modern system of vector analysis, which you learn in college today. Josiah Willard Gibbs, who taught at Yale, and Oliver Heaviside, who worked on electromagnetic theory in England, both were responsible for our modern system of vector analysis. They essentially stripped out the 'vector part' of quaternions and came up with the system we use today. Neither of them liked Hamilton's quaternions and thought that their systems were simpler and easier to use and understand. As a result, over the past 100 years, quaternions have largely been forgotten and are seldom taught in science and engineering courses today. This is too bad, because quaternions clarify a lot about vector analysis. For example, you may have wondered why there are two different ways of multiplying vectors, the dot product, which gives a scalar result, and the cross product, which gives a vector result. Quaternions answer this question – they both show up in a single quaternion multiplication."

"Do you use quaternions in any of your classes?" Peggy asks.

"In my electromagnetics course I taught last winter, I show how the four Maxwell equations that describe all of electrodynamics will reduce to a single equation when written in quaternion form. I've already put that lecture out on your app."

"That sounds to me like there must be something important about quaternions. One equation seems simpler than four. Maybe my Theory of Everything will use quaternions."

"Maybe."

"Have you used quaternions for anything else?"

"A long time ago I taught a virtual reality course, which involves a lot of 3-D graphics. Quaternions are useful in describing 3-D rotations in space, and are used in many computer graphics packages. My book shows how to do this."

Peggy is convinced. "I will definitely make video clips on quaternions."

Wayne and Bill walk into the sunroom.

"Come join us," Sam says. "The American Society for Engineering Education, or ASEE, has its annual conference next June, and the deadline for submitting abstracts was last month. So I submitted an abstract on using the flipping method in my digital design class using my YouTube video clips. The conference also has a large exhibit hall where all of the major textbook publishers will have booths. I think Pearlton Industries should have a booth there where you can demonstrate the Pearls of Wisdom app."

"That's a good idea." Peggy asks, "How do you think most professors will react to it?"

"Who knows? But we might as well shake them up."

"I guess anything for publicity."

"Speaking of publicity," Wayne says, "the TV station in Manchester contacted me and wants to do a human interest story on how our factory in Rochester produces the U-Pen and the PearlPen. They also saw the video of your Dartmouth presentation and they want to include you and the Pearls of Wisdom app in their piece."

"You're kidding," Peggy says.

"No," Wayne says, "they would like to do it a week from tomorrow. You can be there, right?"

"Of course. Bill, too bad you'll be back at RPI."

"You know I like to be in back of the camera, not in front of it."

"You're both going to have to get used to a new public image, I'm afraid," Sam says.

Peggy spends the next week checking on new orders for the PearlPen and Pearls of Wisdom app, orders coming in at a rate of several hundred a day. She makes plans to hire a new, permanent office manager who can oversee the increase in orders and manage the day-to-day operations of the company, including hiring new staff as needed. Revenues are approaching two million dollars and are increasing each week. She also prepares for her TV interview on Friday.

The TV truck, with its satellite dish on top, is parked outside the U-Pen factory in Rochester. Inside, the crew is setting up lights and the program hosts chat with Wayne, Connie, and Peggy. They explain that they will first interview Wayne standing in front of the production line, then have Connie join him. Then they will interview Peggy in the office where she can demonstrate the operation of the PearlPen with a tablet. They will take other close-up shots of the production line showing how orders are automatically filled. They will then go back to the studio and edit it all down to about a seven to eight minute segment. It will probably run sometime in the next two weeks.

"How do you think it went, Peggy?" Wayne asks as the TV truck pulls out of the driveway.

"I feel pretty good about it. It will be interesting to see what they end up using."

"I'll bet Connie gets top billing. They seemed to be intrigued with how the *Name That Face* app is being used by first and second graders to learn to write in cursive and to learn the names of everyone in their class at the same time."

Peggy says, "After the piece airs, we'll have to watch to see if there is an increase in the number of downloads of the free *Name That Face* app, and an increase in sales of the PearlPen."

"You're quite the TV star, Peggy," Dave says as he cuts into his first bite of beef Wellington at Christmas dinner in the farmhouse.

"Connie wasn't bad either," Kate says.

"I think Wayne did a great job explaining how U-Pens and PearlPens are made and all of the different applications that they can be used for," Joe says.

"I'm really pleased with how they edited it," Peggy says. "They really are pros at it. And there was a bump in sales of PearlPens after it aired, plus lots of new downloads of the *Name That Face* app."

"Have you heard from any of your friends who may have seen it?" Eileen asks.

"Yes, I've had lots of reaction on my Facebook page, almost all congratulating me."

"Is Bill coming up tomorrow?" Sam asks.

"Yes, luckily we can run our company from anywhere, including here, but we want to get some skiing in at Gunstock this week."

"Wayne and I will go skiing with you," Connie says.

Bill arrives at the farmhouse the following afternoon. He and Peggy take a walk up to the bridge, a walk characterized by unusual silence. Peggy senses that Bill is upset, probably about her being at Dartmouth, probably about Ryan. *Doesn't he know that Ryan is just a friend, someone I like to talk with, someone who helps me with physics, but not someone I have romantic feelings for? Are all men this possessive? Maybe I should tell Bill how I feel about him, that I can't imagine not being with him, that I can picture spending the rest of my life with him. Maybe I should tell him. Maybe I will. I will. Tomorrow.*

After dinner that night, Sam and Peggy sit in front of the fireplace at the farmhouse. The rest of the families are playing cards.

"Uncle Sam," Peggy says, "I don't think anyone knows what charge is."

"I think you're right."

"Charges are supposed to produce electric fields, but so are changing magnetic fields. So maybe charges have something to do with magnetic fields."

"Well we know that moving charges produce magnetic fields," Sam says.

"But so do changing electric fields," Peggy says.

"And changing electric and magnetic fields are electromagnetic waves, even in the absence of any charges."

"I think somehow we have to get rid of charges, and end up with only fields. That's what Einstein thought."

"You may be right. The idea of a point charge is what causes Coulomb's Law to blow up at the location of the charge where the electric field goes to infinity."

"Do you think a Theory of Everything will involve only fields?" Peggy asks. "Or will it include particles, as in quantum mechanics?"

"That's the 64 thousand dollar question," Sam says. "How about a game of cribbage?"

The next morning, Peggy, Bill, Wayne, and Connie drive to Gunstock for a day of skiing. Peggy hopes that the crisp, cool air will help to clear the air between Bill and her. She has decided that today she will come clean with Bill about her feelings for him, and tell him about the new idea she came up with overnight.

Peggy and Bill move into positions at the bottom of the Panorama chairlift waiting for the next two chairs to move up behind them. They sit down as the chairs lift their skis off the snow, beginning the long ride to the summit.

"Bill, I've got something I want to ask you."

"What?"

"When you're at RPI, do you miss me?"

"Of course I miss you."

"I mean, really miss me, like thinking about me all the time, and wanting to be with me."

"I think about you constantly, and it drives me crazy that Ryan can see you every day, but I can't."

"I've told you that you don't need to worry about Ryan. He's just a friend who helps me out with physics stuff, but I don't have any romantic feelings for Ryan."

"Well, I still don't like you being near him all the time, while I'm a long way away."

"Then why don't you see if you can transfer to Dartmouth, so we can be together all the time?"

"Are you serious?" Bill reaches for his seatbelt to make sure he doesn't fall out of the chair.

"I'm dead serious," Peggy says with conviction. "It would make everything so much easier. We would not have to PearlTime just to see each other and talk. We could get an apartment together near campus."

"That would be fantastic! Are you sure you want to make that commitment?"

"Look, you know I love you. Two years ago you told me that someday you were going to marry me, and I'm going to hold you to it."

"I knew you'd come around," Bill says, poking Peggy with his elbow. "What do you think your parents will say if I move in with you at Dartmouth?"

"We'll wait until you get accepted before worrying about that."

"What do you think my chances are?"

"Well, our Pearls of Wisdom app helped me get in. Just tell them that you were the one that wrote most of the code, and that my grades will suffer if you don't move in with me to keep me calm and focused."

Bill laughs. "I'm sure that will be the deciding factor."

Peggy and Bill step off the chairlift at the summit, kiss each other, adjust their goggles, and ski down Hot-Shot at full speed.

Following the traditional New Year's Eve fondue dinner, Sam suggests a game of Fictionary. He fetches a dictionary, pencils for everyone, and a bunch of 3 x 5 cards. Everyone gathers around the long dining room table as Sam goes over the rules.

"Okay, Peggy will begin by looking up and pronouncing a word that she thinks no one will know. If anyone knows the word, she has to pick another one. She writes the correct definition on her card. The rest of you each make up a definition and write it on your card. Peggy collects all the cards, shuffles them, and reads all of the definitions. We then go around the table and everyone votes for what they think is the correct definition. If no one guesses the correct definition, Peggy gets one point. Anyone who guesses the correct definition gets a point, and you get a point for each person who picks your definition. Is that clear?"

Sam hands the dictionary to Peggy, who flips through until she finds a word.

"Okay, my word is *cateran*." Peggy spells the word and writes the correct definition on her card.

Several moans are heard as everyone writes a definition, hoping to fool the others into believing it is the correct definition. Peggy collects all of the cards, adds hers to the pile, and shuffles them. She then reads the possible eleven definitions, starting at the top of the shuffled pile of cards.

"A mountain lion, indigenous to Central America."

"A geological crack in the earth's surface."

"A small South American bug."

"A Scottish Highlands robber."

"A tool used for sculpturing stone."

"A pastry chef."

"A small cyst, usually found under the skin."

"A hanging toenail."

"A small English pony."

"An ancient Egyptian coin."

"A yellow-leaf plant found in central Africa."

Going around the table, starting at Peggy's left, everyone chooses a definition. Sam summarizes the results.

"Joe, Dave, Connie, and Eileen all picked *A tool used for sculpturing stone*. Whose definition is that?"

"That's mine," Laura says, "so I get four points."

Sam continues, "Kate and Wayne picked *A small cyst, usually found under the skin*. That is my definition, so I get two points. Matt, Laura, and I picked *An ancient Egyptian coin*."

"That's my definition," Bill says, "so I get three points. I picked *A Scottish Highlands robber*. Whose definition is that?"

"That's the correct definition," Peggy says, "so you get another point, for a total of four."

"This is great fun," Bill says. "Now it's my turn to pick a word."

Peggy hands Bill the dictionary and the game continues all evening until interrupted by Auld Lang Syne. Bill, the overall winner of the game, takes Peggy in his arms and kisses her. After everything that has happened this week, Peggy feels that she is a winner too.

23

It is a sunny February afternoon with snow piled high along the roads and sidewalks on the Dartmouth campus. Peggy has just come out of her astronomy class where they were discussing spiral galaxies and how the velocity of the outer stars are much higher than predicted by Newton's laws of motion. The professor told the class that most astronomers believe there must be dark matter in the universe to account for this. Sitting in the class, Peggy realizes that all the moving stars in the galaxy will produce her second magnetic gravitational field. Perhaps the resulting force on the moving stars in the outer galaxy will change in such a way as to account for the observed velocities without the need to invent dark matter. She cannot believe that no one has realized this before. She will have to call Uncle Sam and discuss it with him.

Stopping by the plasma physics lab to find Ryan, Peggy notices all the expensive-looking equipment.

"Is this all your equipment?" Peggy asks.

"Oh no," Ryan says. "There are several other graduate students that work in this same lab."

"So what kind of experiments are you doing?" Peggy asks.

"Let me start by showing you a very simple one that just uses a regular microwave oven."

Ryan explains that he is interested is studying how microwaves interact with ionized gases, or plasmas. He tells her that microwave ovens generate high-powered microwaves using a magnetron of the type originally developed by the British at the beginning of the Second World War for radar that could detect incoming German planes.

"The magnetron is behind the control panel," Ryan says pointing to the keypad on the microwave oven, "and the microwaves go down a waveguide and then spread out into the oven, which is basically a metal box. The frequency of the microwaves is 2.45 gigahertz, which is somewhat above the frequency that your cell phone uses to make calls and just above the Bluetooth frequency used to connect your devices to wireless speakers or headphones."

"What wavelength does 2.45 gigahertz correspond to?" Peggy asks.

"The wavelength is 12.23 centimeters, or a little under 5 inches."

"So what do the microwaves look like inside the oven?"

"Glad you asked," Ryan says, opening the microwave oven door. Inside is a wooden board on which is mounted a rectangular array of about 100 miniature neon Christmas tree light bulbs. The board sits on four blocks and stands about three inches off the bottom of the oven such that it will not rotate when the microwave oven is turned on.

"Now watch," Ryan says as he closes the door and turns on the microwave oven to high.

After several seconds, some of the bulbs light up, but not all of them.

"That's cool," Peggy says, "but some of the bulbs aren't on."

"That's right. The microwaves bounce off all of the walls of the oven, so at any point waves are coming at each other from opposite directions. This creates standing waves where there are nodes of zero electric field intensity, and therefore the light bulb will be off, and places where the electric field intensity is a maximum, which will turn on the lights. The microwave oven behaves like what we call a resonant cavity."

Ryan turns off the microwave oven, opens the door, and removes the four blocks. He then sets the board on the rotating carousal so that the array of neon bulbs will rotate when the microwave oven is turned on. He closes the door and turns the microwave oven on high. This time, as the board rotates, different lights turn on and off as the bulbs move in and out of regions of high electric field intensity.

"We studied standing sound waves in a tube in my physics class," Peggy says.

"That's how all wind instruments make sounds," Ryan explains. "The different notes are just standing waves with different wavelengths. It is the same with string instruments like a violin. In this case, when you pluck the string or run a bow across the string, the body of the violin vibrates and two-dimensional standing waves are created on the violin body. The higher the note means the higher the frequency, so there will be more zero nodes where the violin body isn't really moving, just like some of the neon lights are out in the microwave oven."

"That's pretty interesting. So what are you trying to do with your research?"

"I'm interested in how electromagnetic waves interact with plasmas that are in a magnetic field. Instead of using microwaves, I am using lasers in the visible region of the electromagnetic spectrum. I am studying how light interacts with electrons and positive ions in a magnetic field. The research may lead to new kinds of lasers."

"Thanks a lot for showing me around. Next term I am taking a physics course on Electromagnetic Waves and we have to do a project. Maybe I will measure standing waves in a microwave oven."

"Let me know if I can help."

The following Saturday morning Peggy is PearlTiming with Bill. He has been checking the contributions that have been posted on the Pearls of Wisdom app.

"Peggy, did you see all the new Pearl videos that have been pouring in lately?"

"Yes, and lots of them are coming from overseas. It looks as if our international sales are really picking up."

"That's for sure. But many of these new Pearl videos are getting very low ratings. I don't think we want to keep a lot of these on the app."

"I agree. The app is supposed to keep only the highest rated videos. Maybe we need to shorten the time that low-rated videos stay on the app."

"Right now we keep a new video on for a fixed length of time, but I think I should change that so that if the rating is below, say 4 out of 5, after so many reviews, it is taken off no matter how long it has been up."

"I think that is a good idea," Peggy says. "I would say take down any clip that has a rating below 4 after ten reviews. We need to make sure that the quality stays high."

"I'll make those changes right away and then post the update," Bill says. "By the way, I completed and submitted my application to transfer to Dartmouth."

"Did you tell them that they must admit you so you can move in with me?"

"Yes, I told them that you can't live without me."

Uncle Sam calls Peggy and tells her that the paper he submitted to the ASEE conference in June was accepted. There was sufficient interest in the topic of using the flipping method of teaching that, in addition to the session in which Sam's paper will be presented, they have added a panel discussion on the topic and they wanted to have Sam and Peggy on the panel.

"The conference is in Boston this year," Sam says, "so I think you should come and join me on the panel. This conference will draw hundreds of faculty from around the country so, between our booth and this panel, the Pearls of Wisdom app will get lots of publicity."

Peggy says, "Ok, I guess I'm beginning to get used to these public appearances."

"Don't worry. Just be yourself."

During the spring quarter, Peggy is taking a physics course on Electromagnetic Waves. For her final project, she found a paper in a technical journal, which describes how to detect the standing waves in a microwave oven by using a wet piece of thermal fax paper. She goes to the departmental office and convinces the administrative assistant to tear off a long sheet of thermal fax paper from the roll in the fax machine. She plans to conduct the experiments using the microwave oven in Ryan's lab.

The following Saturday, Ryan helps Peggy do the microwave oven experiment. Peggy cuts a square sheet of the thermal fax paper, wets it, and places it between two pieces of cardboard. She removes the rotating carousal and places the cardboard sandwich on top of an upside down plate that won't rotate when the oven in turned on. She then closes the door and turns the microwave oven on high for 30 seconds. When she opens the cardboard sandwich, the fax paper shows four large black spots representing the standing wave mode pattern. Peggy puts the rotating carousal back in the oven, prepares another cardboard sandwich containing a wet piece of thermal fax paper, and repeats the experiment. This time the fax paper contains a single large black annular ring looking like a donut. The rotating paper causes all parts of the black donut area to pass through the four high-intensity regions of the standing waves.

This experiment has whetted Peggy's appetite to understand the details of how and why microwaves form standing waves inside a microwave oven. She talks to Prof. Anderson, who is teaching her Electromagnetic Waves class, and he agrees to advise her on a special project during the summer quarter, where she can find analytical solutions of Maxwell's equations for resonant cavities.

The following week Peggy walks out of her Electromagnetic Waves class. A short, stocky man approaches her. He is carrying a large, official-looking envelope.

"Are you Peggy Leach?" he asks.

"Yes," Peggy says.

He hands her the envelope. "This is a summons from the Federal District Court in Concord. Have a nice day." He turns and walks away.

Peggy opens the envelope and gasps. "Oh no!"

She hurries to Ryan's lab and finds him at his desk.

"You're not going to believe this; we're being sued by the publisher of the Physics-I textbook."

"What for?" Ryan asks.

"I'm not sure. Something about copyright violation for publishing all the solutions of their problems on our Pearls of Wisdom app."

"How can they do that?" Ryan asks.

"They just did. It says we have 21 days to respond. They're suing us for $100,000 and saying we have to take down our app with their solutions on it."

"That's horrible."

"I know. How will I be able to pay for college if Pearlton Industries goes under? I better call Uncle Sam and ask him what to do. At least we've got three weeks to respond."

Just then, an attractive redhead walks into Ryan's lab.

"Hi Ryan," she says.

"Hi Ashley," Ryan says. "This is Peggy. She is a sophomore physics major."

"Hi, I'm Ashley. Ryan's girlfriend."

Peggy waits for the shock to wear off. "Nice to meet you."

Ryan steps in. "Ashley and I met on a blind date a month ago, and have been going together since. She is graduating this term with a major in biophysical chemistry."

"That's great," Peggy says. "What are you going to do next year?"

"I got a job in one of the labs at the Dartmouth-Hitchcock Medical Center. So I'll be staying in the area."

"Well, I'm sure I'll see you around then," Peggy says as she walks out of the lab.

Peggy snaps a photo of the summons and emails it to Uncle Sam. She then calls him to discuss it. Sam says that he will have Wayne's lawyer look into it, but at this stage, try not to worry too much about it.

Peggy then PearlTimes with Bill and shows him the summons. Bill says that that bad news is offset by the good news that his application to transfer to Dartmouth has been approved and that he can start in the summer term.

"That's terrific!" Peggy says. "Hurry up and get here. I need you. I'll start looking for an apartment."

"When are you going to tell your folks?" Bill asks.

"I'll call them next week and break the news to them."

"What do you think your dad will say?"

"He'll probably be happy that you'll be paying half the rent."

24

Bill has finished his spring term and leaves RPI for the last time. He drives to Dartmouth and drops off his belongings at the apartment Peggy has picked out for them. He and Peggy then continue on to the farmhouse for the long Memorial Day weekend. The whole family is gathering there for a spring cleanup in preparation for another summer season at the lake. The copyright suit is foremost on Peggy's mind when she finds Sam in the lake house living room.

"So what happened when Wayne's lawyer responded to the suit?" Peggy asks.

"He asked that the suit be dismissed as frivolous and harassing," Sam says. "The judge rejected the publisher's demand to take the app down immediately, but did let the suit go forward. He gave both sides ninety days to agree to some type of settlement with the help of a mediator. Otherwise, he would move it to trial."

"What kind of settlement could we agree to that wouldn't screw us?"

"We need to put our heads together and come up with something. But we have time and don't have to rush. Let's think about it a little."

Eileen walks into the farmhouse kitchen. "Say, Kate, I heard that Bill and Peggy are moving in together at Dartmouth. Is that correct?"

"I'm afraid it is. Peggy called us a couple of weeks ago to break the news to us. The good news was that Bill's transfer application to Dartmouth had been accepted. The bad news was that they are moving in together."

"Bad news for you. They probably think it is good news. How's Joe taking it?"

"What can he say? Peggy told him it was the 21st century."

"Did she quiz him about how things were when you and he were in college?"

"Now, Eileen, let's not get into that."

At dinner that night, Connie makes the important announcement that at the end of October she will change her status in the Pregnancy & Birth Department at Portsmouth Regional Hospital from nurse to patient. Everyone is excited at the news of a new Woodbury joining the clan. She says she will not return to nursing after the baby is born, but hopes to become more involved in Wayne and Peggy's companies. Peggy notes that the *Name that Face* app is taking off and selling lots of PearlPens and suggests that Connie can help to push that app. Sam suggests that Connie join the Board of Directors of Pearlton Industries and Peggy and Bill agree. Peggy suggests they hold a board meeting Sunday afternoon.

At breakfast the next morning, Peggy says she had an incredible dream last night.

"What was the dream?" Sam asks.

"There was this new university, called Pearlton University, overlooking Great Bay near Portsmouth. It was unlike any university today. Students didn't come there right out of high school and stay for four years and have the same tenured professors who stay there forever."

"Careful, now," Sam says.

"Instead this university was open to anyone from college age young people to retirees, who have a deep desire to learn something new. There were no permanent faculty, just a Dean of Faculty who was you, Uncle Sam. Faculty from around the world came there for a sabbatical – one year, or two years maximum – and taught what they knew best and made course material and organized the Pearl video clips into dynamic books for the Pearls of Wisdom app. They all received royalties based on the number of 'views' their material gets in future courses around the world just like everyone else. They taught their courses using the flipping method and the discussion groups were streamed live around the world and anyone logged onto Pearls of Wisdom could take part."

"So the people didn't have to be at the university to take the course?" Bill asks.

"No, but they weren't online courses where you are talking to a computer. You could interact with the people who are physically in the discussion group."

"Did the university award degrees?" Wayne asks.

"Not in the traditional sense of a Bachelors or Masters degree. You attend this university for your entire life. You keep taking courses you are interested in forever. The university gave out *Milestone Recognition Certificates*, which became much more valuable and meaningful than traditional degrees. They were based on the number of different courses you completed, the depth of a single area studied, the breadth of interests displayed, and the results of creative and innovative projects produced. They had bronze, silver, and gold certificates."

"Was any research done at this university?" Sam asks.

"Yes," Peggy says. "Associated with the university was the Pearlton Labs for basic and applied research. Again, there was only a skeleton permanent staff, with young faculty from around the world spending their sabbaticals there. In this case, they could stay for up to a maximum of three years. They didn't want to allow burnout, and they wanted to keep new fresh ideas continually coming in."

"That was quite a dream," Sam says. "I would say you dreamed of things that never were."

"Then why not?" Peggy asks.

On Sunday afternoon, Peggy, Bill, Wayne, Connie, Uncle Sam and Aunt Laura sit around the dining room table in the farmhouse for a board meeting of Pearlton Industries. They each have a PearlPen and either a tablet or a notebook computer.

"I've asked Aunt Laura to join us," Peggy says, "and take notes with her PearlPen of everything we go over. We'll all then have immediate copies."

"I think PearlPens should be required in all board meetings for all companies," Sam says.

"Now we're talking," Wayne says.

"Let me write a tentative agenda with my PearlPen," Peggy says. "Of course, it will show up immediately on your screens."

Peggy then lists the following topics: Sales figures, Upcoming ASEE meeting, Status of the Pearls of Wisdom Courses, Budget, Growth.

Peggy says that subscriptions and sales of the PearlPen are now approaching 80,000 and seem to be doubling about every academic term, or quadrupling every year.

"Wayne, can you handle that kind of growth?" Peggy asks.

"For now, we can, but we should probably start making plans to add another manufacturing line."

"The next topic on the agenda," Peggy says, "is the ASEE convention in Boston where we are going to have a booth in the exhibit hall. The convention opens next Sunday evening and goes through Tuesday. Bill and I will be staying here this week and going to Boston on Sunday."

"My talk is on Tuesday," Sam says, "and then the next day Peggy and I are on a panel discussion about teaching classes using the flipping method. Wednesday is the last day of the conference and the exhibit hall is closed that day."

"My people have put together a good booth for Pearlton Industries to have at the show," Wayne says. "Connie will be there with me and we can all take turns at the booth. I will make up a schedule to make sure that at least two people are at the booth at all times."

"I can be there most of the time," Bill says.

"We should have several setups where people can try out the PearlPen and the Pearls of Wisdom app," Sam says. "And I think we should offer a convention discount to people who buy the PearlPen at the show, maybe $30 instead of $50 including a one-year subscription to the Pearls of Wisdom app. Make it worth their while to buy on the spot."

"Good idea," Peggy says.

"They can register their PearlPens right there by just signing their name," Wayne says. "This will let them download the Pearls of Wisdom app onto their tablet if they have it with them, or when they get home."

"Why don't we also give away the *Name that Face* app for their smart phone as a way of capturing their email address for later marketing," Bill says.

"Very good idea," Sam says. "We can also demonstrate that app by taking everyone's photo and capturing their name and affiliation at the same time."

"I love it," Peggy says.

Peggy then goes to the next item on the agenda and shows the courses that are currently on the Pearls of Wisdom app.

"You can see that Uncle Sam has converted three of his books to what I'll call dynamic books, where derivations and examples have been replaced with links to video clips, which show him actually doing the derivation or example with the PearlPen."

"I think these are good examples of what others could do with books they may have written or plan to write," Wayne says.

"I've been thinking about Peggy's dream that she had the other night," Sam says. "I think Pearlton University is exactly what is needed. That would be a game changer."

"But how could we ever start such a thing?" Peggy asks.

"Well, slowly to begin with," Sam says. "But the basic idea of having faculty members spend their sabbaticals at PU developing good course material is sound. To get the ball rolling, however, maybe I should teach a two-week short course on how to develop a dynamic book that will form the basis of a Pearls of Wisdom course. I have already done three dynamic books, and I see what is needed to make the process easier and faster. We need to update our tools for creating the video clips and integrating them into the text of a dynamic book. I've got some ideas and can work with Bill and the other programmers to get them implemented."

"That would be great," Peggy says. "When could you do the first two-week short course?"

"I could probably do a test one with maybe a dozen participants toward the end of the summer. I will put together a flyer that we can hand out in our booth at the ASEE conference and see if we get any takers. We will emphasize the advantages in getting in on the ground floor of Pearls of Wisdom courses, which will mean more royalties for them."

"You could hold the course at our facilities in Newington," Wayne says. "What would we charge them for the course?"

"I would say something like $1500 is what someone might expect to pay for such a course," Sam says. "Of course, we really want them to develop good course material that we can include in the Pearls of Wisdom app."

"I've got an idea," Wayne says. "We could say the cost of the course is $2000, but if you pay cash up front, you get it for half price, or $1000. Otherwise, we would simply treat the $2000 as an advance on future royalties on the Pearls of Wisdom dynamic book they produce. This should be very attractive to them, because they don't have to put any money up front."

"Of course, if their book is no good and doesn't return at least $2000 we lose," Sam says, "but that is a good risk to take."

"Let's do it," Peggy says.

They then go over the budget for the next year.

"The last item on the agenda is Growth," Peggy says. "Uncle Sam has something he wants to say about growth."

"Both of your companies are growing fast, and are poised to start exponential growth within a couple of years. This danger zone kills off many start-up companies. They are not able to handle the growth. At some point, when revenues really start pouring in, you should definitely think about selling the companies to someone like Google or Apple. They would provide immediate worldwide penetration and professional management. The vision of a Pearlton University providing thousands of courses for lifelong learning of the entire population of the world is something that would get Google's attention. Based on what these companies have recently paid for other companies with much less potential than yours, a sales price of over a billion dollars for each company is certainly not out of the question."

"That would be a good thing to aim for," Wayne says.

"Remember what Uncle Sam said at my graduation," Peggy says. "If you aim at nothing, you will hit it every time."

"So let's pin a billion dollar sign on the wall," Bill says.

25

The Westin Copley Place in Boston is the site of the ASEE meeting in June. Sam and Peggy are sitting behind a long table at the front of the ballroom along with three other participants for the panel discussion on flipping methods in teaching, scheduled to begin in about five minutes. It is Wednesday, the last day of the conference, which began on Sunday night with the opening of the exhibit hall. Bill and Wayne had set up the Pearlton Industries booth Sunday morning, and Peggy has spent most of her time at the conference working at the booth, where Connie, Bill, Wayne, and Sam joined her at times. Peggy took a break from the booth on Tuesday to listen to Sam present his paper on using the flipping method in his digital design class.

As Peggy watches the ballroom fill up to hear the panel discussion, she tries to recognize anyone who visited the booth the past two days. Peggy enjoyed meeting people one-on-one in the booth, showing them the Pearls of Wisdom app, the homework videos, the Pearl videos, and the video conferencing feature. Now that everyone in the audience seems to be looking at her sitting behind the front table, Peggy begins to feel uneasy. She wonders, *Why am I here*? She tries to focus on some of the professors who stopped by the booth and had positive things to say about the Pearls of Wisdom app. She tries to forget the particularly obnoxious one who ridiculed the idea of posting the solutions to all homework problems. She chuckles to herself remembering how the book-publishing representative from the adjoining booth worried that the Pearls of Wisdom app might eat into their textbook market. She also recalls how Sam handed out lots of flyers about his two-week short course in August on writing dynamic books of the Pearls of Wisdom app, and how six people have already signed up.

As she looks out at the audience, Peggy is on the far left end of the table, sitting next to Sam. The only other woman on the panel, who is from Michigan, is on the far right end. Peggy figures they have to balance the females on the panel. The moderator, who is sitting in the center, is just starting to introduce the panelists, starting with the Michigan woman at the other end. Everyone gets five minutes to say something, Peggy being the last to speak. She now realizes that everyone else in the room is probably a professor from somewhere, and now she is afraid she is going to make a fool of herself. The moderator has just introduced Sam and is introducing her as the president of Pearlton Industries and a student at Dartmouth College. Peggy tries to force a smile.

The moderator, who is from Kansas, goes first and is saying something about potential benefits of the flipping method. Peggy cannot seem to concentrate on what he is saying. Her eyes scan the audience and she estimates there must be between three and four hundred attendees. Peggy reaches for a glass of water with her trembling hand, trying to quiet the butterflies she feels in her stomach. The Michigan woman at the other end of the table is showing an example of a video clip that she has made for her probability and statistics class, which shows an animated normal distribution graph. *That would be a good addition to the Pearls of Wisdom app.* The next panelist, who is from somewhere in the south, is saying something about how more good video clips are needed to make flipping practical and how textbook companies should be making these. *He doesn't know what he is talking about.*

The moderator asks Sam to go next. Sam gave his paper yesterday, where he showed how he used flipping in his digital design course using his video clips that are on YouTube. Today he is telling the audience how he created video clips in his electromagnetics course by using the PearlPen. Sam says that Peggy will tell them about the Pearls of Wisdom app and show them an example.

Peggy brings up the Pearls of Wisdom app on the big screen behind the panelists and explains how contributors get paid to post homework or Pearl video clips. She then solves a simple integration by parts example on a piece of paper using the PearlPen, showing how it is displayed in real time on the screen, and then converted immediately to a permanent video clip.

The moderator then opens up the floor to questions and comments asking the attendees to wait for a microphone to reach them. The first professor to speak says that he has been giving lectures for thirty years and thinks the students learn pretty well.

"If all my lectures are turned into little video clips," he asks, "why do they need me anymore?"

The moderator says that the professor's role will change from a lecturer to a coach. He says the important thing is that students have a better learning experience.

The next questioner asks Peggy if she thinks it is ethical to post the solutions to textbook problems on her app. Peggy gives the same answer she gave to this question at her presentation at Dartmouth last year. She points out the automatic grading feature of the Pearls of Wisdom app and how students actually have to explain their solutions as they are writing them out using the PearlPen.

Questions continue for another half hour and Peggy senses that a majority of those in the audience are warming to the idea of possibly using the Pearls of Wisdom app. The moderator finally concludes the panel discussion, and Peggy breathes a sigh of relief.

That evening they are all having dinner in the hotel dining room. Bill asks if there has been any progress on the lawsuit.

"I've been thinking about that stupid lawsuit," Sam says. "They are upset that the solutions to all of their problems are on our app. I suppose that the professors who teach the course could be just as upset, because they will find it harder to assign those problems as homework problems. So how about this idea? We pay royalties for people to come up with new problems, together with the solutions. We post the problems without the solutions for a specified time, say two weeks, after which the solutions would be posted. There would always be new problems on the app that professors could assign before the solutions are posted. Professors could register their courses and receive the solutions ahead of time so they would not have to solve the problems themselves. You know professors are as lazy as anyone."

"Why would the publisher drop the lawsuit if we did this?" Peggy asks.

Sam says, "We would agree to arrange the new problems by the chapters in their book, so they could use this new problem feature as a selling point to encourage professors to adopt their book. We would essentially give them free advertising for their textbook on our app."

"We could do this for any textbook whose problems we have solved on the app," Bill says. "We don't want any other publisher suing us."

"That's a great idea," Wayne says. "But I would go even further. In exchange for our advertising of their book on our app, they should explain how to obtain our app in the preface of the next printing of their textbook."

"That sounds like win-win to me," Sam says.

"Do you think they will go for this?" Peggy asks.

"We'll find out," Wayne says. "I'll have our lawyer contact their lawyer next week and see if we can get this behind us. We might even come out ahead."

Bill and Peggy drive back to Dartmouth where they are about to move into their new apartment for the first time. The apartment, within walking distance of campus, is cozy. A sofa, overstuffed chair, TV, drop-leaf table, stove, sink, and refrigerator fill the small living-dining-kitchen area. In the back are two small bedrooms and a bath. The bedroom for sleeping contains a double bed and chest of drawers; the bedroom for studying contains a daybed and two small desks.

Peggy grabs Bill's hand as they walk into the apartment. "Don't you feel strange walking in here with all of your clothes in the closet?"

"It does feel a little bizarre. But in a good way."

They walk from room to room, exploring all of the closets. Peggy puts her arms around Bill's neck and pulls him close.

"Welcome to Hanover!"

26

Bill is taking a numerical methods class and Peggy is working on her project for Prof. Anderson where she is trying to find analytical solutions of Maxwell's equations for resonant cavities. They take a break from their summer projects to spend the 4th of July weekend at the lake house and bring Sam and Wayne up to date. Pearls of Wisdom subscriptions have soared past 100,000 and seem to be on track to double every academic semester. Wayne indicates that he is making changes to keep up with PearlPen orders.

Peggy tells Joe that she can start paying her share of Dartmouth expenses and should be able to begin paying him back for his contributions to her Dartmouth education.

High winds and rain have cancelled this year's 4th of July fireworks in Wolfeboro. Dave agrees to take everyone out in the boat on Labor Day if it is clear starry night. It is still raining the next day as Peggy and Bill drive back to Dartmouth to resume their summer studies.

Peggy stops by Ryan's lab and asks Ryan if he is still going with Ashley. Ryan says that Ashley has moved in with him. Peggy tells Ryan that Bill has transferred to Dartmouth and is living with her. She says that she would like Ryan to meet Bill. They agree to meet for dinner at Murphy's Saturday night. Ryan will bring Ashley.

Ryan and Ashley already have a table when Peggy and Bill arrive for dinner on Saturday night. Peggy introduces Bill to Ryan and Ashley.

"I understand you're studying computer science," Ryan says.

"Yes," Bill says. "Just a computer geek, I guess."

"You've certainly made a big splash with the Pearls of Wisdom app," Ryan says.

"Yes, Ryan showed me your Pearls of Wisdom app," Ashley says. "How did you guys ever come up with that idea?"

"Well, it's a long story," Peggy says. "I'll give you the Cliff's Notes version."

Peggy gives a short history of her relationships with Wayne and Uncle Sam and explains how the idea of using the U-Pen for learning came about.

She says that she is happy with how the app seems to be popular.

"Peggy said that you got a job at the Dartmouth-Hitchcock Medical Center," Bill says.

"Yes, I work in the clinical chemistry lab" Ashley says. "Both Ryan and I work with plasma. He works with ionized gases and I work with blood! At some point I'd like to get into the genetics and molecular biology graduate program at Dartmouth."

Ryan tells Peggy and Bill that they are welcome to use his lab if they want to do any experiments. He says that he will be happy to help them in any way he can. After dinner, the four of them continue to talk for another hour. On the way home, Bill tells Peggy how much he likes Ryan and Ashley.

"Ryan is a really interesting guy," Bill says. "I can see why you liked to be with him."

"I like being with you better," Peggy says as she unlocks their apartment door.

"So what did you learn from doing this project?" Prof. Anderson asks Peggy as she hands in her final report.

"I learned a lot. I learned how to solve Maxwell's equations using the separation of variables to find all the different modes that can exist in microwave waveguides. Then I blocked the ends of a waveguide to form a cavity and I found the resonant modes in such a cavity."

Prof. Anderson flips through the report looking at all of the graphs and computer plots showing the analytical solutions.

"It looks as if you really did learn a lot," he says. "What are you taking next term?"

"I'm taking two physics courses. One is on relativistic electrodynamics and the other is another quantum mechanics course. I'm still trying to make sense of quantum theory."

"Good luck with that," Prof. Anderson says.

On Labor Day, Peggy is sitting on the beach in front of the lake house talking with Sam.

"How did your short course go?" Peggy asks.

"It went very well. I had a dozen faculty members from around the country and they all have great potential to produce good dynamic books."

"What topics?"

"All kinds. There were several mechanical engineering professors. One is doing a book on statics and dynamics, another on vibrations, another on thermodynamics, another on mechanics of materials, and another on fluid dynamics. There was a physics professor doing a book on classical mechanics and another one doing a book on optics. The woman on the panel from Michigan came and is doing a book on engineering probability and statistics.

Finally, there were four electrical engineering professors doing books on circuit theory using Laplace transforms, introductory electronics, control theory, and integrated circuits."

"If they all come through, we should have a good variety of books," Peggy says.

"Yes, and they all agreed that they learned a lot about how to put together a good dynamic textbook and want to get together again next year to compare notes and come up with best practice guidelines."

"So are you going to do it?"

"Yes, I'll have them back and also start a new class with new folks."

"It sounds just like your summer courses for high school students that Bill and I attended."

"Now that you mention it, there are a lot of similarities. Maybe I should run just a single class, so that the experienced book writers can help show the new ones how it is done."

"I think we may have a model for Pearlton University," Peggy says.

Sam also tells Peggy that the textbook publisher accepted their solution to settle the lawsuit. They need to update the app to ask for new problems that will be posted without solutions for a fixed length of time. This needs to be implemented within six months.

That night the sky is clear and the stars are brighter than ever. As promised, Dave takes everyone out in the boat for stargazing. He heads up the lake toward Center Harbor, circles around Five Mile Island, and then comes back to a spot just south of Ozone Island. He turns off the running lights and it looks as if you can just reach up and touch the stars.

"Uncle Dave," Matt says, "you said there are billions of galaxies. Can we see any galaxies other than our own Milky Way?"

"The closest galaxy to our own is the Andromeda galaxy, which is about two and a half million light-years away. It is the farthest object in the sky that you can see with your naked eye."

"Can you show us where it is?"

Dave swings the boat so it is pointing almost due east.

"It is right in front of us, about three quarters of the way from the horizon to directly overhead. First find Pegasus, the four stars forming a big square just over there to the right."

"I see it," Peggy says.

"Now find Cassiopeia, just over there to the left. It looks like a W on its side."

"I see that too." Peggy helps Matt find Pegasus and Cassiopeia.

"Now draw a straight line from the leftmost star in Pegasus to the fourth star down in Cassiopeia. The Andromeda galaxy is just below the midpoint of this line. It looks like a small white smudge."

"I think I see it," Peggy says.

Dave takes a pair of binoculars out of the glove compartment.

"Here, if you look through these binoculars, you should see it clearly."

Peggy takes the binoculars and looks in the direction of the Andromeda galaxy. "Wow! That is fantastic."

The binoculars are passed around until everyone has had a chance to peer into the past two and a half million years.

"How many stars are in the Andromeda galaxy?" Peggy asks.

"About a trillion," Dave replies.

"This is a typical spiral galaxy," Sam says, "where the velocities of the outer stars do not agree with Newton's law of gravity without inventing a lot of dark matter than no one can see."

Peggy is excited. "But my new theory of gravitation might very well explain it."

Wayne asks, "Do you still think that electromagnetic fields and waves are all that is really out there in the universe? What about your new gravitational fields?"

"I've been thinking a lot about that. These gravitational fields satisfy the same four Maxwell's equations as electromagnetic fields, so I think they must be the same kinds of fields. This means that at some basic level mass and charge must be the same thing. And since from Einstein's equation, we know that mass and energy are equivalent, then mass, charge, and energy must somehow be the same thing."

Sam says, "I would say you are on your way to some grand unification theory."

"Peggy's Theory of Everything," Bill says.

Peggy is feeling happy as she prepares for a new fall term at Dartmouth. Ever since Bill moved in with her at the beginning of the summer, things have improved; she is in love with Bill and Bill likes Ryan; she is excited about her classes and progress on the Pearls of Wisdom is moving in the right direction. Peggy senses that she is on the right road to discover her Theory of Everything.

27

Peggy walks into her first fall class in relativistic electrodynamics. During the summer quarter, she had visited Prof. Fitzgerald, who is teaching this class, to ask about its contents. When she learned that they would be discussing the relationship between special relativity and electromagnetism, Peggy showed him Uncle Sam's video clips for his course on the Pearls of Wisdom app, where Uncle Sam shows how to derive Maxwell's equations from Coulomb's law and special relativity. She asked if they would be going through this derivation. Prof. Fitzgerald had not seen those video clips before and said he did not normally use the notation of Cartesian tensors in this class, but said he would look at them and to come back in a week.

When Peggy returned a week later, Prof. Fitzgerald agreed that the derivation was interesting and not found in any textbook he was familiar with. He said he worried that students would not be familiar with the notation of Cartesian tensors. Peggy showed him all of the Pearl video clips that she had made, which went over everything about Cartesian tensors that students would need to know to follow the derivation. Prof. Fitzgerald agreed to begin the course by having the students go over these videos, and then they would discuss the material during class time.

So as Peggy takes her seat for this first class, she wonders how things will go. Prof. Fitzgerald asks how many students are familiar with the Pearls of Wisdom app and is surprised when everyone raises his or her hand.

"I guess I'm a little behind the time," Prof. Fitzgerald says.

He shows the students which video clips to go over if they are not familiar with Cartesian tensors. He says he will review special relativity during the next class and a good preparation would be to go over the very good video clips on special relativity, which are on the Pearls of Wisdom app. Peggy had not told him that she made those video clips during the summer after she graduated from high school.

Prof. Fitzgerald then shows the students Sam's video clips on the derivation of Maxwell's equations and tells them to go through those videos in detail and they will discuss them in class a week from today.

A week later, Prof. Fitzgerald asks if anyone has questions or comments about the derivation of Maxwell's equations from Coulomb's law and special relativity. One student says that it seems to her that the magnetic field was almost an optional definition related to the electric field in the frame of reference moving with a charge. There was a lively discussion on this point and on how the Lorentz force falls out of the derivation.

Peggy asks how Maxwell's equations can be valid for accelerated charges inasmuch as the derivation is based on special relativity, which assumes uniformly moving charges. They spend the rest of the class discussing this point and reach no satisfying conclusion.

"You've really stirred up a hornet's nest, Peggy", Prof. Fitzgerald says as Peggy is leaving the class.

He doesn't know what a hornet's nest is, Peggy thinks as she walks into her quantum mechanics course, taught by Prof. Taylor. If Maxwell's equations are suspect, she thinks that Schrödinger's wave equation in quantum mechanics is outright subversive. First of all, as far as she can tell, Schrödinger just pulled it out of the air. Prof. Taylor "derived" the equation by making up rules to convert classical mechanics equations to this wave equation. Now she realizes that scientists have been arguing for almost a century about what it means. She decides to visit Prof. Taylor during his office hours.

The next day Peggy knocks on Prof. Taylor's office door.

"Come on in, Peggy."

Peggy tells Prof. Taylor about her interest in a Theory of Everything and about the conversations she has had with Uncle Sam. She tells him about Uncle Sam's doubts about the big bang, the expanding universe, how their preconceived notions may blind scientists. She asks why physicists cannot explain dark matter and how Uncle Sam thinks that plasma theory might explain the universe better than general relativity.

"You really are a rebel, aren't you Peggy," Prof. Taylor says.

Prof. Taylor has no satisfying answers to many of her questions, but tells her that most faculty in the physics department believe that general relativity is correct, even though only a few actually work in that area. He tells her that her chance of discovering a Theory of Everything is highly unlikely. She would first have to get a Ph.D. in physics and then study under one of the top theoretical physicists in the country to gain an adequate background.

"But that approach hasn't worked for all of the people who have taken that route," Peggy says.

Prof. Taylor has to agree. "It is obviously not an easy problem."

Peggy tells Prof. Taylor about how, in one of her other classes, they derived Maxwell's equations from Coulomb's law and special relativity, and how this derivation raised more questions as to the validity of Maxwell's equations. She also tells him about her doubts as to the validity of the Schrödinger wave equation.

"Well it certainly isn't valid in the relativistic case," Prof. Taylor says. "For that you need to use Dirac's equation."

"Are we going to cover Dirac's equation in this class?" Peggy asks.

"Yes, we'll start covering it in about a week."

"That's good," Peggy says, "maybe that will satisfy me."

"I doubt it," Prof. Taylor says.

Peggy goes back to the apartment and reviews Uncle Sam's videos from his electromagnetics class. She realizes that after the derivation of Maxwell's equations, Uncle Sam shows how to reduce Maxwell's four equations to a single quaternion equation. She knows all about quaternions because she made Pearl video clips about them along with all of her vector analysis videos. She goes through the derivation of a single quaternion Maxell equation and realizes that it is very elegant. She wonders if Prof. Anderson knows about it. She will visit him during office hours tomorrow.

In his office, Peggy shows Prof. Anderson how Maxwell's four equations can be written as a single quaternion equation. She says that L. Silberstein did this in a book on the theory of relativity over 100 years ago, and that this book is available free online. Prof. Anderson admits that he does not use quaternions for anything and has not seen this derivation. They talk about how the single equation involves the Greek symbol *psi*, ψ, which contains both the electric and magnetic field vectors in terms of a complex quaternion. They talk about what it may mean. It is a cute shortcut trick to write the four equations as a single equation, but does it have any deeper meaning? They are not sure.

A week later, in her quantum mechanics course, Prof. Taylor starts talking about the Dirac equation. Instead of a single ψ, there are now four of them. Peggy notes that the ψ in quantum mechanics is a probability amplitude and does not have anything to do with the ψ in her quaternion version of Maxwell's equations. Or does it?

On October 23rd, Peggy's cell phone alerts her to a text message: "Olivia Pearl Woodbury arrived at 9:06 am. 6 lb., 12 oz."

It is Saturday morning, and Peggy and Bill are studying for their final exams. Peggy realizes that she does not understand the Dirac equation very well. All of these matrices and talk about spin are making her head spin.

"I don't understand my textbook's description of Dirac's equation," Peggy says. "I'm going to walk up to the physics library and see if I can find better discussions in other books."

"Ok," Bill says, "have fun."

Fifteen minutes later Peggy is moving slowly through the stacks of the library looking for quantum mechanics books. She finds one that has a good detailed solution and discussion of the Dirac wave equation and sets it aside to bring home. She keeps looking for other books, kneeling on the floor to check out the bottom shelf. Suddenly, her eyes focus on a small book about half an inch thick, tucked in between two larger books. Along the spine is the title of the book and its author: *A Unified Field Theory* by Miles V. Hayes. Peggy removes the book from the shelf, stands up, opens the book, and starts to read. Her heart almost stops – and then seems to be racing. *This cannot be true*! She takes the book, along with the quantum mechanics book, to the circulation desk and checks them both out. Peggy runs out of the building, sits on a bench, and immediately calls Bill.

"Bill, you are not going to believe what I just discovered!"

28

Peggy rushes into the apartment and shows the book to Bill. The first paragraph of the Preface, called a Summary, reads:

> The universe consists of a complex quaternionic field which is a function of space-time such that, in the sense defined by the algebra of complex quaternions, its rate of change is proportional to the square of its magnitude.

In the next paragraph is a single equation, which the author calls the field equation and which he asserts describes all of physical reality.

Peggy opens the book to page 1 where the author, who was an associate professor of engineering at Dartmouth when he wrote the book in 1964, explains how he came to write the book. He says he came up with the theory at the end of 1961 and then writes

> In the following year I developed the theory and submitted three papers to the Physical Review. They were rejected on the grounds that the theory is 'speculative'. Had all scientists refrained from speculation there would be no physics and no Physical Review. I have decided to publish the theory privately.

> The difficulty in gaining any acceptance or even consideration for the theory is not, I think, that it fails to explain physics but that it explains too much too simply. It seems incredible that a short simple equation $D\psi = \frac{1}{2} \psi^* \iota \psi$ should be adequate to explain all of physical reality. I don't blame physicists for being skeptical, since I have a great deal of trouble believing it myself.

> But I have even more trouble believing the theory is false when it explains so much. What other theory is proposed that better explains, or indeed explains at all, the existence of classical electromagnetism, classical mechanics, quantum mechanics, electric charge, matter and anti-matter, special relativity, the conservation laws, and promises to explain elementary particles? I am open to conversion, but until someone shows that the theory leads to

fallacious results, which no one has done, or someone produces a simpler and broader theory, which no one has done, I propose to accept on a tentative basis the unified field theory, and I recommend that others at least consider doing likewise.

The book is small – only 70 pages long. On the copyright page, it states, "Four hundred copies of this book have been printed in Bulmer type on Curtis Rag paper. This is copy no. 230." In the appendix is a distribution list, showing where all 400 copies went. He sent 33 copies to the leading physicists of the day, including de Broglie, Heisenberg, and Dirac. He sent 166 copies to the Chairs of the Departments of Physics of major universities around the world. He sent 89 copies to various libraries around the world, including four to different Dartmouth libraries, 15 copies to various publishing houses, 47 copies to a variety of other people, and he gave 39 copies to members of the Dartmouth faculty.

"Can you believe this?" Peggy exclaims. "I wonder if my physics professors know about this book. I'm going to have to show it to them on Monday."

Bill Googles the book and only comes up with Amazon, which has two used copies for sale, both from obscure bookshops.

"We should order both of these books," Bill says.

"Yes. Have one sent here and have the other one sent to Uncle Sam. We can talk with him about it at Thanksgiving."

"I'm ordering them right now."

"Look," Peggy says, "the left-hand-side of his field equation is identical to the left-hand-side of my single quaternion equation version of Maxwell's equations, which I showed to Prof. Fitzgerald this term. The variable ψ, is the same complex quaternion involving the electric and magnetic fields. The right-hand-side of his field equation is a quadratic factor of this variable, whereas in Maxwell's equations this is just a constant quaternion. I've got to let Uncle Sam know."

Peggy texts Uncle Sam: "Made huge discovery today. It will arrive in the mail from Amazon soon."

"That should perk his attention," Bill says.

"I can't wait to read the book," Peggy says. "I wish finals were over so I had the time."

On Monday, Peggy shows the book to Prof. Taylor and to Prof. Fitzgerald. Neither one has ever heard of the book.

29

Everyone is excited to see Olivia Pearl Woodbury when they arrive at Dave's for Thanksgiving dinner. Connie has the baby in the sunroom overlooking the ocean when Peggy and Bill arrive.

"Can I hold Olivia?" Peggy asks.

"Of course. I just finished feeding her, so you can burp her."

"You better show me how. I don't want to screw things up."

"You'll be fine."

After Olivia gets passed around, Connie puts her down for a nap, and Sam and Wayne join Peggy and Bill in the sunroom.

"This is quite a book you sent me," Sam says holding up his copy of *A Unified Field Theory*. "I'm just getting into it."

"I know," Peggy says. "I brought my copy too. I just finished finals so I have only had a chance to flip through it quickly. I can't wait to read the whole thing."

"On the jacket flap is a brief biography of the author," Sam says. "He got undergraduate degrees in mathematics from Yale and in electrical engineering from MIT. After the Second World War, he earned a master's degree in physics from Harvard and a Ph.D. from Harvard in applied physics and engineering science. He then worked in industry before joining the faculty at Dartmouth in 1960. So the guy doesn't seem like a quack."

"I Googled his name," Bill says, "and found from an MIT obituary that he died in 1995."

"I like the way he dedicated the book to the memory of Albert Einstein," Peggy says, "who he quotes in the dedication as writing the following:"

> 'There will be no place in the new physics,' Einstein wrote, 'for both fields and matter, that is, particles, because fields will be the only reality.'

"Do you think that's so, Uncle Sam?" Peggy asks.

"Well, he makes a good case for it. As I was flipping through the book, I found on page 52 that he talks about what led him to this approach. Let me read it to you."

I was first led to the field equation by the following line of thought. My point of departure was a scientific hypothesis or artistic feeling or religious faith that the universe is both unified and simple. Physics has reduced it to fields and elementary particles, but this is dualistic, not unified. Fields can exist, as empty space, without particles, but particles cannot exist without space, which is a field, in which to exist, so fields are more fundamental than particles. A unified theory of physics therefore should attempt to explain particles in terms of a field.

"That's a good point," Peggy says. "If you can explain everything with just fields instead of fields and particles, it must be simpler and more fundamental, just like Einstein thought."

"It makes sense to me," Wayne says.

"Me too," Bill says. "Remember Occam's Razor!"

Peggy says, "I can't believe that the variable ψ used in his field equation is the same complex quaternion involving the electric and magnetic fields that we use in the single-equation version of Maxwell's equations."

"That really got my attention," Sam says.

"You always told me that quaternions were probably going to be important in a Theory of Everything."

"He also said that he chose the electromagnetic field as a starting point because it was best understood, and that he dismissed the gravitational field as being a much smaller order of magnitude and therefore probably a second-order effect."

"Just like we have talked about," Peggy says.

"The other thing that got my attention," Sam says, "is that if you set the right-hand-side of his field equation to a constant, it reduces to Maxwell's equations. And if you set the right-hand-side of his field equation to a linear function of the variable, ψ, then it reduces to the Dirac equation of relativistic quantum mechanics."

"So all of classical electrodynamics and all of quantum mechanics would be approximations of his field equation," Wayne says.

"If you look on pages 2 through 4," Peggy says, "you see that he expands the field equation into eight coupled nonlinear partial differential equations. I'm going to have to go through that math in detail, but it looks like just a bunch of quaternion multiplications, which we are all familiar with now, thanks to our Pearl videos that I made."

"Once all this gets out," Bill says, "the hits on those videos should skyrocket."

"Ok, all you geeks," Eileen says, "Thanksgiving dinner is on."

Everyone moves into the dining room and finds a seat at the long dining room table.

"Well, Peggy may have discovered her Theory of Everything," Wayne says.

"Really?" Eileen asks, "How did you discover it?"

"It was sitting out in plain view on a Dartmouth library shelf," Peggy says, "where it has been sitting for over 50 years."

"How come no one else has found it before now?" Matt asks.

"Woodbury's Law," Bill says.

"So Matt, how do you like your first year at UNH?" Wayne asks.

"It's fun. I'm having a great time."

"Are you doing anything other than partying?" Peggy asks.

"Of course, I study a lot."

"What are you majoring in?" Dave asks.

"I started out as undecided, but I think I may become a music major. I play trumpet in the marching band and also play the guitar."

"Do you think you can make a living as a music major?" Dave asks.

"I don't know," Matt says. "I like to compose my own songs."

"You should write an app that helps you to compose songs using the PearlPen," Peggy says.

"I'm not good at programming."

"That's ok, we've got lots of good programmers. We just need lots of good ideas on how to use the PearlPen."

"You should think about it, Matt," Sam says. "There might be a lot of possibilities here."

"Ok, I'll think about it."

"Speaking of apps," Joe says, "what has become of that *Name that Face* app that we played on New Year's Eve?"

"It's doing really well," Bill says. "We have a free version that holds only 10 faces and has limited capability. About 20,000 people have downloaded that one. Then we have the full version for both smart phones and tablets, which we sell for $2.99, and interfaces with your contact list. We've sold about 6,000 of those so far by just word of mouth."

"That's pretty good," Sam says. "I think that app will really take off."

"I tried using the PearlPen to make a pen and ink drawing," Laura says. "I needed a finer tip and Wayne was able to put one on for me."

"How did it work out?" Peggy asks. "I'd like to see one."

"I brought a couple with me. I'll go get them."

Laura brings back two pen and ink drawings; one of the farmhouse and one showing a pair of loons near the shore.

"These are really nice," Peggy says.

"I like having them automatically in my tablet where I can print out any number of copies," Laura says.

"Once they are in the app," Bill says, "it is easy to add other effects such as printing them in sepia tone."

"That could make some of them striking," Laura says. "I would like to try it."

"I can show you how to do it," Bill says. "It is pretty easy."

"Uncle Sam," Peggy says, "there is a building at Dartmouth called Woodbury Hall. Do you know if it is named for one of your relatives?"

"It is named for Levi Woodbury, and actually he is my fourth cousin five times removed. Our common ancestor is Peter Woodbury, who was born in 1640 and the son of the immigrant John Woodbury."

"How come Woodbury Hall is named for him?"

"Levi graduated from Dartmouth and became quite famous. He was governor of New Hampshire and served in all three branches of the federal government. Your dad probably knows more about him than I do."

Joe responds, "He was the 9th governor of New Hampshire for a couple of years in the 1820s, and was then elected to the U.S. Senate from New Hampshire and served for six years until appointed by President Andrew Jackson to be Secretary of the Navy. He served as President Jackson's Secretary of the Treasury in the late 1830s. He was then re-elected U.S. Senator from New Hampshire and served until appointed an Associate Justice of the Supreme Court by President James Polk. He died in Portsmouth in 1851 at the age of 61 and is buried in the Harmony Grove Cemetery not far from the high school. Woodbury Avenue in Portsmouth is also named for him."

"I guess you're not the only accomplished Woodbury, Uncle Sam," Peggy teases.

"I met an interesting guy last week," Dave says. "His name is George Harrington, and he works for one of the large banks in New York. He's getting ready to retire in a couple of years, and I'm going to design a big oceanfront home for him on the cape. The interesting thing is that his specialty is mergers and acquisitions."

"Did you tell him that we want to sell our companies for a billion dollars each?" Wayne asks.

"As a matter of fact, I did tell him about both companies. He told me that he has worked closely with both Google and Apple in buying other companies. He is a nice guy and told me he would be happy to meet with you guys any time and fill you in on how these kinds of sales usually go down. He also said that when you get to the point where you are serious about selling, he can put you in touch with the right people to get you the best deal."

"That sounds terrific," Wayne says. "Maybe we can have him up to the farmhouse sometime between Christmas and New Year's to get acquainted."

"Not a bad idea," says Dave. "I'll ask him if he and his wife can join us for a New Year's Eve party at the farmhouse."

Peggy is excited, determined to read her new book cover to cover, determined to go through each derivation step-by-step in detail, determined to understand everything, determined to uncover her Theory of Everything.

30

It is two days after Christmas and Peggy, Bill, and Sam are sitting in front of the farmhouse living room fireplace after dinner.

"So did you two have fun skiing at Gunstock today?" Sam asks.

"We did," Peggy says, "the conditions were excellent."

"I see you brought your copy of the unified field theory book with you. Did you get a chance to read it all and go through the derivation to expand the field equation?"

"Yes, we both did," Peggy says. "I can't believe this book."

Sam says, "What I can't believe is that this book just seemed to drop off the radar screen 50 years ago. I can't find any reference to it on the web."

"Another example of Woodbury's Law," Bill says.

"So Peggy, what's your big take away from the book?" Sam asks.

"Well on page 52 where he is talking about how he came up with the field equation, he says that he postulated that particles are standing light waves. This really got my attention because I know all about standing electromagnetic waves in a microwave oven, so I just picture the inside of a microwave oven shrinking down to the size of an atom, and that's what he says particles really are."

"But it is the walls of the microwave oven, which reflect the microwaves to produce the standing waves," Sam says. "So how does he get standing light waves in free space with no walls to form stationary particles?"

"That's why he had to modify Maxwell's equations to make them nonlinear," Bill says.

"Exactly," Sam says. "Using the linear Maxwell's equations, if two wave packets approach each other from opposite directions, they will simply add up temporarily when they meet but then just pass through each other so no standing wave can occur."

"But according to the book," Peggy says, "if you square the sum of these two wave packets, it can lead to stationary standing waves, and this is what he says particles really are."

"That's correct," Sam says. "In his chapter on the natural system of units, he makes an interesting point about why the field equation must be nonlinear when he writes the following."

The field equation, being non-linear, accounts for the fact that physical phenomena, particles, and constants are of fixed and specific sizes, cannot be scaled up or down, and do not depend on the initial conditions of the differential equation. The experimental fact is that the world is that way, and no linear theory can explain it. For that reason, if for no other, it seems to me axiomatic that any fundamental equation of physics must be non-linear.

"The problem was," Peggy says, "that when he wrote the book 50 years ago, no one knew how to solve the eight coupled nonlinear partial differential equations, which the field equation expands into, and computers in those days were not powerful enough to solve them numerically."

"But today they are," Bill says. "In fact, the computer program I wrote last term in my numerical methods class to solve hyperbolic partial differential equations could easily be modified to solve this nonlinear field equation."

"We've got to do it," Peggy says. "No one else has ever done it before. What if we found solutions that corresponded to the electron, or hydrogen atom? We would be on the way to explaining everything!"

"You would be on your way to Stockholm to pick up your Nobel Prize," Sam says.

"So what problems do you think we will run into when trying to solve these equations numerically?" Peggy asks.

Sam says, "The author talks about how to do this on page 37 where he writes:"

I propose to try to solve the eight scalar equations which constitute the field equation by straightforward numerical methods. The differential equations would be replaced by finite difference equations on a finite mesh in four-dimensional space-time. For selected initial conditions and zero boundary conditions the equations would be iterated or allowed to propagate.

"He then talks about at least three difficulties," Sam says. "The first is that the number of mesh points varies as the fourth power of the number of points along each axis, so for 100 points along each axis, this would be 100 million mesh points or 800 million equations to solve per iteration. This was beyond the capabilities of computers 50 years ago, but not today, as Bill has already shown."

"The second problem he mentions," Bill says, "has to do with the kind of solutions we're looking for, namely standing waves that must be stationary in space if they are to constitute elementary particles. There can be no boundary conditions to constrain the standing wave as in a resonant cavity. He suggests that certain symmetry conditions might help here."

"Finally," Sam says, "the biggest problem may be knowing when you've found a solution and what it means. The nonlinear equation is supposed to be a Theory of Everything, so there will be innumerable solutions depending on the initial conditions. So it will be important to pick initial conditions that are close to the desired solution. This won't be easy, because we really don't know what the solutions will look like. The author suggests that by just plunging in and trying different initial conditions you may obtain and learn to recognize physically significant solutions."

"I would say we have our work cut out for us," Peggy says. "When I get back to school I'm going to meet with my professors and see if I can get any on them interested in this problem. I'm going to suggest that Bill and I do our senior project on this topic. If we start next term, we'll have over a year to get some results. Wouldn't it be a hoot if it works?"

"It is so contrary to conventional wisdom," Sam says, "don't expect your professors to jump on board. If this field equation turns out to be the Theory of Everything it will turn physics on its head. As you read in the book, it means no expanding universe, no big bang, no dark matter and no dark energy – all of these things that astrophysicists have staked their careers on. Many of them won't be happy. You might have better luck working with a younger faculty member who isn't so invested in the status quo. On the other hand, you might want to find someone who has recently gotten tenure, so they don't get blackballed by their more senior faculty members."

"I can't believe there would be that much politics among college professors," Peggy says.

"Oh, the stories I could tell you," Sam says.

George Harrington and his wife, Isabel, arrive at the farmhouse around noon on New Year's Eve. Dave and Eileen show them to their upstairs room.

"As soon as you get settled," Eileen says, "we'll drive down to the lake house and meet the rest of the family. It's a little too slippery to walk down through the snow."

"What a great view across the frozen lake," George says.

Dave introduces George and Isabel to everyone.

"Why don't you all just sit here in the living room," Eileen says, "and I'll bring in sandwiches and drinks for everyone."

"Perfect," Dave says. "We can all start picking George's brain about mergers and acquisitions in the banking business."

George regales everyone with stories of corporate buyouts and takeovers. He tells how a large computer company bought one small computer software company with only ten employees for over a billion dollars worth of cash and stock. He explains how potential buyers will value such small companies.

"For someone looking to buy your company," George says, "the question is how much profit will your company generate over the next few years, what will you add to growth and market penetration, and do you help protect their core business."

Peggy gives George a brief demonstration of the Pearls of Wisdom app and shows him the sales figures for the past two years. She tells him about their plans for starting Pearlton University and how this will generate ongoing dynamic books and course material for the Pearls of Wisdom app, with the goal of replacing traditional textbooks for not only most college courses, but for lifelong learning on a global scale.

"That's the kind of vision that is likely to get the attention of someone like Google," George says. "They're already in the knowledge dissemination business and have scanned lots of old books from various libraries. But making new textbooks available at very low cost to millions of people is a challenge that might intrigue them. The question is what value do you have that others couldn't easily duplicate?"

"You're right to focus on that," Sam says. "I've told Peggy from the beginning that it is all about quality content. Outstanding traditional textbooks are rare, but I think we have identified a mechanism to continually produce dynamic books for the Pearls of Wisdom app that are of the highest quality."

Sam goes on to tell George about the short course he taught for faculty who want to write dynamic books for the Pearls of Wisdom app, and how he is going to teach a follow-up course this summer. This would be a kind of test run for how Pearlton University would work. Sam explains the special authoring tools they have developed for creating all of the course material for the app.

"My advice," George says, "is to grow sales as much as possible in the next year or so, and add as many new dynamic books and course material as you can to the app. I would put together a complete business plan with projections and plans for the next two to four years. Say a year from now, I could make sure that such a plan got in the hands of the right people at Google. Their typical way of hiring people is not to wait for applications to come in, but to seek out exceptional people who may not even be looking for a new position. If they find exactly what they think they need, or could exploit, they will often go out and hire an entire team or even buy the entire company."

Sam says, "That gives me an idea for finding good candidates to come to Pearlton University for their sabbatical to work on writing a dynamic book. At most universities, faculty members are promoted based on their research, not on their teaching. Their research-devoted peers often look down on those who are good teachers and write textbooks. The thing to do is to find good teachers who have not yet written a textbook, but already have tenure and have taught for say ten years. Find the ones who love to teach and whose students rave about them on 'Rate My Professor'. They may have excellent notes they have developed over a number of years, which they could turn into an outstanding dynamic book for the Pearls of Wisdom app. The idea would be to check them out, and then approach them about becoming a pioneer in the future of higher education. Those who would respond to that vision are the type of people we are looking for, and would guarantee the success of the Pearls of Wisdom."

"That's great," George says. "Put it all in your planning document. If your sales are increasing exponentially next year at this time, I think it may be time to put out feelers."

"Ok," Eileen says, "it is time to go back up to the farmhouse for our fondue dinner and New Year's Eve party."

By the time the strains of Auld Lang Syne fill the farmhouse, Peggy's head is spinning, with talk of billion dollar deals, her Theory of Everything coming into focus, Bill becoming a permanent part of her life; it is almost too much to absorb; it is time for another glass of champagne.

31

It is two weeks into the winter term as Peggy and Bill walk into Wilder Hall for their weekly meeting with Prof. Fitzgerald. He has agreed to advise them in their Undergraduate Research course where they will try to solve the field equation in the book that Peggy discovered. On the bulletin board in the hall, is the announcement for next week's Physics Seminar. It says that the speaker will be Prof. Ogden Sallows from the physics department at Dartmouth, who will talk about his current research on the nature of black holes.

"We better go to that seminar," Peggy says. "If we find that our field equation is the Theory of Everything, then that will do away with Einstein's general theory of relativity along with Prof. Sallows' black holes."

"I doubt that will make him very happy," Bill says. "He must have been here working on them for at least thirty years."

"Let's ask Prof. Fitzgerald about him."

"Come on in, guys," Prof. Fitzgerald says as Peggy and Bill come through his office door.

Prof. Edward Fitzgerald, recently promoted to Associate Professor with tenure, earned his Ph.D. at Purdue and worked at NASA for three years before coming to Dartmouth six years ago. Peggy and Bill like him because he is easygoing, did a good job teaching the relativistic electrodynamics course last term, and seems to have an open mind about the shortcomings of physics. When they told him about their desire to try to solve the field equation in the book, *A Unified Field Theory*, and showed him the project that Peggy did the previous summer with Prof. Anderson, he agreed to be their advisor on this undergraduate research project. Peggy and Bill meet with him weekly, trying to convince him of the validity of the field equation and seeing if they can come up with any numerical solutions that make sense.

"So, Peggy, what other physics courses are you taking this term?" Prof. Fitzgerald asks.

"I'm taking another Quantum Mechanics course with Prof. Taylor. I took one from him last term and we got into Dirac's equation a little bit, but I need to study it in more detail. I've got to figure out where Dirac went wrong."

"Dirac wrong?" Prof. Fitzgerald asks.

"Yes," Peggy says, "look at page 14 of my little unified field theory book here, where the author, Hayes, writes the following:"

> In my opinion, it is impossible to represent a non-linear universe exactly by a linear equation since all the non-linear properties are necessarily lost, so Dirac's equation cannot be better than an approximation.

"He says that Dirac had two goals in coming up with his equation. The first was to obtain a relativistically invariant equation, which Schrödinger's is not, and the second was to obtain a linear differential equation to represent a non-linear relativistic Hamiltonian. This is why Dirac had to introduce those four 4×4 alpha matrices to get rid of all the cross-product terms so his equation would be linear. Hayes says this was Dirac's mistake, and that Dirac's linear equation is just an approximation of his non-linear field equation. Here's what he says on page 18:"

> It is the hopeless quest for linearity that leads to the obscure and complex representation instead of the clear and simple quaternionic representation.

"Don't you think that Hayes' nonlinear field equation makes more sense?" asks Peggy. "After all, it reduces to Dirac's equation if you make the right-hand side linear, and it reduces to Maxwell's equations if you make the right-hand side a constant."

"It is intriguing," Prof. Fitzgerald says. "I will give you that."

Peggy says, "Essentially, what he did to get the field equation was to take Maxwell's equations and replace the charge density with the electromagnetic energy density and the current density with the electromagnetic momentum. Look how he puts it on page 5:"

> The field equation $D\psi = \tfrac{1}{2}\psi^{*}\iota\psi$ states that the source of the field is the field itself. It states that the linear field $D\psi$ has its source in the quadratic field $\tfrac{1}{2}\psi^{*}\iota\psi$, which defines energy, charge, mass, and momentum, and is what we mean by matter. The field has its source in matter, and matter consists of the field.

> The field equation is expressed in the natural system of units obtained by selecting the size of two of the three fundamental units of measurements of length, time, and mass, so that the velocity of light $c = 1$ and the ratio of charge to mass of the electron $e/m = 1$. In such a system of units, energy, charge, and mass are identical. The size of the third fundamental unit is determined by the solution of the field equation.

"So you're going to try to find solutions to the field equation, right?" Prof. Fitzgerald asks.

"Yes," Bill says.

Peggy and Bill go on to explain how they will develop the difference equations from the eight coupled nonlinear partial differential equations obtained from the field equation. They describe all of the potential problems that Hayes mentions in the book.

"If I were you, I would begin by solving Maxwell's equations in free space with no boundary conditions, just initials conditions," Prof. Fitzgerald says. "See if you can solve for travelling wave packets in both positive and negative directions."

"That's a good idea," Peggy says, "because in the nonlinear case, two such wave packets from opposite directions are what should combine to form particles."

"We saw that Prof. Sallows is giving a seminar next week on black holes," Bill says.

"That's right," Prof. Fitzgerald says. "He has been doing research on black holes for years. He is one of the old-timers here."

"Is he a nice guy?" Peggy asks.

"Well, how should I put this? Let me just say, he has his own ideas about things and he doesn't suffer fools gladly."

"So are you saying if I told him there were no such things as black holes, he may not take it well?" Peggy asks.

"No black holes?" Prof. Fitzgerald seems surprised.

"Well, in this book Hayes offers a hypothesis that the universe is not expanding. He suggests that the redshift may not be due to the Doppler effect, but the nonlinear interactions of light waves. Look what he says about it on page 8:"

> The theory predicts that light waves interact with light waves, or photons with photons. The frequency, amplitude, phase, and other characteristics of light waves are modified by interaction with the other light waves through which they pass in coming from the stars. The greater the distance travelled the greater the modification.

"Later, on page 59," Peggy continues, "he concludes an interesting chapter, where he offers a hypothesis that a creation-annihilation reaction exists, with the following:"

> We have already postulated that the universe is not expanding but that the astronomical red shift is due to the non-linear interaction of electromagnetic waves in space. The fact that the shift is always to a lower frequency indicates that the energy has been lost from the observed wave to space. Where does the lost energy go? We

suggest into the creation reaction.

To summarize, we postulate that a creation-annihilation reaction exists which is not subject to the second law of thermodynamics, and that the reaction is the primary and continuing source of energy in the stars and of the rest mass in space.

The universe is non-expanding, conservative, self-renewing and eternal, without beginning and without end.

"If we can solve the field equation and show that such a reaction exists," Peggy continues, "it would be goodbye expanding universe, goodbye dark matter, goodbye dark energy, and goodbye black holes."

"And goodbye general relativity," Bill says.

"And Prof. Sallows just finished writing a book on general relativity and cosmology," Prof. Fitzgerald says. "It took him ten years to write it. He would not take such news well."

The following week, Peggy, Bill, and Prof. Fitzgerald sit together as Prof. Sallows begins his seminar on black holes. Prof. Sallows is short with Einstein-like, bushy white hair. He goes through a PowerPoint presentation, showing many pretty pictures of galaxies. He says that black holes are formed from supernova explosions and stellar collisions. He brings up some equations representing a particular solution of Einstein's general relativity equation, and points out where a particular term goes to zero, resulting in a singularity, which he claims corresponds to a black hole. Peggy decides that she must take his general relativity course, which is offered in the spring term.

Prof. Sallows goes on to describe some of the properties of black holes and shows the results of some of his recent research on rotating black holes. When he finishes his presentation, he asks for questions. Peggy raises her hand.

"It seems to me that the existence of black holes is inferred from the solution of Einstein's general theory of relativity field equation."

"That's correct," Prof. Sallows says.

"My question is," Peggy continues, "why do astrophysicists think that gravity is the only, or major, force driving the universe?"

"Are you a student here?"

"Yes, I'm a junior physics major."

"Then you should know that Newton's law of gravitation has been shown to accurately predict how the earth, and all planets, moves around the sun."

"I know, but you are talking about galaxies that are millions of light years away."

"Well gravity doesn't go away out there," Prof. Sallows says.

"But it doesn't accurately predict what you see," Peggy says, "without introducing mysterious dark matter and dark energy."

"Now are you the expert?" Prof. Sallows asks. "I've been doing these calculations for thirty years. If you want to learn more, you should take my general relativity course."

"I plan to."

As they leave the seminar, Peggy hears a voice behind her, "I think you really got under his skin."

She turns to see Ryan catching up with them.

"I didn't see you there," Peggy says.

"I try to come every week."

Peggy tells Ryan about discovering the book, *A Unified Field Theory*. She says that she will stop by his lab next week to fill him in on all the details.

The following week Peggy and Bill are in Ryan's lab showing him the book and explaining what the field equation means. She explains that particles are standing light waves. She shows him that if the right-hand side of the field equation is set to a constant, it reduces to Maxwell's equations with charged particles. She shows Ryan a paragraph on page 9 that reads,

> To summarize, the field equation accounts for the existence of Maxwell's equations as the constant approximation to the field equation. It accounts for the existence of the three apparently separate realms of physics, namely classical electromagnetism, classical mechanics, and atomic and nuclear physics. It accounts for the failure of Maxwell's equations in the atomic and nuclear domain where the constant approximation is invalid. The exact field equation eliminates the need for classical mechanics, and unifies the hitherto separate domains of classical electromagnetism and of atomic and nuclear physics.

Peggy explains to Ryan how the field equation accounts for the two possible signs of charge in terms of the handedness of the ψ-field. "Look at the following quotes from page 11."

> The field equation accounts for the existence of particles of matter and anti-matter as ψ-wave distributions having right- and left-handed asymmetry, and accounts for the fact that such particles appear to have opposite signs of charge.

> The handedness of the ψ-wave constituting a particle and the sign of charge of that particle are one and the same thing.

Peggy continues, "The field equation also explains neutral particles. Look at these quotes from page 12."

> Neutral particles might exist...because even though they are unsymmetrical the total amount of left-handed field energy equals the total amount of right-handed field energy, as in a proton-electron pair.

> It takes an unsymmetrical pair like electron and proton, or positron and anti-proton to be stable, I suspect because they cannot disintegrate without violating the conservation of angular momentum.

"This is a pretty interesting book," Ryan says. "And you tell me that it has been sitting on the library shelf right here at Dartmouth for over 50 years?"

"Exactly," Peggy says, "Can you believe it?"

Peggy goes on to explain how the field equation is consistent with the fundamental postulate of quantum mechanics, and how you can resolve Einstein's big complaint about quantum mechanics that God does not play dice.

"The ψ in quantum mechanics doesn't have to be a probability amplitude vector," Peggy says. "Look at what the author says on page 13."

> This forces one to identify the probability amplitude vector with the complex electromagnetic vector $\mathbf{H} + \mathbf{\mathcal{E}}$.

"Don't you see," Peggy says, "all those pretty spherical harmonic pictures of the probability distribution modes in a hydrogen atom are just the sums of the squares of the electric and magnetic field distributions, the electromagnetic energy density. I am beginning to think that it might be possible to make sense of quantum mechanics after all. Here's one more quote on the bottom of page 13."

> The field and the field equation depend only on the properties of a complete vacuum. They create matter out of the properties of a vacuum. They are not created by the properties of matter. This is the final dematerialization of physics:
> Existence depends only on the properties of a complete vacuum.

"Boy, this does require you to reevaluate what you think you know about physics," Ryan says. "Imagine, physics without particles! I'm glad I didn't go into particle physics!"

"Don't worry," Peggy says, "your plasmas still have electrons and positive ions, we just now know what they are. They are standing electromagnetic waves."

"We still have to prove that," Bill says, "by solving the field equation for the case of an electron."

"How can you do that?" Ryan asks.

"I have no idea," Bill says. "That's the problem. I have the set of eight coupled nonlinear partial differential equations and I have written a computer program to solve them, but I have no idea what to put in for initial conditions so that the nonlinear solution might converge to a stable set of limit cycles corresponding to the configuration of an electron. This is what we are supposed to be doing for our Undergraduate Research course."

"Wow," Ryan says, "that's some undergraduate research topic! How long do you think it will take you?"

"We have no idea," Peggy says. "We're going to keep working on it through the summer and through the fall term of our senior year. Then we'll see where we are. We'll have to write something up after that in order to graduate the following June."

"Well, keep me informed on how you are doing," Ryan says. "I'll be happy to help you in any way that I can."

"Does anyone have any questions?" Prof. Taylor asks at the beginning of the Quantum Mechanics class the following week.

Peggy raises her hand. "You say that photons are particles of light."

"That's right," Prof. Taylor says. "Light sometimes behaves like particles that we call photons."

"My question is, What is the size of a photon?"

Prof. Taylor responds, "Well, photons are normally described in terms of their energy or frequency. We don't really think of them as little billiard balls. Remember, photons also have zero rest mass."

Peggy is still not convinced. "If photons don't have any size or any mass, isn't it sort of stupid to call them particles?"

"Well, they certainly have both energy and momentum," Prof. Taylor says.

"So do all electromagnetic waves," Peggy says.

"That's true."

"So why do physicists think that light is both a wave and a particle?"

"One reason is Einstein's successful explanation of the photoelectric effect. Another is an explanation of the Compton effect where a photon interacts inelastically with an electron."

"But don't these just assume that light energy is proportional to frequency, not that it has to be quantized into little particles called photons?"

"Yes," Prof. Taylor says, "but Planck's explanation of blackbody radiation assumed that light energy could have only discrete values, some integer multiple of a tiny unit of energy proportional to the frequency of the light."

"But that's what might have gotten everything off on the wrong foot at the beginning," Peggy contends. "After all, Planck didn't really believe light behaved that way. He thought his equation was just a mathematical trick to agree with the experimental result."

"But how would you explain the blackbody radiation results?"

"Actually, I found a paper in the Physical Review from 1969 that explains blackbody radiation completely in classical terms using the theory of random electrodynamics."

"I read that paper," Prof. Taylor says. "Where do you think the random background radiation comes from?"

"Maybe it is a solution to the field equation in the book I showed you, which has been on the library shelf here at Dartmouth for over 50 years."

"That would be something if it was."

Peggy says, "I'm beginning to think that Planck took the wrong path way back in 1900, and that all the quantum mechanics that has followed for over a century is a bunch of nonsense."

"Well, Peggy, if you want to pass this class, you're going to have to learn some of that nonsense."

After class, Peggy meets Bill in the Collis Café in the Student Center for a hot chocolate.

"I just told Prof. Taylor in class that I think quantum mechanics is a bunch of nonsense."

"He must have loved that," Bill says.

"He told me that I have to learn it anyways. I don't mind that, but I'm determined to prove him wrong."

"I'm making some progress solving Maxwell's equations for plane wave packets, but finding good initial conditions for the nonlinear field equation is proving to be very difficult."

"The book talks about possible experiments using lasers, which could verify the field equation. Maybe we should talk to Ryan about it."

"Sounds like a good idea," Bill says.

That night Peggy dreams of experiments, climactic experiments that verify her Theory of Everything.

32

Right after the winter term finals, Peggy and Bill go to Ryan's lab to talk with him about possible experiments, which might verify the field equation. Surrounded by lasers and oscilloscopes, they join Ryan around a small, square table. Peggy shows Ryan the following quote from page 36 of the book, *A Unified Field Theory.*

> An intense modulated radio or light beam should produce transformer action by the revised Ampere's Law. An intense, coherent light beam, split and mirrored to pass through a region in opposite directions, should produce a zero $\mathbf{E} \times \mathbf{H}$ but a non-zero $1/2\left(H^2 + E^2\right)$ and so according to the revised Gauss' Law should produce an electrostatic field.

Peggy asks Ryan, "Do you think there is any way we could devise experiments, using these ideas, to verify the field equation?"

"Well, let's take the second sentence first," Ryan says. "The idea would be to produce a standing wave of the laser light in as small a region as possible. A concentric spherical optical resonator configuration might work."

Ryan goes to the white board on the wall, draws two spherical mirrors facing each other, and draws a dot along the centerline halfway between the mirrors.

"This is the focal point of each mirror," Ryan says. "If two collimated laser beams are incident on the mirrors, they will both be focused to the same focal point at the center and produce a standing wave."

"How can we get the two plane waves to be incident on the mirrors?" Bill asks.

Peggy has an idea. "Why don't we put a double-sided flat mirror at 45 degrees with a small hole at the focal point, like this?"

Peggy adds this mirror to the drawing on the white board, and then draws collimated light waves coming in from the top and bottom to the mirror.

"See, the light coming from the top will be reflected from the mirror to the left spherical mirror and the light from the bottom will be reflected to the right spherical mirror."

"That just might work," Ryan says. "We could produce the two collimated beams by passing the laser beam through a microscope objective, pinhole, collimating lens, beam splitter, and extra mirrors."

"How would we measure any resulting electrostatic field?" Peggy asks.

"That will probably be tough," Ryan says. "In principle, we could put some type of conducting surface near the focal point spot of light, where any electric field should be strong, and measure that voltage to ground. It is probably best to use a high-powered pulsed laser to get the maximum energy over a short pulse, and then amplify any voltage pulses at the laser repetition rate."

"Of course," Peggy says, "we don't know if we will generate right- or left-handed standing wave configurations corresponding to positive or negative charges, or if we'll get some combination corresponding to neutral particles, in which case we'll see nothing."

"That's right," Ryan says. "We better do some calculations to see what kind of numbers we are talking about. In the meantime, let's take a look at that first sentence in the quote from the book."

Bill asks, "What does the book mean by 'transformer action by the revised Ampere's Law'?"

Peggy says, "Well, the field equation essentially replaces the current density in Maxwell's equations by the electromagnetic momentum, or Poynting's vector. So if current produces a magnetic field, then the field equation says that an intense light beam should also produce a magnetic field."

"This is not predicted by current physics theories," Ryan says. "So if you can measure such a predicted new result, it will add a lot of credence to your field equation theory."

"The book talks about modulating a light beam to produce transformer action," Peggy says. "How could this be done?"

"I have an infrared pulsed laser," Ryan says, "that produces over a joule of energy in a 10 nanosecond pulse. It can produce about 10 of these pulses per second. We need to figure out how we can replace the current in the primary windings of a transformer with this pulsed laser beam and then measure an alternating voltage in the secondary windings."

"Could we use fiber optics for the primary windings around an iron toroid?" Bill asks.

"It would be easier if we could keep the laser beam going in a straight line," Ryan says.

"I've got an idea," Peggy says. "Could we make a regular transformer by running a wire down the bore of a small diameter iron pipe? If we run alternating current through the wire, it will produce a circular alternating magnetic field around the circumference of the pipe. If we now wrap insulated wire through the pipe and around the outside, we should measure an AC voltage across this wrapped secondary winding."

"I think I see what's coming," Ryan says. "Replace the wire down the bore with the pulsed laser beam."

"Exactly," Peggy says. "And if we measure an output voltage, that's game, set, match!"

Bill has another idea. "If we put a mirror outside the end of the iron pipe so the pulse gets reflected back through the pipe, then the magnetic field will change direction and we'll get a real positive and negative output voltage."

"I think you guys have two good experiments to design," Ryan says. "We need to do some more calculations. Let's get together again after the spring term gets underway and see where we stand."

"I'm psyched!" Peggy says.

33

Today is Peggy's 21st birthday and the spring term begins in two days. Sam and Laura have come to Hanover with Peggy's parents, Joe and Kate, to celebrate the milestone by having lunch with Peggy and Bill at the Hanover Inn across from the Dartmouth Green. The waiter pours a glass of champagne for everyone from a bottle that Sam ordered.

Sam offers a toast. "Happy Birthday, Peggy. May the coming year be as eventful as the last, with lots of progress on many fronts."

All concur as they take a sip.

"My first legal drink," Peggy says.

"So, how's your Pearls of Wisdom app doing?" Joe asks.

"It is doing great," Peggy says. "Subscriptions have really picked up lately. I think we are over 400,000 now and should probably have half a million by the end of this spring term."

Joe is impressed. "I admit that I was wrong about your ability to get your company up and running. I should have known you would succeed. After all, any time you really wanted something, you would be bullheaded about it, never giving up until you got what you wanted. I should not have doubted you."

"Thanks, Dad. I am glad to be able to pay you back all the money you had to spend on my education. This summer I will have everything paid back with interest."

"Did that lawsuit get settled ok?" Kate asks.

"Yes," Peggy says. "In fact, we ended up getting a big boost from it. The latest edition of the physics textbook now mentions our app in the preface to the book, so this has resulted in many more subscriptions."

Bill says, "Not only that, but our new feature of having people submit their own new homework problems has proven to be very successful and popular. Professors love it because they can assign different homework problems each term without having the answers posted until after the due date. There are always fresh homework problems on the app."

"I've noticed that many of these homework problems are very good and innovative," Sam says.

"Yes," Peggy says, "I think people try to compete with each other for the best homework problems."

"Peggy is really shaking up the faculty in the physics department," Bill says.

"In what way?" Sam asks.

Peggy tells Sam about her confrontations with Prof. Sallows and Prof. Taylor.

"I am determined to show them that quantum mechanics and general relativity are screwed up and that my field equation better explains things."

"Any progress on finding solutions to it?" Sam asks.

"Not really," Bill says. "It is really tough picking initial conditions and knowing what scale we are talking about."

"Let's think about units for a minute," Sam says. "The field equation assumes that the value of the speed of light is unity, or one, which really defines a new time unit. The author also states that the ratio of charge to mass of an electron is probably also unity, which could define a scale of mass."

"But he also assumes that mass, charge, and energy are all the same thing," Peggy says. "So isn't it redundant to say that the ratio of charge to mass of an electron is one?"

"He suspects that Planck's constant might be one in the field equation," Sam says, "but you would need a third constant to be equal to one in order to fix the units of length, time, and mass."

"I was thinking about that," Peggy says. "Remember my new gravitational theory came about by recognizing that Newton's law of gravitation looks just like Coulomb's law for charges, where the mass replaces the charges and the constant of proportionality is the gravitational constant, G. Maybe G equals one in the field equation."

"That's an interesting observation," Sam says. "Setting G equal to one makes Newton's law of gravitation have exactly the same form as Coulomb's law that we combined with special relativity to derive Maxwell's equations. This means that a generalized law of gravitation, consistent with special relativity, should look just like Maxwell's equations with the charge density replaced with mass density."

"That's just my new theory of gravitation, which means that we wouldn't need to buy into Einstein's warped space theories," Peggy says.

"It would also show how gravitation is naturally included in your field equation," Sam says, "which makes it more likely to be a Theory of Everything."

"But just like Maxwell's equations are an approximation of the nonlinear field equation," Peggy says, "these new gravitational field equations would still be just an approximation. The nonlinear field equation would still describe everything."

"So we may be able to fix all units in the field equation by setting the speed of light, the gravitational constant, and Planck's constant all equal to one," Sam says. "Setting Planck's constant to one makes sense when you realize that the field equation itself basically sets the energy density equal to the rate of change of the field vectors and Planck's constant is the ratio of energy to frequency. It will be easy to calculate the basic units of time, length, and mass based on setting these three constants to one."

"Let's do it," Peggy says.

Peggy and Bill tell Sam about how Ryan helped them design two experiments that might be able to verify the field equation.

"Let's see if Ryan is in his lab," Peggy says. "We can show you our proposed experiments and calculate the sizes of the basic units."

"Sounds good," Sam says. "I'd like to see Ryan again."

"Kate," Laura says, "I think that I will explore some of the shops here in Hanover while they are visiting Ryan's lab. Would you like to join me?"

"That sounds like much more fun to me."

Peggy smiles. "Mom, you don't know what you will be missing."

Joe has his own idea. "I'm going to take advantage of being here and visit the Baker-Berry Library while you techies are in the lab."

"Ok," Sam says. "I'll text you when we are done and we'll meet back here at the Inn."

Looking out of the window of the Hanover Inn, Peggy watches students cross the Dartmouth Green, realizing how much she loves it here, how much it has changed her life, how happy she is that Bill transferred here, how lucky she was to stumble on the *Unified Field Theory* book in the library, how nice it is to be twenty-one.

34

Sam holds out his hand. "Ryan, it is good to see you again."

"Glad you could visit my lab. Your niece is beginning to shake up the place around here."

"I'm not so sure about that," Peggy says.

"I would be disappointed if she didn't make some waves," Sam says. "Peggy says that you have all come up with a couple of plausible experiments that might help verify the field equation."

"That's true."

Ryan goes to the whiteboard and sketches the diagram showing the two spherical mirrors. He explains how a high intensity laser standing wave might be generated at the central focal point.

Sam studies the diagram. "Depending on the size of the spherical mirrors and the distance between them, the diffraction limited size of the central spot could be as small as a few wavelengths. Let's do a quick calculation of the energy densities we are talking about for your infrared pulsed laser."

After doing the calculations on the whiteboard, Sam notes that the energy density associated with an electron is about 13 orders of magnitude greater than the energy density of their laser standing wave.

"I would say your chance of creating a single charge equal to that of an electron is pretty much nil. Perhaps a standing wave made up of gamma rays would be closer to the mark."

Ryan nods in agreement. "In particle physics a gamma ray near a nucleus can produce an electron-positron pair. They think it needs to be near a nucleus to conserve momentum, but your field equation conserves both energy and momentum, so two gamma rays blasting into each other with enough energy might very well create an electron-positron pair, contrary to conventional physics."

"I've already concluded that conventional physics is all wrong," Peggy says with a smile.

"Any chance of producing a high-energy gamma ray standing wave in the lab?" Bill asks.

"It would be very difficult," Ryan says.

"But it may be happening all the time in outer space," Sam says.

"Our new laboratory – outer space," Bill says.

Peggy perks up. "That reminds me, Ryan, remember I told you about my new theory of gravity. Well, I'm pretty sure that the explanation of gravity in the unified field theory book is correct."

Peggy reminds Ryan about how the similarity of Newton's law of gravitation and Coulomb's law means that Maxwell's equations must apply to gravity where mass replaces charge. She shows Ryan that in a system of units where the gravitational constant is set to one, the exact same derivation of Maxwell's equations from Coulomb's law and special relativity that they have on their Pearls of Wisdom app can be carried out with Newton's law of gravitation without any changes.

"This means that gravity really has two fields," Peggy says, "corresponding to the electric and magnetic fields, and the magnetic field only exerts a force on moving objects."

"You know," Ryan says, "you are absolutely right. I wonder why no one has thought of that before."

"Actually, Heaviside thought about it in 1893, but only as an analogy to Maxwell's equations. Einstein didn't invent special relativity until twelve years later, so Heaviside didn't know that you could derive Maxwell's equations from Coulomb's law and special relativity like Uncle Sam does in his book."

Sam interrupts. "And once Einstein explained gravity in terms of his general theory of relativity, it took nearly 100 years for others to pick up on Heaviside's analogy of gravitational and electromagnetic fields – something they call gravito-electromagnetism."

"You should see if the gravitational version of Maxwell's equations predicts the precession of the perihelion of Mercury," Ryan says. "It was this prediction from general relativity that helped make Einstein a household name."

"I did a quick calculation," Sam says, "and it doesn't look as if the extra forces from the moving sun and planets will give the exact answer for Mercury's precession. Remember, however, that Maxwell's equations are only an approximation of Peggy's field equation, so we should probably look at the full nonlinear field equation."

Peggy had posted a sign on the wall showing the four equations obtained by expanding the nonlinear field equation.

Sam continues. "Look at the equation for the divergence of the electric field. Normally that is equal to the charge density, or in the case of gravity, mass density. However, in the nonlinear field equation, it is equal to the electromagnetic energy density. That is, the source of the field is the field itself."

"Does this mean that the mass density of the sun continues all the way to the planets?" Peggy asks.

"Exactly," Sam says. "But remember that mass and energy are equivalent by Einstein's famous formula, so mass is really just a convenient fiction. The universe if filled with only electric and magnetic fields, forming waves that interact in a nonlinear way to produce standing wave packets we call particles, ending up as stars and planets."

"The fact that the gravitational field of the sun, and therefore its mass density, extends to the planet Mercury could easily explain Mercury's precession," Ryan says.

"Instead of mass causing the curvature of space-time as Einstein suggests," Sam says, "it is much simpler to think of mass as being high-intensity standing wave electromagnetic fields, influencing all of space through waves travelling at the speed of light."

"And interacting with waves from other bodies in a nonlinear way to produce new standing wave particles," Peggy says.

"You certainly wouldn't have to invent dark matter," Ryan says, "to explain why the speeds of the outer stars in a galaxy are as high as they are. The mass density of the galaxy core isn't just concentrated there, but extends in a weaker form throughout all of space."

"You know," Sam says, "I think Peggy may have just put the first nail in the coffin of Einstein's general theory of relativity."

"Peggy – a household name," Ryan says.

"No one will ever believe it, though," Bill says.

"You've got to get your computer solutions to the field equation working," Peggy says.

"I'm trying, but I don't know what to look for."

"I'm putting another sign on the wall," Peggy says. "It will read, *It's the nonlinearity, stupid.*"

"Ok," Sam says, "let's see if we can identify the sizes of the three basic natural units of time, length, and mass in the field equation."

"Maybe energy should be a basic unit rather than mass," Peggy says.

"Either would work," Sam says, "since from relativity we know that energy is just mass times the speed of light squared."

"Ok," Peggy says, "at lunch Uncle Sam said that if we set the speed of light, the gravitational constant, and Planck's constant all equal to one, then we can calculate the three basic unit values of time, length, and mass."

"Looking at the field equation for a plane wave," Sam says, "it looks as if energy will be proportional to frequency if we choose Planck's constant divided by 2π to be one. So let's try that."

Sam goes to the whiteboard and writes the three constants – speed of light, gravitational constant, and the reduced Planck's constant – in terms of the three basic units of time, length, and mass. He then solves these three equations for the three basic units of time, length, and mass in terms of the three constants with known values.

"So, let's see what we have for the values of the natural system of units in the field equation," Sam says. "The basic unit of length is about 1.6×10^{-33} centimeters, which is called the Planck length. The basic unit of time is about 5.4×10^{-44} seconds, which is called the Planck time and is the time it takes light to travel a distance equal to the Planck length. Finally, the basic unit of mass, called the Planck mass, is about 2.2×10^{-5} grams, which corresponds to an energy of about 2×10^{16} ergs, or about a ton of TNT.

"That energy is huge," Ryan says. "The first atomic bomb had an energy of about 15 thousand tons of TNT and the biggest hydrogen bombs have energies around 50 million tons of TNT."

"So, let me see if I get this," Bill says. "To get to the size of a hydrogen atom, I would have to scale up the natural unit of length by about 25 orders of magnitude."

"That's right," Sam says, "and you would scale the mass or energy density down to values corresponding to the hydrogen atom. By the time you get to sizes bigger than molecules," Sam says, "the values of the electric and magnetic fields will have diminished to the point where the nonlinear terms are no longer significant, and we're back to Maxwell's equations and ordinary radio waves."

"And Peggy's new theory of gravitation based on Maxwell's equations might come into play," Ryan says.

"I'm taking the general relativity course with Prof. Sallows this term," Peggy says. "It starts in a couple of days, so I should be able to compare my new theory of gravitation with general relativity soon."

Sam has some advice for Peggy. "I recommend you get a head start on that course by studying the chapter on general tensor analysis in my *Vectors and Tensors* book. You are going to have to come to grips with the metric tensor, Christoffel symbols, and covariant differentiation. It is all there, including the curvature tensor."

"I'm going to get started on it right away," Peggy says, "and I'll make video clips of the material for our Pearls of Wisdom app."

"So what was the second experiment you guys came up with?" Sam asks.

Ryan goes to the whiteboard and draws a diagram that shows an iron pipe with wire going down through the core and then wrapped around the outside.

"If we send a pulsed laser down the center of the pipe and reflect it back through the core, a changing magnetic field around the circumference of the pipe should induce a voltage across the wrapped wire."

Sam studies the diagram.

"How fast can you pulse the laser, and with what power?"

"We have a 5 watt pulsed laser," Ryan says, "which can generate pulses as short as 3 nanoseconds with a repetition rate of a megahertz."

Sam does a quick calculation. "If we make the pipe about a meter long and put the reflecting mirror a half meter beyond the end of the pipe, then the reflecting pulse won't interfere with forward propagating pulses, and any generated magnetic fields in the pipe will change direction at a megahertz rate."

Ryan says, "And the induced voltage across the windings will be a megahertz signal that we can filter and amplify to detect a very weak signal."

"We need to do some more calculations," Sam says, "to see if this laser power has any chance of producing a detectable signal."

"More work to do," Peggy says.

"We've made a lot of progress today," Sam says, "but I need to head back to Durham. I've got a class to teach tomorrow."

"And I've got to get ready for my general relativity class coming up in a couple of days," Peggy says.

Sam reminds Peggy, "You've really got to go through that derivation of Maxwell's equations using Newton's law of gravitation and special relativity. It will certainly predict gravitational waves, which I'm sure you will cover in your general relativity course. You could really shake things up with an alternative derivation."

"I can't believe all the stuff I have to do in the next few days," Peggy says.

Sam sends a text to Joe, Laura, and Kate telling them he will meet them at the Inn in fifteen minutes. As Uncle Sam leaves the lab, Peggy begins to get excited. *I am going to shake things up. Gravity is beginning to make a lot more sense. So is quantum mechanics. My theory of everything is coming into focus.*

35

It is four weeks later, and Peggy is sitting in her general relativity class with Prof. Sallows, who is reviewing the material on covariant differentiation and the curvature tensor, which he covered last time. So far, the course has all been about tensor analysis, and Peggy is happy that she had Uncle Sam's book on *Vectors and Tensors* to fall back on, because it was so much easier to understand than the class textbook or Prof. Sallows' lectures. Peggy has already posted video clips on the Pearls of Wisdom app from the material in Uncle Sam's book covering contravariant and covariant components of a vector, the metric tensor, covariant differentiation including Christoffel symbols, and the curvature tensor. She is thinking to herself, *so far, so good in this class. I wonder what's coming next.*

Prof. Sallows begins his discussion of general relativity by explaining how Einstein introduced his principle of equivalence. This principle assumes the complete physical equivalence of a gravitational field and a corresponding acceleration of the reference system. Prof. Sallows says that in this class we will develop Einstein's field equation, which includes the Ricci curvature tensor and the stress-energy tensor, and look at simple approximate solutions. The upshot is that mass causes space to curve, and then bodies in free-fall follow the shortest path, or geodesics, in this curved space.

Peggy thinks she sees where Einstein might have taken the wrong road over 100 years ago. It sounds as if he took his own principle of equivalence too literally. Another student, Michael, asks Prof. Sallows if space really is curved, or is this just a cute mathematical trick to calculate some answers to gravitational problems. Prof. Sallows assures the class that space really does become curved in the presence of massive bodies. It is all in Einstein's field equation.

Knowing Prof. Sallows' reputation, Peggy hesitates to ask a question. She does not want to start a big controversy. Nevertheless, she can't help herself and raises her hand.

"Do you have a question, Peggy?"

"Yes, if space is really curved, how come the equations of electromagnetism and quantum mechanics don't assume that?"

"They operate in different regions of space-time, which is essentially flat,"

Prof. Sallows says. "On larger scales we know that the gravity of the sun will bend light coming from a distant star, as predicted by Einstein's general relativity equation."

"But couldn't other theories of gravity that assumed flat space-time predict the same thing?" Peggy asks.

"No," Prof. Sallows says, "there have been a lot of quack theories over the years, but none of them agree with experiment like Einstein's general relativity field equation."

Peggy thinks she should probably give up, but decides to give it one more try.

"Newton's law of gravitation and Coulomb's law are exactly the same form. Do you think this is just a coincidence, or would you expect that gravity could be explained with equations similar to Maxwell's equations?"

"The gravitational force and the electrostatic force are two different forces, and Maxwell's equations do not describe gravity, Einstein's field equation does."

Peggy realizes that Prof. Sallows has no idea that a set of equations identical to Maxwell's equations can be derived from Newton's law of gravitation and special relativity. She just did it last night. Uncle Sam was right, he has drunk the Kool-Aid, and there will be no convincing him.

As Peggy leaves class, Michael, the student who asked Prof. Sallows about curved space-time, runs to catch up with Peggy. Michael is puffing due to his overweight.

"I see you have doubts about general relativity too."

"Yes," Peggy says, "I think it is a crock."

"I just don't get all these Christoffel symbols and the curvature tensor stuff," Michael says. "The math is really complicated."

"Do you have the Pearls of Wisdom app? I've posted some video clips on tensor analysis from my Uncle Sam's book that makes it a lot clearer."

"Are you the Peggy who wrote the app?"

"Yes, my boyfriend, Bill, and I did. In fact, I am on my way to have a snack with him in the Collis Café now. Our friend, Ryan, will also be there. Want to join us?"

"Sure, sounds like fun."

"Michael, this is Bill and Ryan," Peggy says as they sit at the rectangular table in front of the fireplace in the Collis Café. "Michael is in my general relativity class."

"And suffering," Michael says.

"Are you a physics major?" Ryan asks.

"I'm a junior and was planning to major in astrophysics, but the more I get into it the more I think I'll switch to engineering physics so I can do something useful."

"I'm a graduate student doing research in plasma physics," Ryan says, "and I'm not sure how useful that is going to be."

"Well, I'm doing something useful," Bill says. "I'm majoring in computer science."

They order some food and drinks and bring them back to the table. Peggy tells Michael about how she and Bill came to write the Pearls of Wisdom app. She also tells him how she discovered the *Unified Field Theory* book in the physics library right here at Dartmouth and how the field equation in the book puts a big question mark on general relativity and conventional quantum mechanics. She tells Michael that after Einstein got special relativity right he made two big mistakes. One was inventing the photon to explain the photoelectric effect, and the other was the principle of equivalence, which led to his general relativity field equation in terms of all these nasty tensors.

"I'm convinced that physicists have been going down these two wrong roads for the past 100 years," Peggy says.

"Wow," Michael says, "that is unbelievable!"

"I know, but nobody will ever believe me."

"I've got a great idea."

"What's that?"

"I'm the president of the student debating club here at Dartmouth. I should set up a public debate between you and Prof. Sallows on how his precious general relativity is all screwed up."

"I could never debate him on general relativity."

"But you wouldn't debate him on general relativity per se," Ryan says, "but on how Einstein went down the wrong two roads and how you discovered the unified field theory book."

"I can see it now," Bill says. "The great Dartmouth debate: Einstein was Wrong and Peggy Discovered a Theory of Everything. Peggy Leach in the affirmative, squaring off against Prof. Ogden Sallows."

"Now just wait a minute," Peggy says. "Let's not get carried away."

"Actually, it is a great idea," Ryan says. "It would be a good way to get people to pay attention to your Theory of Everything."

"Well, Prof. Sallows would never go for it anyways," Peggy says.

"I'm not so sure," Michael says. "I had him for another course and he really is bullheaded. I think he might just jump at the chance to smack you down."

"So now you're leading me to the slaughterhouse," Peggy says.

"If I can ever get my computer solutions to the field equation working," Bill says, "then maybe you'll have some surprises in store for him."

"Now that would be worth buying a ticket for," Ryan says.

"You guys are all dreaming," Peggy says.

"Look," Michael says, "it is too late to schedule a debate this term anyways, so it would have to be in the fall. Let's see how our general relativity class goes and at the end of the term, I will approach Prof. Sallows and tell him that the debating club would like to sponsor a debate between you and him in the fall on how Einstein was wrong. I bet he would jump at it, just to show you up."

"Well, let me think about it," Peggy says. "We have got until the end of the term."

36

Peggy and Bill sit on the beach at the lake house and watch Connie swing 8-month old Olivia back and forth in the water while grabbing the baby's waist. At times Connie dunks Olivia's head completely under the water.

"Connie is going to have Olivia swimming before she is a year old," Peggy says.

Peggy and Bill arrived yesterday for the long 4th of July weekend. It has been almost a month since Peggy took her final exam in the general relativity class. She smiles as she remembers the last four weeks of the course, with almost the entire class engaged in heated discussions about black holes, an expanding universe, dark matter, and dark energy. Prof. Sallows had his hands full beating back objections from one student after another. Michael was one of the most vocal critics in these discussions. After finals were over, Michael went to see Prof. Sallows and brought up the idea of a debate between Peggy and him on the issue of Einstein being wrong. Michael told him that the debating club would sponsor such a debate in the fall and that it would be in the highest tradition of Dartmouth's proclaimed ideal of open debate on crucial issues. Prof. Sallows was initially reluctant to entertain the idea, but Michael apparently laid it on thick, implying that Prof. Sallows had a moral obligation to maintain and promote academic freedom, because Prof. Sallows eventually agreed to participate. Michael has already booked the Moore Theater in the "Hop" – the Hopkins Center for the Arts – for the event to take place during the first week in October. He has also started a campus-wide publicity campaign with posters and signs all over the place and a notice already appearing in the student newspaper.

Sam pulls up a chair next to Peggy on the beach. "So tell me more about this debate."

"I'm not sure what I got myself into," Peggy says.

Bill hands Sam a piece of paper. "Here's the announcement that was in the student newspaper."

Sam starts to read.

Coming in the Fall –
The Great Dartmouth Debate
Resolved:
Einstein was Wrong and Peggy Discovered a
Theory of Everything.
For the affirmative:
Peggy Leach, Dartmouth senior majoring in physics.
For the negative:
Prof. Ogden Sallows, Professor of Physics, Dartmouth
College.

"This is going to be fun," Sam says. "I'll definitely be there."

"I think your idea of fun is sick," Peggy says. "I am just going to make a fool of myself."

"No you won't," Sam says. "What is the worst thing that can happen? First of all, you did discover a Theory of Everything – right on the library shelf at Dartmouth. The fact that Prof. Sallows did not even know it was there is one strike against him. He is the one who should be on the defense. After all, most physicists agree that dark energy is their biggest embarrassment. They don't have a clue what it is. At least you can claim that it's not necessary."

"I know; but I can't help feeling that I am taking a big risk."

Sam looks directly at Peggy. "Remember, taking risks is what leads to big payoffs. It is important to become comfortable taking risks. Not reckless risks, but thoughtful risks that you can manage. You can manage this one. You have the facts. You have done your homework. If you get some positive results from the experiment you are doing this summer, or from Bill's computer solutions of the field equation, then you will even have an edge over Prof. Sallows. In any event, no one is going to expect a college senior to beat a senior professor in a debate about the foundations of physics, so you really have nothing to lose."

"I guess you're right," Peggy says. "At least it will be a challenge."

The sky is clear and full of stars on the night of the 4th as Dave drives his boat at headway speed in the middle of the broads on their way back from the fireworks in Wolfeboro.

"Another beautiful night for stargazing," Wayne says. "This looks like the year that Peggy may have cracked the code on her Theory of Everything."

"Wait until she spills the beans to Prof. Sallows in their big debate in October," Bill says.

"I'm not sure I like what you guys got me into."

"So what is your Theory of Everything?" Dave asks.

"Well, the book I found on a library shelf at Dartmouth filled in my missing piece. I was right about everything in the universe being only electric and magnetic fields. The book presents a nonlinear field equation that describes the behavior of these fields. In special cases, the equation reduces to Maxwell's equations of electrodynamics and to Dirac's equation of quantum mechanics."

Connie is confused. "How can everything in the universe be just electric and magnetic fields? This boat looks like a boat to me."

"If you look inside all of the materials in this boat, you find everything is made up of atoms. These atoms are made up of electrons, protons, and neutrons. If you probe these deeper, you find that all of the sub-atomic particles are just standing electromagnetic wave packets – just bundles of energy made up of electric and magnetic fields. That is all there is in all of the stars and galaxies in this beautiful sky we are looking at."

"This is going to be a great debate in October," Sam says.

During the three weeks before coming to the lake, Peggy had been working in Ryan's lab wrapping thin, insulated wire down through the bore on a meter-long iron pipe and around the outside. It was a tedious job, and she wanted to get over a thousand loops of wire wrapped around the pipe to increase the chance of detecting a signal when a pulsed laser beam is sent down the center of the pipe and reflected back. Ryan had ordered a more powerful pulsed laser, which he will be able to use in his research, and Bill took a digital signal-processing course last term and was working on some special filtering techniques that will help detect any small, induced voltage among the noise.

Peggy and Bill go back to Dartmouth and spend the rest of the summer trying to get the experiment working and looking for computer solutions to the field equation. Toward the end of the summer, Peggy, Bill, and Ryan have been working steadily all day in Ryan's lab, searching in vain for any small output voltage from the iron pipe experiment. It is late afternoon when Ashley walks in carrying a large pizza and soft drinks.

"Time for a break," Ashley says as she sets the pizza on a large table.

The smell of the warm pizza makes Peggy realize how hungry she is.

"That looks good," Bill says. "Thanks for rescuing us."

Everyone grabs a piece as Ryan brings over a roll of paper towels.

"So have you guys had any luck today?" Ashley asks.

"Not really," Peggy replies. "But we are getting good at using all of the equipment."

It doesn't take long before the pizza box is empty.

"Have you guys decided what you're going to do after you graduate next year?" Ashley asks.

"Well the first thing we're going to do is get married," Peggy says.

"Really!" Ryan says. "Congratulations. Does your family know? Have you made an official announcement?"

"Three years ago, Bill told me he was going to marry me someday."

"Did he tell your folks?" Ryan asks.

"No, but I did. So I don't think they are going to be that surprised."

Bill laughs. "They'd be more surprised if I didn't marry her."

"So Peggy, are you going to graduate school?" Ryan asks.

"No, I don't think graduate schools could handle me. I'm too much of a non-conformist."

"Peggy's going to start her own university instead," Bill says.

"You are?" Ashley asks.

Peggy tells Ashley and Ryan about her dream of starting Pearlton University and how it will be unlike any university in the world. None of the restrictions and constraints of conventional universities will hamper her university from being truly revolutionary.

"How are you going to fund this university?" Ryan asks.

"By the sale of millions of PearlPens and Pearls of Wisdom apps."

"That sounds exciting," Ashley says. "Maybe I'll take courses at your university rather than going to graduate school at Dartmouth."

"Ryan, what are your plans when you graduate?" Peggy asks.

"It will probably be at least two more years before I get my Ph.D., and then I'll look for a teaching position somewhere."

"Ryan and I have already decided to get married before then, though," Ashley says.

"No kidding," Peggy says. "That didn't take long."

"We've been going together for a year," Ryan says.

"Gosh, that is long," Peggy says. "My cousin Wayne got engaged to Connie after knowing her for only six months!"

"I have known Peggy since we were in kindergarten together," Bill says.

"I guess that is long enough," Ashley says.

Back at the lake house for the Labor Day weekend, Peggy is coming to grips with the fact that the debate is only a month away. The iron pipe experiment is ready to go as soon as Ryan unpacks the new laser and gets it tested out. Bill has succeeded in getting his computer program to produce wave packets propagating in free space to either the right or left with an arbitrary elliptical polarization. He is now ready to introduce the nonlinear terms, and he and Peggy think that perhaps different handedness standing waves, corresponding to charges with different signs, might be produced by interfering wave packets with different combinations of right- and left-handed polarizations. He is going to try this out as soon as they get back to Dartmouth.

Michael was busy all summer promoting the upcoming debate. Interest grew across campus and Michael realized that the Moore Theater was not going to be big enough to hold all those who might want to attend. He decided that it should be televised and shown on a large screen in the Alumni Gym. He then contacted N.H. Public Broadcasting to see if they might be interested in recording the debate. They agreed not only to record it, but also to broadcast the 7:00 p.m. debate live. They also contacted all PBS outlets across the country and offered to provide them with a live feed of the debate. Many students at Dartmouth posted news of the debate on social media and the news quickly spread across the country. A week ago, Peggy received phone calls from reporters at both the Wall Street Journal and the New York Times asking for an interview or comments. Peggy referred both of them to the Pearlton Industries website, and said she was not giving any interviews until after the debate. The Manchester TV station also plans to cover the debate for its local news broadcasts.

Peggy is incredulous. "I can't believe that Michael now has this debate being televised live across the country on PBS."

"Don't worry," Matt says. "No one watches PBS. I don't think that any more than two million people will be watching."

"Thanks a lot. I should have you get up and play your trumpet in front of two million people."

"I'll play taps at the end."

37

The debate begins in fifteen minutes. Peggy is back stage getting last-minute TV makeup put on by the PBS staff. Sam and Laura are with her for moral support along with Bill, who will be sitting with Peggy on the stage.

"Don't worry," Sam says, "you'll do fine. Remember, you've got nothing to lose."

Sam kisses Peggy on the forehead and he and Laura leave to join the rest of the family in the front row, which Peggy has reserved for her entire family. The makeup person touches up Peggy's forehead with a little more powder.

The PBS director comes backstage. "Starting in five minutes. Please take you places on the stage."

Two rectangular tables are set at an angle on each side of the stage with a smaller table in the center for the moderator. Two lecterns with microphones stand just off the ends of the two rectangular tables nearest the moderator. Peggy and Bill take the two seats behind the table on the audience's right, with Peggy nearest the lectern. Behind the opposite table, sit Prof. Sallows next to his lectern and Prof. Williamson, another astrophysics professor at Dartmouth. The moderator sits behind the center table with a microphone in front of her. Behind each rectangular table is a large screen on which each speaker can project computer screen images. Three TV cameras will record the event – one at the center back and one about half way up each outside aisle. The overhead lighting is bright and hot.

"Ten seconds," the director yells.

The red light on the center TV camera comes on.

"Good evening. My name is Virginia Kimball and I am an Assistant Professor of Government here at Dartmouth. I will be the moderator for tonight's debate. Our goal tonight is to have a wide-open debate. Both participants have agreed that Prof. Sallows and I will refer to Peggy Leach as Peggy, and Peggy and I will refer to Prof. Sallows as Prof. Sallows. The following is the agreed upon format for tonight's debate. Peggy will begin by giving a 6-minute opening statement for the affirmative. Prof. Sallows will then give his 6-minute opening statement. This will be followed by a 6-minute rebuttal by Peggy and then a 6-minute rebuttal by Prof. Sallows. We will then have an extended free-format dialog between the two speakers, where each will have the opportunity to ask the other any question. Peggy will be the first to ask a question and I will attempt to keep things moving without a lot of filibustering. Following this free-format dialog, each participant will give a 2-minute closing statement starting with Prof. Sallows. There is a timer on the floor at the front on the stage that will show how much time you have left for a particular statement. A yellow light will come on when you have 30 seconds left, and a red light will come on when time is up. During the question and answer period, I will turn on the yellow light if I think you should wrap up an answer."

Suddenly, Peggy feels a calm descending upon her, a calm created by confidence, confidence gained by knowledge, knowing that she knows something that Prof. Sallows doesn't know. She waits patiently for the moderator to complete her opening remarks.

"Each speaker is allowed to have one assistant seated with them on the stage. These assistants may not speak, but can pass questions and comments to each speaker. Peggy's assistant is Bill Parker, a senior computer science major at Dartmouth, and Prof. Sallows' assistant is Prof. Williamson, a professor of astrophysics at Dartmouth."

Peggy squeezes Bill's hand as the moderator wraps up.

"The question for tonight's debate is, 'Was Einstein wrong, and has Peggy discovered a Theory of Everything'? When each member of the audience entered the hall tonight, they voted on this question. The results of that vote are as follows: 18% yes, 82% no. Following tonight's debate the audience will vote again by a show of hands. We are now ready to begin. Peggy, you have six minutes for your opening statement."

Peggy gets up and stands behind her lectern, stunning in her new, black, above-the-knee dress, bought for her by her mom on a recent shopping spree, the cap sleeves and architectural cutout neckline providing the perfect framing for the single pearl necklace, given to her by Bill that first Christmas at the lake. From the front row, her mother, Kate, beams with pride, and Joe does not think he has ever seen his little girl look so striking. George Harrington is watching Peggy on the 60-inch TV in the family room of his Long Island home. Watching with George is Thomas Zorello, head of acquisitions at Google.

Peggy smiles and looks at the red light on the TV camera on the far side aisle. She then turns to the moderator. "Thank you Prof. Kimball, and thank you, Prof. Sallows for agreeing to debate me tonight on what I think is a very important question. That question is, 'Was Einstein wrong, and have I discovered a Theory of Everything'? Tonight I will show that the answer to both questions is yes. Einstein *was* wrong and I *have* discovered a Theory of Everything."

Sam smiles. He has never seen Peggy look more confident. *Just keep it up.* Bill is beginning to sweat under the hot lights. He is much more nervous than Peggy appears to be.

Peggy continues. "I will dispose of the second question first. I most certainly have discovered a Theory of Everything. In fact, I discovered it almost one year ago, less than 500 yards from where I am standing now. I found it just sitting on a bottom shelf in the Kresge Library on the third floor of the Fairchild Physical Sciences Center. Shockingly, the book had just been sitting there, unread, for over 50 years. The book was written by an engineering professor who taught right here at Dartmouth 50 years ago. The title of the book is *A Unified Field Theory* and the author's name is Miles V. Hayes. Here is the book."

Peggy holds up the small, 70-page book, and pauses for maximum effect.

"This book is small, but the contents describe a single equation, which explains all of physical reality. You may wonder why almost no one has read this book, and why the author did not publish his results in refereed journals. Well, he did try to publish his results. He sent three articles to the Physical Review and all three were rejected as being speculative. As he points out in the book, without speculation there would be no physics and no Physical Review. Tonight, Prof. Sallows will undoubtedly tell you a lot about what physics has to say about how the universe works. When he does, I ask you to think about how much is really just speculation. Is the big bang theory speculation? Is it speculation to think that the universe is expanding? Are black holes speculations? Is dark matter speculation? Is dark energy speculation? Miles Hayes was right. Without speculation there would be no physics."

Peggy still finds Miles Hayes' reaction to his paper rejections remarkable. Would she have bounced back and published her own book? Would she have given away all the copies Hayes did? She looks directly at Prof. Sallows.

"And so, following the Physical Review rejections, Miles Hayes decided to publish this little book himself. He printed 400 copies and numbered each copy. In the appendix, he lists who received each of the 400 copies. He sent copies to the leading physicists of the day, including de Broglie, Heisenberg, and Dirac. He sent copies to the Chairs of the Departments of Physics of major universities around the world. He sent copies to various libraries around the world, including four to different libraries here on the Dartmouth campus, and he gave copies to members of the Dartmouth faculty. This is copy number 309, which originally belonged to one of his Dartmouth faculty colleagues. I bought it from an obscure used bookstore on Amazon."

From the look on Prof. Sallow's face, Peggy is pretty sure he knows nothing about this book. She has only talked about it with Ryan, Prof. Fitzgerald, and Prof. Taylor. None of them has mentioned it to Prof. Sallows.

Peggy continues. "Now you may wonder, if de Broglie, Heisenberg, and

Dirac all received copies of this book, and if the unified field theory described in it is correct, why didn't any of them vouch for its validity? But that is exactly the point. It shows why they are all wrong. No one of their stature, particularly if they have been working on their own theories for years, is going to admit that they are wrong, particularly based on the theory of some obscure Associate Professor of Engineering at Dartmouth. If they even opened the book, they probably looked at all the quaternion mathematics, realized it was not the kind of mathematics they were using, and just threw the book away."

Peggy knows she must bring up Einstein to lay the groundwork for how he took a wrong turn.

"Einstein died nine years before Miles Hayes published this book. I'd like to think that Einstein would have taken it seriously. After all, it is exactly the kind of unified field theory that Einstein tried to figure out for the last thirty years of his life. But the reason that Einstein was unsuccessful in his search for a unified field theory, or a Theory of Everything, is that he took a wrong path when he introduced his principle of equivalence in 1907, which led him to develop, what I believe to be his erroneous general theory of relativity in 1916. Einstein was right about Special Relativity, but wrong about General Relativity."

The yellow light on the timer just came on. Peggy needs to wrap up.

"Unfortunately, astrophysics today is based almost entirely on Einstein's general theory of relativity. Prof. Sallows will tell you about all of the exciting things that that theory predicts. The only problem is that that theory is wrong."

Peggy takes her seat and Bill squeezes her hand.

The moderator turns to her right. "Prof. Sallows, you have six minutes for your opening statement."

Prof. Sallows goes to his lectern and turns on a PowerPoint presentation, which is displayed on the large screen behind him. The first slide is titled Albert Einstein – Significant Contributions. On this and the next eight slides is a list of two dozen papers Einstein wrote on a wide range of topics from relativity to quantum mechanics. It becomes clear to Peggy that Prof. Sallows' strategy is to show what a genius Einstein was and how his contributions to physics are unassailable. Prof. Sallows is stressing how experiments have validated many of Einstein's predictions.

Bill slides a paper to Peggy, on which he has written, "Einstein – 1905 – photoelectric effect, photon, mistake." Peggy nods.

Prof. Sallows is saying that our knowledge of the universe is based in large part on Einstein's general relativity theory. He says that we have measured a background microwave radiation in the universe, which is a remnant of the big bang. He says the universe really is expanding and that black holes are real. In his summary, he says that while Peggy is well meaning, when she learns a little more, she will realize that Einstein was right after all.

Pretty condescending, Peggy thinks, as she steps behind her lectern for her six-minute rebuttal.

"Prof. Sallows showed you a long list of papers that Einstein published over the years. Let's talk about some of those papers. I would argue that the most important one was his paper on special relativity, actually entitled *On the Electrodynamics of Moving Bodies*, which he wrote in 1905 when he was only five years older than I am. It is typical that many of our greatest physicists did their best work when they were young. Why is this? One reason is that they have not been contaminated by the mistakes of others. In the case of Einstein, he developed his theory of special relativity when he was working by himself in the Swiss Patent Office. It was not until 1909 that he obtained his first academic position at the University of Zurich. Now while Einstein may have been a genius in some sense, he was still human, with a turbulent family life. But once he successfully changed our understanding of space and time with his special theory of relativity, I think he became sidetracked when developing his general theory of relativity. How did this happen? Well, special relativity is really about having the laws of physics the same in all, so called, inertial reference frames. That is, frames of reference moving with constant velocity. In other words, if you are moving on a train going at constant speed down a straight track with no bumps, there is no experiment you can do that will tell if you are on a moving train."

Peggy figures this is the time to cast some doubt on Einstein.

"But now Einstein wanted to extend his idea of an inertial reference frame to accelerated systems. And this is where I think he went down the wrong road. He assumed that free fall was the equivalent inertial frame for accelerated reference frames. In other words, if you jumped out of an airplane and there was no air resistance – you would have to hold your breath – you are really not accelerating toward the earth, but are following the shortest path in a curved space created by the earth. You would not be able to do any experiment to tell if you are falling to the earth. Until you hit the ground, of course. Then you go thud, and are dead.

"This is exactly what happens in Prof. Sallows' black holes that he told you were real. If you enter a black hole, you feel nothing. You think everything is fine. Until you hit the singularity, then everything goes pop, and you are dead. I think you'll agree with me, this is madness."

Peggy waits for the chuckles in the audience to subside. She takes a quick look at Prof. Sallows. He is not smiling.

Peggy continues. "So was Einstein wrong? Yes, he was wrong on general relativity. Gravity is gravity and acceleration is acceleration. They are not the same thing. They are not equivalent."

I will come back to gravity later. Better start skewering quantum mechanics now.

"I think Einstein was also wrong when he introduced the idea of the photon in his 1905 paper on the photoelectric effect. In 1900, Planck introduced the idea that light energy comes in discrete bundles of energy in order to derive an equation that accurately explained blackbody radiation. However, Planck never thought that light really behaved this way. He thought it was just a clever mathematical trick to find an equation that agreed with the experimental results. But Einstein went further and said that this is the way that light works. That it is a particle, a funny particle with no mass and no size that you can identify. But it is an even funnier particle. It sometimes behaves like a wave. This so-called wave-particle duality has been frustrating quantum mechanics for over 100 years. All because Einstein was wrong."

Time to push my unified field theory.

"My Theory of Everything, based on this *Unified Field Theory* book, replaces the wave-particle duality with the wave unity. Everything in the universe is a wave – waves made up of electric and magnetic fields. All matter in the universe is made up of particles, which are standing electromagnetic wave packets. The single nonlinear quaternion equation in this book describes all of physical reality. In the constant approximation, the equation reduces to Maxwell's equations of electrodynamics. In the linear approximation, the equation reduces to Dirac's equation of quantum mechanics. Therefore, all of electrodynamics and all of quantum mechanics are approximations to this single nonlinear field equation. This Theory of Everything also explains gravitational and nuclear fields.

"So I think it is quite clear – Einstein *was* wrong, and I *have* discovered a Theory of Everything."

As Peggy sits down, Bill hands her a PearlPen and a pad of paper. They both have Android tablets and when Peggy returns to the lectern for the question and answer session after Prof. Sallows completes his rebuttal, Bill will be able to send her messages on her tablet by writing on his pad of paper with his PearlPen. Bill has set up the system so that Peggy will be able to switch to a mode where everything she writes on her pad of paper will be displayed on the large screen behind her.

Prof. Sallows has started his rebuttal. He first attacks Peggy's claim that Einstein was wrong on general relativity. He says it correctly predicts the precession of Mercury's orbit about the sun. He says it correctly predicts the bending of starlight when it passes close to the sun. He says that general relativity is used to correct errors in GPS systems because gravity causes clocks in the GPS satellites to run at a slightly different rate than clocks on the surface of the earth. He says that scientists have actually measured gravitational waves as predicted by Einstein's general relativity theory. He says that Peggy's little field equation would have to predict all of these observed facts.

Prof. Sallows goes on to say that Einstein was right about photons. He says that experiments show that light really is made up of particles and that you can detect a single photon. He goes on to say that Einstein worked for 30 years trying to find a unified field theory without success and that lots of very smart people have spent the last 30 years developing string theory, which may well lead to a Theory of Everything. He concludes by saying that it should be obvious to the audience that a Dartmouth senior is not going to discover a Theory of Everything.

The moderator turns on her microphone. "We now come to the question and answer portion of the debate. This will be a wide-open back and forth dialog between the two speakers. We will begin with Peggy asking the first question."

Peggy and Prof. Sallows both stand behind their respective lecterns. When Peggy was preparing for this debate over Labor Day weekend at the lake with Uncle Sam and Bill, they wondered whether Prof. Sallows had ever read the Hayes book on *A Unified Field Theory*, or if he even knew about it. They planned two different lines of attack, depending on the answer to this question. So they agreed that this should be Peggy's first question to Prof. Sallows.

Peggy holds up the book. "Prof. Sallows, have you ever seen this book before?"

"No."

"So you have never read this book?"

"No, I have never heard of that book."

"Even though this book has been sitting on the shelf in the physics library for all the years you have been here, you never came across it?"

"That's correct; there are a lot of books in that library I haven't read."

"So if the field equation given in this book really did describe a Theory of Everything, you wouldn't know that, would you?"

"I really doubt that a field equation that some non-physicist came up with over 50 years ago would have any relevance in modern-day physics. You would have to show me the equation for me to tell you what is wrong with it."

"I would be happy to."

Peggy writes the equation on her pad of paper with her PearlPen. It shows up on the large screen behind her as she writes it. Peggy says that this is a quaternion equation involving complex quaternions. She says the *Psi* variable in the equation is a complex quaternion containing both the electric and magnetic field vectors. She writes down the equation for *Psi*. She says that the D operator is also a complex quaternion containing derivatives with respect to both space and time.

"There are two important special cases," Peggy says. "If you set the right-hand side of the equation to a constant, equal to the current quaternion, the equation reduces to Maxwell's equations of electrodynamics. If you set the right-hand side to a linear function of the variable *Psi*, the equation reduces to Dirac's equation of relativistic quantum mechanics. So all of electrodynamics and all of quantum mechanics are approximations to this nonlinear field equation."

Prof. Sallows interrupts. "But this equation is not a tensor equation, so it is not at all clear that it would be valid in all inertial frames of reference, and therefore could not be a law of physics."

"Actually," Peggy says, "Hayes proves in this book that this nonlinear field equation is invariant under a Lorentz transformation. That is, it is the same in all inertial reference frames. We know that Maxwell's equations and Dirac's equation – but not Schrödinger's equation – also have the property of relativistic invariance, but they are both approximations of this field equation."

"Well, no mainstream physicist uses quaternions to describe physical theories," Prof. Sallows says.

"That may be the problem. Einstein wasn't the only one who was wrong. Gibbs and Heaviside were the ones who, over a hundred years ago, separated out only the vector part of Hamilton's quaternions, which he discovered in 1843. Hamilton spent the last 22 years of his life studying quaternions and believed that they were the best way to describe all physical theories. Perhaps if Gibbs and Heaviside had stuck with the full quaternions, we wouldn't have had to wait for more than 100 years for this Theory of Everything to be discovered."

"I don't see how you get Maxwell's equations out of your field equation," Prof. Sallows says.

"First of all, you just plug in the definitions of *Psi* and D into the field equation and carry out the quaternion multiplications. The details of how to do this are all on our Pearls of Wisdom app, which most students here at Dartmouth have been using for the past two years."

Peggy pulls up the Pearls of Wisdom app on the large screen and shows how anyone can learn all about quaternions by going through several short video clips. She then fast-forwards through the expansion of the field equation into eight coupled nonlinear partial differential equations. She shows how if the electromagnetic energy density term is replaced by the charge density, and if the electromagnetic momentum term is replaced by the current density, the equations reduce exactly to Maxwell's equations.

"So you see," Peggy says, "that this theory states that charge and mass are the same thing, and are equal to the electromagnetic energy density in terms of only electric and magnetic fields. All particles are just standing electromagnetic waves in very small regions of space where the electric and magnetic field strengths are very high, and the nonlinear terms in the field equation become important."

Prof. Williamson hands Prof. Sallows a piece of paper.

Prof. Sallows looks at the paper and turns to Peggy. "The right-hand side of your field equation is quadratic, and therefore always positive. But in your Maxwell equations approximation, this quadratic term becomes the charge density. But we know that both positive and negative charges exist, so your field equation cannot be correct."

Peggy responds. "This actually bothered Hayes for some time until he realized that if he changed the sign of *Psi*, the left-hand side of the equation involving the space and time derivatives changes sign, but the quadratic term on the right-hand side doesn't. Therefore, it only appears that the charge density must be positive. There is another whole set of solutions in which you can make the right-hand side negative by changing the sign of *Psi*. Hayes shows that this actually corresponds to the electric and magnetic fields having a right- or left-handed sense."

Prof. Sallows tries a different attack. "You say that in the linear approximation, your field equation reduces to the Dirac equation. But the Dirac equation includes four values of its *Psi*, which are probability amplitudes and don't seem to be the same as your *Psi*."

"Hayes shows in detail in this book how his linear approximation is related to all of Dirac's 4 x 4 matrices. But there are two main problems with Dirac's equation. The first is that he insisted on getting a linear equation from a nonlinear Hamiltonian, which is what led to his 4 x 4 matrices. But no linear equation can describe all of physical reality. The second is that he wanted his equation to reduce to Schrödinger's equation in the non-relativistic limit, with the same interpretation of *Psi* as being a probability amplitude. However, this is the wrong interpretation of *Psi*. It is a complex quaternion involving the electric and magnetic fields. What you think is a probability density is really just the electromagnetic energy density. This is one case where Einstein was right. God does not play dice."

Prof. Williamson hands Prof. Sallows another piece of paper.

"Ok, let's assume your field equation might be a different way of looking at electrodynamics and quantum mechanics. It says nothing about gravity, which is what general relativity is all about. So how does your field equation handle gravity?"

"I'm glad you asked. Let's take a look at these two equations."

Peggy brings up a slide on the large screen, which shows Coulomb's law for the force between two charged particles and Newton's law of gravitation for the force between two masses.

Peggy looks at Prof. Sallows. "If you were to ask any high school student if these two equations look similar, what do you think they would say?"

Prof. Sallows nods.

Peggy continues. "Not only are they similar, if you just change the names of the variables, they are identical. Does anyone really believe that electrostatic forces and gravitational forces are fundamentally different when their force equations are identical? Yet physicists have been telling us forever that these are different types of forces. We are led to believe that electromagnetism as described by Maxwell's equations is one thing, taught in its own separate course, and that gravity as described by general relativity is completely different and taught in its own separate course."

Peggy brings back up the Pearls of Wisdom app on the big screen.

"Here are a series of video clips that have been out on this app for over a year. My Uncle Sam, who is sitting here in the front row, recorded them when he taught an electromagnetics course at UNH a couple of years ago. In these video clips, he derives Maxwell's equations from Coulomb's law and special relativity. That is, if you assume the force equation for electrostatics that I just showed you, and you assume that special relativity is correct, then Maxwell's equations follow just by mathematical manipulation. No further assumptions are needed. The Lorentz force, which includes the force on a moving charge in a magnetic field, falls out of the derivation. The meaning of the magnetic field, in terms of an electric field in a moving frame of reference, also falls out of the derivation."

Peggy flips back to the slide that shows Coulomb's law for the force between two charged particles and Newton's law of gravitation for the force between two masses.

"Now if you had just gone through this derivation using this force equation for electrostatics, and someone asked you to come up with a general theory of gravitation that would be valid for moving bodies as well as static masses, what would you do?"

Peggy looks at Prof. Sallows, holds out her hands and shrugs.

"Would you do what Einstein did and spend several years constructing a 4-dimensional curved space described by a curvature tensor with lots of Christoffel symbols? Or would you simply do the exact same derivation using Newton's law of gravitation for the force between two masses? This would lead to equations identical with Maxwell's equations except that the mass density replaces the charge density. You would then realize that there is a second gravitational field, analogous to the magnetic field, which exerts a force only on moving bodies. You would realize that this force adds to the normal gravitational force acting on all moving bodies in the universe, perhaps explaining some of the observed abnormal behavior of planets and stars. But if you had come across the Hayes book in the library, then it would become obvious to you that there needs to be only one set of Maxwell's equations; that the much weaker gravitational force is a second-order effect of electromagnetic forces; that there really are only electric and magnetic fields; that mass and charge really are the same thing; that all particles are standing electromagnetic waves created by the nonlinear field. You would realize that all the particles in the stars and galaxies are just very high-intensity electromagnetic fields and that these fields propagate throughout all of space. You would realize that the energy density of these electric and magnetic fields are equivalent to a mass density extending from the core of a spiral galaxy. You would realize that this would account for the velocity of the outer stars in the galaxy and you would not have to invent dark matter to explain it. You would realize that it is unnecessary to assume that masses in the universe change the curvature of space-time. You would realize that electric and magnetic fields fill the entire universe, connecting all objects together in a unified way. You would realize that even very smart people, like Einstein, when they come to a fork in the road, can end up taking the wrong road."

Peggy pauses and there is not a sound in the hall. She waits.

The moderator breaks the silence. "Prof. Sallows, do you have another question?"

"Well, this is all very interesting speculation, but you have no evidence that solutions to your field equation can be found, or would lead to any physical reality."

Since returning to Dartmouth after the Labor Day weekend, Peggy and Bill have been working around the clock trying to find solutions to the nonlinear field equation. They have also been working in Ryan's lab trying to get some results from the iron pipe experiment. Two weeks ago, they began to get some standing wave solutions to the field equation. And two nights ago, they celebrated with Ryan in his lab. This is the moment Peggy has been waiting for.

Peggy brings up a slide showing the eight coupled nonlinear partial differential equations. "Actually, Bill and I have been trying to solve these equations numerically for almost a year now. A couple of weeks ago we got some interesting solutions which I can show you."

The big screen shows two wave packets approaching each other from the right and left of the screen. As they meet, their amplitudes get added and then go away as the wave packets continue across the screen.

"This is what is predicted by Maxwell's equations," Peggy says, "because the equations are linear. However, something different happens when we solve the nonlinear field equation."

A second animation appears on the screen. This time when the two wave packets meet, they do not just pass through each other, but form a stationary standing wave.

"This is how particles are formed. Depending on the polarizations of the two wave packets, the resulting particle could be negatively charged, positively charged, or neutral."

Peggy puts up a figure of several color photos, which appear similar to the spherical harmonics solutions of Schrödinger's equation for the hydrogen atom.

"These are exact solutions of the field equation, representing the hydrogen atom. The different energy levels are actually stable limit cycles in a nonlinear field. While they look similar to the spherical harmonics solutions you are familiar with, the interpretation is quite different. The different intensities shown are not the probabilities of finding an electron there. Rather, they are simply the electromagnetic energy densities – the sum of the squares of the electric and magnetic fields. We can actually look inside to see what the electric and magnetic fields of an electron orbiting the nucleus of a hydrogen atom look like."

Peggy puts another image on the screen. The title of the image is, *It's the nonlinearity, stupid.*

"It is a little more difficult to visualize this because we have six values to display at every point in space – the three components of the electric field and the three components of the magnetic field. Nevertheless, I have done the best I can by plotting various components of the electric field versus components of the magnetic field. This way you can see the limit cycles and how the handedness of the fields represents the negative charge of the electron."

Peggy waits as Prof. Sallows stares at the image on the screen.

"Prof. Sallows, do you have another question?" the moderator asks.

Prof. Sallows thinks for a moment. "To be taken seriously, a new theory needs to predict new phenomena, which can be verified by experiment. What does your field equation predict that we don't already know?"

Peggy points out that the theory says that charge density is just the energy density of electric and magnetic fields, so that strong enough standing wave electric and magnetic fields should produce measurable charge. She says that the calculations show that the energies would need to be at least those of gamma rays to be measurable. She suggests that two gamma rays colliding head on to produce a standing wave might very well produce an electron-positron pair, the reverse of what has already been measured.

Peggy goes on to say that the electromagnetic momentum, in the form of the cross product of the electric and magnetic fields, plays the role of current density in the new unified field theory. Therefore, high intensity laser beams should be able to produce some type of transformer action. She brings up a schematic diagram of their iron pipe experiment.

"Prof. Sallows, if a pulsed laser beam is sent down the center of this pipe, would you expect a voltage to be measured across these terminals?"

"Absolutely not. That would violate all known laws of physics."

"So if I show you the results of this very experiment, and if those results show that a voltage is indeed measured, you would say what?"

"I would say that your experiment was wrong, and there would have to be some other explanation for the result."

Peggy brings up a photograph of the iron pipe experiment.

"This is a photo of an experimental setup that is currently in the plasma physics lab in Wilder Hall. Two nights ago, we ran an experiment where we sent a pulsed laser beam down the center of the pipe at a repetition rate of one megahertz. Our calculations showed that based on our field equation, an induced voltage across the windings would be produced, and the output of our spectrum analyzer would show a peak at one megahertz of two major grid markings on the screen. Here are the results we obtained."

Peggy brings up a photo of the spectrum analyzer screen, which shows a peak at one megahertz, two major grid markings high.

"I think it is clear that my Theory of Everything is correct."

Prof. Sallows just stands there. Finally, he addresses Peggy. "New results like this should not be presented in a public forum. They should be submitted to the Physical Review so they can undergo peer review."

"Sorry," Peggy says. "The Physical Review had their chance 50 years ago and they blew it. Hayes submitted three articles to the Physical Review on this field equation and they rejected all three articles. They do not get another chance. A video of this entire experiment with all of the details on how to reproduce the results was posted this afternoon on our Pearls of Wisdom app. Anyone, anywhere in the world, can do exactly the same experiment, and will get exactly the same result."

The moderator interrupts. "Unfortunately, we've come to the end of our open dialog period. Each speaker will now give a 2-minute closing statement. Prof. Sallows will go first."

"I think tonight's debate has been very interesting and informative, but I think it may be going too far to say that Einstein was wrong. General relativity has been recognized as the correct theory of gravitation for a hundred years. I don't think it is going to be overturned in one evening here at Dartmouth."

Prof. Sallows goes on to give a defense of quantum mechanics, and while admitting that there are a lot of unanswered questions when it comes to trying to find a Theory of Everything, he thinks that the current work on string theory will eventually lead to some useful results. He finally thanks the audience for attending.

Peggy begins her closing remarks. "I want to thank the Dartmouth Debating Club for organizing this debate, and thank Prof. Sallows for agreeing to participate. The question we have been debating, 'Was Einstein wrong, and have I discovered a Theory of Everything,' is an important one. When you walked into the hall this evening, the vast majority of you voted *No*. You did not think Einstein was wrong, and you did not think that I had discovered a Theory of Everything. If I had walked into this hall not knowing what we have covered in this debate, I most likely would also have voted *No*. After all, how can Einstein be wrong? Almost everyone believes that he was right. Is it possible that almost everyone can be wrong? Four years ago, my Uncle Sam Woodbury told me about his Woodbury's Law. It is that *conventional wisdom is wrong most of the time*. Therefore, it really is possible that Einstein was wrong, and that everyone is wrong who thinks that he was always right.

"Even Einstein himself thought that his general theory of gravitation was probably wrong, when he wrote the following to Felix Klein in 1917."

Peggy reads the following quote that she has projected on the screen.

> But I do not doubt that sooner or later the day will come, when this way of conceiving [of gravitation] will have to give way to another that differs from it fundamentally, for reasons that today we cannot even imagine. I believe that this process of deepening of theory has no limit.

"That day has come. I find it remarkable that a single equation – a single equation that has been sitting in a book, unread, on the library shelf right here at Dartmouth for over 50 years – can describe all of physical reality. But I think I have shown you tonight that that is the case. Einstein *was* wrong, and I *did* discover a Theory of Everything. I ask you to vote *Yes* on tonight's debate question. Thank you."

"That concludes tonight's debate," the moderator says. "We will now take a second vote on the question. The question is, 'Was Einstein wrong, and has Peggy discovered a Theory of Everything'? All those who wish to vote in the affirmative, or *Yes*, please raise your hand."

The vast majority of hands go up.

"Those who wish to vote in the negative, or *No*, please raise your hand."

Perhaps a dozen hands go up.

"The affirmative vote wins this debate. Thank you and good night."

Peggy nearly collapses as applause fills the hall. Prof. Sallows comes over to congratulate Peggy. Uncle Sam is on the stage hugging her. "You did it," he whispers.

Michael comes up to Peggy. "The PBS anchors want you backstage for a live, nationwide, on-air interview."

38

The ocean waves crash on the beach in front of Dave's home as the entire family sits down for Thanksgiving dinner.

"I can't believe that it was four years ago today," Connie says, "that Kate invited me to Thanksgiving dinner at her home in Portsmouth. What a four years this has been."

"We certainly have a lot to be thankful for," Kate says.

"You're telling me," Peggy says.

"Were you able to get any studying done after your debate?" Sam asks.

"It has been hard. I have been swamped with requests for interviews from all over the country. It has been surreal."

"Sales of PearlPens and subscriptions to the Pearls of Wisdom app have skyrocketed," Bill says.

"George Harrington told me that Google has noticed this," Dave says. "They have started the ball rolling on making an offer to buy both of your companies. He told me that some of the board members are out of the country now, but they were supposed to contact them by yesterday or today. He told me he would let us know as soon as he learned anything."

"That reminds me," Sam says. "You know the Johnsons who own the small cottage next to us at the lake. They have decided to retire and move to Florida permanently, so they are selling their property on the lake. He offered us first refusal, and I told him that I was sure that you would want it for the time when you and Bill are ready to settle down."

"I sure will," Peggy says. "By the way, Bill and I have set the date for our wedding next June as soon as we graduate. And Uncle Dave has agreed to have the wedding right here, just like Connie and Wayne's."

"That cottage you're going to buy on the lake is a tear down," Dave says. "For a wedding present, I'm going to design you a real home for that lot. You will look right across the lake to Gunstock."

"Oh my gosh," Peggy says, "I don't believe it."

"And it is in a little cove," Sam says. "I am going to call it *Peggy's Cove*. By the way, did you ever hear from Prof. Sallows after the debate?"

"Actually, a couple of weeks ago, he sent me a very nice hand-written letter. I have it in my purse. I'll go get it."

Peggy returns with the letter and starts reading it.

Dear Peggy,

You are a remarkable young lady. I underestimated you when I agreed to participate in the debate, and I was a little miffed after the debate. However, I went to the library and got the Hayes book and I have read it. You are right; it is mystifying how this book could have fallen below the radar for all of these years. After reading this book and going over your solutions to the field equation and reviewing the results of your experiment that you have posted online, I realize that all the work I've been doing for the past decade has been going in the wrong direction. This first made me angry, but then I realized that I had become complacent and had just kept working on the same old stuff. I also realize that you have given me an opportunity to be one of the first to explore this whole new understanding of what physical reality is all about, and for that I thank you.

You have a bright future ahead of you, Peggy, and you have my very best wishes for continued success.

Yours very sincerely,

Ogden Sallows

"It took a big man to write that," Sam says.
"I told you how important hand-written letters are," Laura says.

"So Peggy, has the Theory of Everything taught you anything?" Sam asks.
"I don't know; it is hard to say. I am sure that the infinite ways that electric and magnetic fields can arrange themselves could, in principle, explain everything, but we will never know. How can it explain that hard work is fun? How can it explain why our family is the most important thing in my life? How can it explain why writing those video clips that help other people to learn gives me so much satisfaction?"
"I think if we keep working on it, we can learn a lot more," Bill says. "The fact that the high intensity fields that make up an entire person depend to some small degree on all the other fields in the universe can begin to explain a lot."
"Like why I often know what Sam is going to say before he says it?" Laura asks.
"Yes, there are tons of examples like that," Peggy says.
"The chapter on *Consciousness* in the unified field theory book was thought-provoking," Sam says.

"Yes," Peggy says. "The author makes sense when he postulates that the field is truly unified and encompasses all of existence: matter, mind, and spirit. I like his view that consciousness is a universal property of the field everywhere, including the field in a complete vacuum. When your particular brain moves into a certain region of space, that region becomes conscious and the old region becomes unconscious."

"His view of death also gives you a lot to think about," Sam says.

"I agree," Peggy says. "He talks about human consciousness being a wave in the field, which is born, lives, and dies. Just like the ocean waves crashing on the beach outside. But the field is immortal, just like the ocean, and goes on producing wave after wave."

"He has a lot to say about that," Sam says, "as well as how the field equation implies both a principle of evolution and that free will exists."

"There's one more thing that we learned from solving the field equation, which the author of the book didn't know," Peggy says.

"What's that?" Sam asks.

"The self-similarity properties of the solutions. How the standing waves tend to group themselves into clumps, and how this structure is preserved at all scales very much like fractals."

"It is too bad we can't see deep inside the nucleus of an atom to see what it really looks like," Bill says.

"But we can," Peggy says. "Just look up in the sky. The general structure of the solar system is repeated at a larger scale in galaxies, and at an even larger scale in clusters of galaxies. It is all in the field equation."

Looking out at the ocean waves crashing on the beach, Peggy cannot believe that everything she sees, everything she does, everything she thinks, everything she feels are the result of just six numbers, six numbers representing the three components of the electric field and the three components of the magnetic field at every tiny point in space, points separated by incomprehensively short distances, the values of the six numbers fluctuating widely at incredible speeds, billions and billions of times per second, just six numbers dancing to different tunes, growing to new horizons: a jitterbug growing to elementary particles, a foxtrot growing to atoms, a samba growing to molecules, lots of waltzes growing to flowers, trees, kittens, babies, oceans, planets, solar systems, galaxies; just six numbers dancing a polka, producing a theory, a theory of everything – Peggy's Polka.

Peggy's phone beeps, indicating a text message.

"Who is the text message from?" Bill asks.

"George Harrington."

Epilogue

10 Years Later

It is a sunny June morning on the Dartmouth Green and the commencement ceremony is underway. The President of Dartmouth College steps to the lectern and speaks.

"Will Peggy Leach Parker and William James Parker please step forward."

Peggy and Bill get up from their seats, and stand next to the president facing the audience.

The President continues,

"Whereas, Peggy Leach Parker and William James Parker were both undergraduate students at Dartmouth a decade ago, and during that time discovered a single equation, which explains all of physical reality, notwithstanding the fact that the equation had been sitting on library shelves here at Dartmouth for over 50 years, and

Whereas, through diligent efforts and persistence, you found solutions to this equation, which have changed the face of science, and

Whereas, these solutions have completely changed our understanding of the universe, and

Whereas, you conducted experiments, which verified new predictions of this single equation, and

Whereas, the company you formed while college freshmen, Pearlton Industries, was sold to Google for over a billion dollars, and

Whereas, your Pearls of Wisdom app is now used for teaching almost all college and university courses worldwide, and

Whereas, your establishment of Pearlton University in southeastern New Hampshire was an innovative and groundbreaking accomplishment, where people of all ages, from right out of high school to retirees, can meet, study, think, and invent, and where you have abolished traditional degrees and broken down all barriers between narrow disciplines, and

Whereas, as a result, scores of new companies have been formed and New Hampshire has become the fastest growing economy in the country, and

Whereas, your contributions to society at large are immeasurable, and Dartmouth is proud to have you as distinguished alumni,

Therefore, by the authority vested in the Board of Trustees of Dartmouth College and delegated to me, I hereby confer upon each of you the degree Doctor of Science, honoris causa, with all of the honors, rights and privileges pertaining thereto."

The Dean of the Faculty of Arts and Sciences and the Dean of Engineering assist the President in putting a doctoral hood on Peggy and then on Bill. Peggy then steps to the microphone.

"It is a real privilege and honor to be here today. Thank you so much. This campus brings back so many happy memories. I wish I had the time to recall all of them with you today. I wish I had the time to give you the many pearls of wisdom that helped me when I was a student here and since. I wish I had the time to thank everyone who has helped us along the way. However, there are two people who I must thank. The first is my dad, Joe Leach, who is here today along with other members of our families including our two children, 6-year-old Sam and 4-year-old Connie. After some discussion, my dad agreed to let me transfer to Dartmouth after my freshman year at UNH. A year after we graduated, he interrupted his European tour, celebrating his 25th wedding anniversary, to give Bill and me a personal tour of historic Rome. He now enjoys his new home overlooking Great Bay, where he serves as Dean of Pearlton University.

"The other person who I must thank is someone who has provided me with an inexhaustible supply of pearls of wisdom, and without whom, I know I would not be here today. That is my Uncle Sam Woodbury, who retired a few years ago after teaching engineering at the University of New Hampshire for over 40 years. Since his retirement, he has written a novel, and in that novel is everything I wish I had the time to tell you. Therefore, my gift to each of you today is a copy of that novel. They are available on the tables in the rear, so please take one when you leave. Thank you all. Congratulations and best wishes."

As she takes her seat, Peggy looks up and winks at Miles V. Hayes.

Author's Note

All of the characters in this book, except one, are fictional. The poem, *Time*, on page 35 was written by my daughter, Debbie, when she was fourteen. The one real character in the book is Miles V. Hayes, who actually did write the book, *A Unified Field Theory*, in 1964. All of the passages quoted from that book are exact quotes. Of the four copies of this book, which Hayes donated to Dartmouth libraries, three still exist. Two are in the Rauner Special Collections Library, still in pristine conditions, complete with dust covers, appearing not to have been opened in fifty years. The book that Peggy found on the bottom library shelf is still on the bottom shelf of the Kresge Physical Sciences Library on the third floor of the Fairchild Physical Sciences Center. It was last checked out in 1975.

About the Author:
Richard E. Haskell grew up in New Hampshire and is Emeritus Professor of Engineering at Oakland University in Rochester, Michigan, where he taught electrical and computer engineering for 46 years. He is the author of over thirty books ranging from plasma dynamics to digital design. He currently lives in New Hampshire.

Website: www.richardhaskell.com
Email: richardhaskellbooks@gmail.com

Related Books by the Author :
(available from Amazon.com and other retail outlets)

Those who wish to pursue a more technical approach to the topics described in this book will find the following two books useful:

Richard E. Haskell, *Vectors and Tensors By Example – Including Cartesian Tensors, Quaternions, and Matlab Examples*, ISBN: 978-1515153115, 2015.

This book covers all of the material described by Sam in his book, *Vectors and Tensors*.

Richard E. Haskell, *Understanding Special Relativity and Maxwell's Equations – With Implications for a Unified Field Theory*, ISBN: 978-1516864744, 2016.

This book includes Sam's derivation of Maxwell's equations from Coulomb's law and special relativity, Peggy's alternate theory of gravitation, and the expansion of Miles Hayes' quaternion field equation into eight coupled, nonlinear, partial differential equations.

Acknowledgments

My colleague, Darrin Hanna, read early versions of this book and each time made important suggestions for improving the plot and characters. My journey from writing non-fiction, technical books to writing a novel has been an interesting one, made easier by helpful criticisms and suggestions from members of my neighborhood writing group, especially Norm Phillips and Sharon Fish, as well as from Shelby June and Donald Kohler. My brother, Phil, and my son, Jeff, were both good sounding boards for early drafts and provided important feedback. I thank them all for their helpful inputs. Finally, my wife Edie has been my best critic, forcing me to try to keep Peggy from being a complete geek. Her love and encouragement made the book possible.

Made in the USA
Charleston, SC
01 April 2016